I0743720

Canadian Cataloguing in Publication Data
A. Tarrant
Pursuing Pagan
978-1-895166-21-7
1. Fiction. I. Title.
Printed and bound in North America.
First published in 2022
by Inconsequential Diversions

PURSUING

PAGAN

A. TARRANT

How dare I say that I have seen
These lovely, faery things..?
Because I have … I know I have…
Else what is this that sings..?
– Anne Brigman, 'Enchanted'
in *Songs of a Pagan*

The Myth of the Megumawaach

Infinitude

There are people living near the Megumawaach River, on the east coast of New Brunswick, who scoff at the theory of what happened the day that Grace went into the waters of Faery Lake. They're not inclined to believe what they refer to as 'fairy stories', or as one cynical journalist referred to it: 'The Myth of the Megumawaach'.

There are many others though—a surprising number—who nod affirmatively when they discuss the matter, even though the theory is not the sort of thing they ascribe to in their day-to-day lives.

Every outlandish theory has its believers of course, but in this instance subsequent events have tilted things in their favour.

One of these events involved the search for Henry's horse. As it turns out, no one living along the river, in the area he liked to paddle past, owned the black horse he claimed to have seen—or any horse at all for that matter.

I let the truth of the theory remain an open question. Who can say what's real and what's not? It's up to each of us to decide.

1

Grace hated this cottage—or 'Grace O'Malley's Castle' as she dubbed it—but she wouldn't have to put up with it much longer.

It was the spot where her family deposited everything broken in their lives that they chose not to discard. Their cast-off furniture that creaked and groaned in its misery, begrudging its every use, the junk passed down through generations that could not be discarded—and of course Grace.

For days it seemed that all she'd done in the evenings was pace from one end of the cottage to the other.

It would soon be time to begin the adventure of a lifetime and she could hardly wait.

The cottage was seldom used anymore, since her mother and step-father had sold their house in town and bought a large place overlooking the ocean. They had held on to the cottage for the day when Grace or one of her two younger step-siblings—the children of her mother and step-father—would marry and produce grandchildren. An increasingly unlikely prospect in Grace's case given that she hated children. And lately, Grace's parents were more inclined to accept her reluctance to have any offspring because her boyfriends were inevitably useless layabouts and criminals.

This place had bad memories for Grace. When she was a kid the family would come here for a month every summer. They'd play with kids from the neighbouring cottages.

"Something always happened to me," Grace would say later, "the sort of things that happen to girls and not boys." She refused to say anything more on the subject except that she hated kids and would never have any of her own.

The therapy started when she was thirteen, after an incident at the cottage.

The raccoons in the area were always around, scouting for scraps and turning over garbage cans. They were clever things who could get into anything, no matter what you did to shut them out. And there was a huge population of the critters.

One day Grace looked out her bedroom window to see eight raccoons on the lawn in front of the cottage. They fascinated and disgusted her. It was a war between us and them she decided. Hadn't her step-father always said that? "In the end it'll be them or me. One of us has to go."

The family was out but Grace knew where her step-father kept his .22 rifle and she took it from his bedroom closet. The shells were on the closet shelf. She inserted a clip holding ten bullets into the rifle and went outside.

Within three minutes the bodies of eight dead raccoons were strewn about the lawn. Grace was pleased with herself and stacked the corpses in a corner of the yard to show her family that she'd found a remedy to their raccoon problem. It had been easy enough to come up with a solution. All it took was the desire to act instead of just talking to no effect.

When the family came home and saw the pile of dead raccoons, Grace received no praise. Her mother was horrified and went to her bedroom to be alone.

Her step-father said nothing and looked shaken. Over the course of that day he carted the raccoons, two at a time, far back into the bush on the other side of the road and heaved them into the undergrowth.

That night, and the next day, Grace's parents huddled and discussed what to do. She wouldn't return to school. She would be home schooled by her mother. When they returned to the city there would be therapy.

Her step-siblings were told not to discuss Grace's problems with their friends.

The fist therapist declared that it was simply a phase of Grace's mental development and not to worry. A kind of temporary insanity as it were. And the therapist may have been correct, as nothing like the raccoon incident happened again.

Grace felt deserted however. No one understood. No one was there for her. Her step-siblings avoided her like she was a freak.

Grace's first arrest, for break and enter, came when she was fifteen. She was sentenced to juvenile detention.

Her step-father hoped that the police wouldn't find out that Grace had psychiatric issues and resented authority. It might end up leading to an extended incarceration and he wouldn't do that to Grace. If she got caught up in the system with specialists trying to change her nature she might be trapped for life. Grace would never be good.

2

*Drawing of the Irish
Mythological Hero*

Henry Hebert stripped off his clothes and plunged into the water. It was still summer but the stream remained frigid.

He swam twenty metres upstream, responding to the cold with furiously kicking feet and stabbing arms. His heart pounding and his blood pumping, he soon adjusted to the icy temperature.

Henry reversed course and swam downstream at a more leisurely place.

The stream was a fast-moving tributary of the Megumawaach River and emptied into it a kilometre downstream. Henry's daily immersion began in late March when he moved to the area. It wasn't based on some machismo notion about conquering nature, taking all that it could throw at you and withstanding it. Nor was it based on wanting to 'feel alive'. In Henry's words, his swimming was about "adapting my life to being in this place and this environment."

That was a fair enough reason, but it hadn't changed the fact that he was still afraid of nature. He was especially spooked by the forest noises he'd hear as he made his way along the bush trail between the river and his house.

This fear wasn't a bad thing for a romantic to confront. Nature can kill you at almost any moment without so much as a twinge of guilt. It's brutality wasn't an aberration. Nature was seldom idyllic.

Pagan's mother, Aisling, had her own take on that. She was known to say that the inhabitants of the forest are a brotherhood to which we belong, but in spite of that, "Nature is cyclic. For there to be rebirth there must first be death. That too is part of nature. You must accept that everything adheres to its true nature in the end; to its authentic spirit. If animals kill one anther it's not from a lack of mutual respect."

Sometimes Henry's swim was followed by an exploratory canoe trip up or down the stream. He liked to spot nesting birds high up in the trees, to watch eagles and ospreys soaring, and to glimpse the flash of a salmon in one of the ponds as it fled from him, ever elusive.

Is it any wonder that, in the Irish myths that Aisling often cited, a salmon was the repository of all knowledge?

Henry had been quickly disabused of any notion that there was peace and quiet in nature, away from the city. As he slid along the stream or river he would listen to the threats and seductions of the songbirds and to the chirps, buzzes, trills and other noises, all of mysterious origin to a young man who'd spent his entire life in Toronto.

Gliding down the stream, as it meandered through the bush, provided Henry with a new sense of awe at the slow daily transformation of the flora as it went from buds to impassable sprawl.

On the side of the stream opposite his house, the trees that crowded its banks gave way to a grassy hill. On more than one occasion, as Henry passed by, he'd seen a black horse that had wandered over the crest of the hill to graze on the down slope leading to the water's edge. On seeing Henry the creature always stood still—except for its tail, busily swishing away bugs—and locked eyes with him. Henry had never seen anything so breathtaking.

It was for exactly this that he'd left Toronto.

Henry climbed from the water and dressed, his clothes having been fastidiously laid over his upturned canoe resting on the bank.

As he usually did, Henry then sat down on the bank to take a breather before walking home. He loved being able to observe nature in this close proximity. He plucked a fern and —not for the first time—marvelled at the lattice threads that ran through it. All nature, he had come to realize, was unique, complex, miraculous, and beautiful, coming in all shapes, sizes, colours, textures, and smells. Sometimes he reflected that this applied to women too since they were also part of nature. Those wistful thoughts occurred at moments when he was ruing his lack of companionship to share these moments with.

Henry began the walk back to his house, a two-story farmhouse of indeterminate age with wide oak baseboards and moulding, and with scratched and worn hardwood floors. He'd been determined to restore it to its former glory but had quickly realized that the wood-framed windows would be insufficient to keep out the cold in winter, so he replaced them himself.

He had rescued old furnishings to fill the house. The furniture was worn, but by life being lived. A corner of the Persian carpet that he'd found in a thrift shop was nearly bald but it was likely the result of passing footsteps or of children playing. The sofa, that had been left in the house by the previous owner, had threads torn lose at its corners courtesy of some rude cat or other. As a result, the house felt full of life.

Henry's ambition, in moving to this area, was to be a homesteader. In spite of the fact that his initial garden was pathetic, at best, he hoped that someday he'd be able to grow his own food and generate his own power. Ideally, he'd eventually get right off the grid.

He knew that he'd also have to either work part-time, have a sideline business, or generate some income as a writer.

After breakfast, with the latter thought in mind, his plan was to work on his mystery novel. For four months he'd bounced between renovations and writing. Both long term projects. Both stopping him from socializing.

Henry would eye the vendors at the farmer's market—especially the small scale producers of crafts or organic food—and wonder if some of them might be fellow travellers; people like himself who were interested in the environment and self-sufficiency.

His isolation wasn't complete, however, because he had the company of the fictional people he wrote about. But fictional acquaintances can only take you so far.

In the morning he'd be driving to Moncton for a

convention of the Union of Atlantic Mystery Writers. When he registered for the event it had occurred to him that—along with getting some help with writing—he might make a new friend or two.

3

Pagan had an image of her flatmate Darla in mind when she'd described one of the characters in the novel she was currently working on as 'statuesque'.

She was now wavering. The word, to some, might imply 'voluptuous' and that wasn't right. It was Darla's manner of carriage and height that Pagan had been thinking of.

Observing Darla, at this moment, it occurred to Pagan that 'stately' might be a more apt adjective. 'Regal'? 'Majestic'?

By contrast, Pagan had once heard herself referred to as 'diminutive'. If she was describing herself she might instead opt for a synonym implying both small of stature and magical, like 'fairylike', 'spritelike', 'brownieish', 'elfin', or even 'pixieish'.

"I thought you'd settled on driving down?" Darla said. She was washing dishes with her back to Pagan who was standing in the kitchen doorway.

"I said I was thinking about it," Pagan replied, in reference to attending the next day's mystery writer's convention.

Darla paused, her hands still immersed in soapy water. She turned her head sideways to display a profile of natural animal nobility. "Well, none of my business, but this thing sounds like a good idea for getting out of the house and meeting some new people. You dumped Patrick because he was too boring but you haven't ..."

"Did I say Patrick was too boring?"

"Oh, not in so many words I suppose."

"And I didn't dump Patrick. It was a mutual decision."

"Okay, well, I thought you wanted more variety in your life. Or was it excitement? I thought that's what you said."

Pagan didn't reply. It was true. She remembered now that she'd indeed said it one evening. "I badly need some excitement in my life," were her exact words.

The two years of living with Patrick had been mostly dull routine. Every night he'd go off to the gym while she wrote. She'd had enough time to herself to complete her first two novels. That in itself might not have been a bad thing since she loved writing and the solitude—she was a bard after all, as her mother Aisling often said—but it led to a need for some adventure and intellectual stimulation the rest of the time, and that had gone lacking.

It had seemed okay in the beginning but life gradually came to feel like living in a closet, hidden away from the world. An existence without fun or magic. This was worsened as Pagan ceased having any social life of her own.

In time, Patrick had come to control both the what and the when regarding their shared, and very meagre social life. That he was controlling didn't occur to Pagan for a long time because his control wasn't overt. If there was a new restaurant she wanted to try, instead of going to Patrick's favourite, he'd agree and then moan about how awful the food was. Same thing when they went to Pagan's choice of movie. No reasons were given for his disapproval in either case. He even mocked her preferences.

Pagan eventually submerged her own tastes. It was easier that way; to just do Patrick's favourite things. She'd allowed it to happen.

In an act of bravery, she eventually ended up online looking for a new place to live. Seven months ago she'd answered Darla's ad for a flatmate and moved in.

Ironically, given Pagan's desire for a life free from boredom, since leaving Patrick she'd filled her time with writing her third novel. It was a way to understand and sort through her recent life. It was a means of self-discovery. Something that she was compelled to do.

The result was that she now needed some excitement in her life more than ever. It was dawning on her though, that she'd forgotten how to find it.

Darla's cell phone rang. She vigorously shook the soap suds from her wet hands. Rather than drying them, she self-consciously fluffed up her short-cropped hair before snatching up the phone from the table.

Pagan retreated to her bedroom but left the door open because she'd been trying lately to stop shutting herself off from the world.

She walked to the window, drawn to the sunshine perhaps, or to the outdoors. But there wasn't much of either to be seen here, since the window faced north.

She looked out on the backyard of the century home. The lawn had been paved over for use as a parking lot for the tenants of the four apartments. The only vehicles in it at this moment were her black Honda Civic and her roommate's blue Sentra, parked on opposite sides of the lot.

Pagan slowly walked a well trodden route around her room—her path when she wanted to think—letting her fingers lightly drag across the front of her desk and then over a shelf in her bookcase where they traversed the spines of the books there. Her fingertips delighted in the sensual pleasure of *Mi'kmaq Landscapes*, *The Poetry of Sappho*, *Irish Fairy Tales* by James Stephens, *Medea and Other Plays*, *Norse Mythology*, *The Second Sex*, *The House of the Spirits*, and *William Blake: Visionary*.

She sat down at her recently acquired IKEA desk and automatically opened her laptop, but she then just stared off into space, listening. She didn't mean to eavesdrop. Darla's voice, delightedly conversing with her boyfriend Wolf, was just there.

"Uh huh. Uh huh. No, no, just talking to Pagan, trying to convince her to go to a writer's convention tomorrow and take a break from scheming about ..." Darla dropped her voice an ominous octave, "the perfect ... bank ... robbery." She laughed at her own joke which referenced an unpublished mystery novel written by Pagan—her first—about a couple who pulled off what Pagan described as a perfect bank heist.

At that same moment, as if trying to live up to the

lascivious and predatory implications of his name, Wolf—a policeman stationed in Megumawaach—was locked in eye contact and smiles with a curvy, blonde, lady constable. Darla's words flowed in and out of his brain like spilled water.

"So I should be home by seven but if I'm late just let yourself in," Darla concluded.

There was still no reply.

"Wolf?"

"Er … yeah, yeah I'm here. He was convinced that the attractive lady constable had "a thing" for him. He thought it was why she was hanging around the exit instead of leaving. "Gotta go. See ya tomorrow."

When Darla ended her phone call she went to the picture window in the livingroom, at the front of the apartment, and craned her head to the right so she could see all the way to the end of the street.

The little red car wasn't there. Not surprising. It was usually only there on Saturday or Sunday mornings, and Darla hadn't seen it at all for the last several weeks.

A vehicle parked on the street was in itself no surprise. Drivers unloaded their dogs here then took them along the bush trail that began where the street ended. But the driver of this car never left his vehicle.

It had been her "intuition," she said, since she didn't know where the idea came from, that started Darla wondering if the driver was watching someone, and that someone was Pagan.

Wolf ran the car's license plate and they had their answer. Darla's intuition was correct. Yet she didn't tell Pagan about her stalker, based on Wolf's advice.

Wolf was now logging all the times the red car was spotted parked out front; building a case against the driver.

4

The Fomors (or The Power of Evil Abroad in the World)

Grace had driven all the way to Maine from Megumawaach to purchase the pirate masks. They'd taken awhile to source online but they were perfect.

And the long drive to a place where she was unknown was worth it too because no one would be able to name her afterwards as the woman who bought the masks. They likely wouldn't even remember her.

She'd immediately dubbed the mask with a female face, "Grace O'Malley," recalling the notorious Irish pirate whose name she'd adopted.

When she was a teenager, Grace and her small circle of close friends had given themselves the names of famous pirates as nicknames. It was a game that reinforced their sense of being an exclusive gang.

Since none of them shared their first name with a famous pirate they went with second names. Grace's given name was Elizabeth Grace. Others took the pirate names of Mary Read and Calico Jack Rackham. And there was even a Blackbeard, because the boy who adopted it shared the pirate's Christian name of Edward. When Grace again became close to her step-sister, she named her Anne Bonny and began to call her Annie.

They all agreed that matching second names was better than matching first names since it made for a secret bond. It was the first thing in Grace's life that had ever felt exactly right.

Of the group, Grace was the most enamoured with the game, so much so that she took to using the name Grace at all times. She felt that it expressed her essential nature.

The second pirate mask, the one featuring masculine features—christened Calico Jack—was named after Grace's soon to be kidnapping accomplice.

Rounding out their disguises for the crime were the green gloves that Grace discovered in the gardening section of a dollar store in Sussex on her drive back home. That they had to be green had been drummed into her head by Calico Jack. No other colour would do.

Grace didn't like being bossed but she went along with it —this one last time. Those occasions of being a follower, of being unappreciated and unheard, would soon be remnants of a forgotten past. Life was about to change. She knew it.

It felt as if she was on a precipice about to leap off. And she badly wanted to make that jump.

There was something else that had always stirred in her nature, but it had been suppressed. Grace couldn't identify what it was precisely but she knew she was close to being transformed and fulfilling her destiny. She merely had to let go and let the spirits take over.

The impending kidnapping and robbery was the second time in her life that something felt exactly right. She'd known it since that day when she met Pagan and heard the story of the pirate robbers. Everything fell so perfectly into place that she knew it was meant to be.

The plan demanded waiting for the right moment, but that time was now at hand. Before long, everyone would know about Grace O'Malley, the notorious and brutal pirate of the Megumawaach River.

5

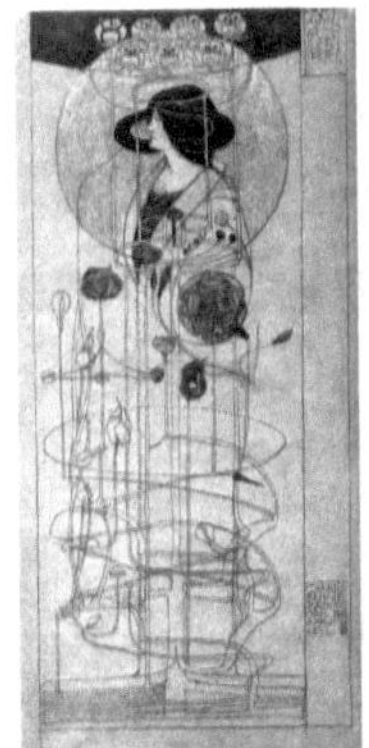

Part Seen, Part Imagined

Henry was running late. His trip down the two-lane coastal highway had begun well enough but he soon ended up as the caboose in a long train of cars trailing a driver who was puttering along at the speed limit.

Peering ahead he couldn't see anyone overtaking the lead car. The other drivers seemed to be reconciled to the idea that one pokey driver would set the speed for everyone else.

Henry was antsy at first. He wanted to speed up. A car from Quebec and another from Ontario managed to pass the line by leapfrogging multiple cars at a time. Henry's impulse was to follow suit, but he hesitated. The out of province license plates had suggested something. Perhaps, he thought, his desire to have his foot heavy on the gas pedal, with the world whizzing by, was due to his Toronto upbringing. Torontonians were constantly frustrated from sitting in traffic jams. It led to the normalization of irrational and dangerous driving.

Maybe the sanguine attitude of the New Brunswick drivers was a reflection of living life at a different rhythm. He decided to be patient and embrace the slower pace. Another instance of "adapting my life to being in this place and this environment." He opened his truck window and breathed deeply.

Henry occupied himself during the rest of his plodding drive by marvelling at the lush forests and sea vistas. He closely observed the palatial homes overlooking the ocean. He'd been given to understand that many of these houses were the summer homes of rich Québecers.

He wished the houses gone. They were obstructing his view.

Toronto with its intensity, crowding, and anxiety inducing atmosphere, had sometimes left him feeling like the veneer of civil society could disappear at any minute in an explosion of animal ferocity. Toronto was thankfully receding in his consciousness.

Living out of the city, his perception of nature was shifting, just a bit at a time. It was never seismic.

He was well versed in the environmental science that spoke about the sea as a climate sink and trees as oxygen factories. Protecting the earth had led him to demos at Queen's Park and Parliament Hill.

But the reality here, away from Toronto, was to be overwhelmed with the realization that there was magic and wonder in the ocean and forests. Some unidentifiable quality had begun to make its presence felt.

When Henry arrived at the Moncton Library he couldn't find a nearby parking space. A festival had taken over the whole of the downtown and there was also some sort of convention at the arena up the road.

The parking space he finally found was six blocks away. It struck him as an odd place to locate the city's only library. Since it was downtown, almost no one lived nearby so school-aged kids couldn't walk there on their own after school as he had done when he was young. An act that instilled a permanent love of reading. And on Saturdays like this—with all the congestion—he imagined that even adults with small children would stay away.

Henry had to sprint to get to the library on time. He managed to slip into the main floor conference room just before the doors closed to begin the daylong convention of mystery writers.

There were five rows of tables in the room and almost all the chairs were taken. Henry found a vacant spot in the last row.

He didn't notice Pagan, seated in row two. She was deep in conversation with a young man in a baseball cap so she didn't notice Henry either.

The session began with every person in attendance standing and stating who they were and where they were from and, in a sentence or two, telling the group about their current book project. In spite of that direction, some people excitedly went on at great length about their work in progress until the moderator had to halt them.

One person indicated that the genre he was writing was 'mind fiction'.

Instead of talking about her current effort, Pagan mentioned that the novel she'd finished the year before was about to be published and she hadn't gotten far on her new novel.

When Henry's turn came around he explained that his initial project was doing its best to convince him that he had no discernible writing talent whatsoever so he wouldn't dream of boring anyone with details of the project. Most people laughed.

The moderator eventually thanked everyone and introduced the first speaker, a wizened old man who spent fifteen minutes bragging about himself, his historical mysteries, and his non-fiction books, before giving his take on the question of whether to lay out a plot before starting a book or to let it develop as you go along.

"Don't begin with a plot," he told the group. "People think of it as a skeletal structure, so they assume it must come first, but, if you do that, you may end up throwing away your best ideas. Plot is what your characters do over a period of time, so begin by creating characters, flesh them out a bit, then put them in scenes to develop them further. Pretend you're a child with some new dolls. You name them, dress them, figure out who they are, and then invent situations where they interact with each other. They might agree and they might argue. Sure enough, eventually, one of them will stab or shoot another one of them."

Henry was jotting down notes but his eyes began to drift over the convention participants. They were, almost without exception, senior citizens. He imagined that, like him, they were readers who'd always nurtured the idea that when they had the time they'd try their hand at writing; to share their voices and wisdom. He decided that their presence affirmed his decision to take a serious stab at being an author while still in his late twenties.

He began to watch Pagan.

Sitting, listening attentively to the speaker, she continuously twisted her longish hair round and round through her fingers then let it slide liquidly over them. Henry was hypnotized.

He'd first noticed her when she stood up to talk about her current project. Oddly, her jeans also caught his eye. What Henry knew about women's clothing amounted to pretty much nothing but he did recognize the name on the tag on her jeans. His last job had been managing a store owned by an environmental charity to raise funds for their operations and their inventory included a small collection of clothing. Part of his job had been to order the clothes so he knew the jeans were from a company that made "eco-friendly and organic" clothes, said to last twenty years or more.

He'd heard a theory. People don't express themselves in their choice of clothing; they disguise themselves. They dress to try and to control what other people think of them.

The theory popped into his head. Was this woman environmentally conscious or had it become a trendy enough stance for people to pretend to be that way?

He stopped this line of thought wondering how he'd gotten so cynical.

Henry continued to watch Pagan twirling her hair until he suddenly chastised himself. It's like I've never seen a woman before, he thought. Four months on an isolated hobby farm and here I am, acting like a man dying of thirst who spots an oasis, or a scientist who discovers a specimen he's never seen before and puts it under a microscope. Pathetic.

His shame prompted him to re-focus on the speaker.

The afternoon session of the convention was a series of workshops. It kicked off with attendees sitting in small circles, critiquing photocopied two page samples of each other's work.

Pagan's and Henry's groups were on opposite sides of the

room. Within his circle, Henry's chair faced the front of the room. Pagan's chair was aimed directly towards Henry.

He might be good looking, Pagan thought, but he obviously hasn't had a haircut in a long time. Was he a mountain man, too lazy to cut his hair, or a heavy metal singer? The possibilities rolled through her thoughts.

And even short beards like this guy's always made her wonder if its purpose was to disguise the lack of a chin.

His wavy locks however, would undoubtedly please Aisling.

Pagan always told her friends that her mother was a hippie but she now wondered if that was precise enough. Pagan sometimes struggled with words in her love affair with them.

How about 'unreformed hippie'? But then, wasn't 'unreformed' meant for sinners? Might 'incurable' be a better choice? No, that suggested sickness. 'Obsessed'? Did that suggest a mental aberration?

Pagan thought of her mother's interest in astrology, tarot cards, witchcraft, veganism, and all things Celtic. She settled on the phrase 'committed Neo-Pagan'. She liked it. It invoked the idea of someone adhering to a set of spiritual beliefs and a certain sort of life.

She continued watching Henry, trying to read him the way one reads a mime, from movement alone. Pagan often studied people as they interacted with each other with this in mind. She also liked to watch television with the sound muted. It left her free to imagine the plot of the show and the nature of the characters, and their inter-relationships.

The young man with the bushman's hair that Pagan had focused her attention on smiled and laughed lightly at things said by the other participants in the group. He looked shy, and possibly uncertain of himself. One of the older woman in the group—well they were all old—so the one with reddish-brown hair with grey flecks—would you call that 'roan'?—seemed to be, no, was definitely speaking solely to the mystery guy alone, like he was an object of fascination, or had charms she wanted to suss out. Was she flirting? Lonely?

The word "flinty" came to mind as an adjective to describe

the man. She'd used it once in regards to a character. "The door-darkening Bruce studied Effie with a flinty expression on his face." So no, 'flinty' meant unkind and cold. It wasn't the right word at all. 'Stony'? No, that was too much like 'flinty'.

She'd write her imaginary version of this guy across the room as something like a stone however. Ordinary in a way, but when cracked open, some rare and precious elements were revealed. "Sparkling flecks of gold and silver glinted in the sun." Yes, that would do.

6

from *Irish Fairy Tales*

Wolf parked his car in front of a house in downtown Megumawaach. He was there to pick up Darla for their dinner date.

Pagan and Darla's two-bedroom apartment was on the second floor of a converted Victorian house. It was situated in a once affluent neighbourhood; likely the former home of someone of prominence.

The flat had character. Its wide oak baseboards and window frames had been stripped of paint at some point and refinished. Its hardwood floorboards that creaked under your feet had gotten the same treatment.

Wolf hadn't intended on arriving so early. If things had gone the way he hoped, at this moment he'd be chatting up the curvy blonde cop at the station, pretending to be a nice single guy—his usual scam—but she'd been detained on a domestic call.

He swore to himself on getting the news and then, with nothing else to do, he came straight to the apartment despite knowing it would be up to an hour before Darla arrived home.

Wolf let himself in.

Pagan would have been distressed about what was happening back home had she known about it.

She hated the fact that Wolf had an apartment key so he could get in to wait for Darla when nobody was home. She imagined that if he ever made use of the key he would soon be rummaging through her room and her things—and she was creeped out by the thought. It wouldn't do.

She toyed with the idea of telling Darla that she was uncomfortable with Wolf having access to their flat when they weren't at home but how could she go about that? If she said anything, Darla would likely jump to her boyfriend's defence and the end result would be a strain on their friendship.

Pagan didn't like Wolf. He was a creep. Three times he'd made suggestive comments to her when Darla wasn't nearby and this past week he'd positioned himself about a centimetre behind her. Pagan had felt his stale breath on her neck. She'd slipped off sideways rather than back up into the predator.

She'd decided at that moment that in the future she would remain acutely aware of Wolf's location whenever he was anywhere in close proximity to her.

When Pagan told her mother that Darla's boyfriend was named Wolf, Aisling had said, "Beware of him. In Celtic myth, wolves can be shape-shifters to disguise their evil hearts."

Wolf's disguise was somewhat less than perfect.

Soon after entering the apartment, looking decidedly flinty, with a stony expression on his face, Wolf was wandering about as if he owned the place.

In Darla's bedroom he did a rigorous scan to suss out any secrets.

Next, he went into Pagan's room, poked around and looked through her dresser drawers. He opened the closet door and nosed about. He ran his hand lightly over the clothes on hangers in an act of further violation. Noting the two handgun cases on the closet shelf, he took one down and had a look. It was locked with three small dollar store locks. Easy enough to break into.

His sole judgment of Pagan was that, while she dressed conservatively, she was still 'hot'. He was sorry that she wasn't there. He'd told himself that one of these days when the two were alone he'd press his amorous attentions. I don't buy the prim and proper act, he thought, sitting down on her bed, she's repressed and just needs the right encouragement.

In front of him, in the desk drawer, was a spiral bound notebook. Not for the first time, he took it out and opened it.

On the cover, Pagan had written: "Plot Outline For <u>The Pirate Robbers</u>."

Wolf flicked through the pages and began reading bits here and there—as he always did. But when he came to the detailed description of the bank robbery, he began reading in earnest.

The robbery began with a home invasion and the abduction of the two small children of a bank manager. The manager was told that if she ever wanted to see her kids again that she must go into work and divert a huge amount of money from her bank to an offshore account.

The kidnapper/robbers intended to then shuffle the money through several other bank transactions so that it was untraceable.

Wolf got up off the bed and sat down at the desk, committed to his task.

He spent the next ten minutes carefully reading the rest of the outline, nodding at each step in the story and each financial transaction. Bloody genius, he thought, but he quickly qualified his judgment. It wasn't as brilliant as the robbery plan he'd come up with if he chose to design one himself, being a trained cop and all.

Just as he finished reading the outline, the sound of Darla's key in the apartment door lock caused him to flip the notebook closed, put it back in the desk, return the desk chair to its previous position, and exit the room before Darla was fully inside the flat.

Darla heard the creaking of the floorboards, and may have known that Wolf had been in Pagan's room, but either she had something else on her mind or she didn't have any concern about where he'd been because she smiled when she saw him.

7

The Bridesmaid

The final segment of the convention began around 5:00 PM in the ballroom above a restaurant. It was intended to be an informal get-together. A chance to meet and mingle, and to make contacts.

The lights in the ballroom were dimmed. Individual tables with chairs encircling them were spaced along the west side of the room. The middle of the room was open.

Small groups of conventioneers clustered here and there, especially in front of the cash bar. The buzz of their conversation was audible over the wallpaper music being emitted by a spectacular sound system sitting off in a corner, seriously underused except for an initial ear-splitting blast that was immediately quelled.

Either by chance or design, Pagan and Henry found themselves side-by-side in one of the two lines of people shuffling towards the first of two buffet tables set end-to-end in front of the stage.

They exchanged smiles and said hello.

"What did you think of the talks?" Henry asked.

"I thought they were good," Pagan replied. "I'm thinking about offering to give a seminar on guns next year. People were talking about pistols and revolvers as if they're the same thing, for example."

"So you know your firearms."

"Of course. I'm a mystery writer so I like to shoot people. … Actually I'm no expert, I just know the basics. I took the firearms training courses with my dad, years ago, and we did a lot of shooting. I still have our semi-automatic handguns on the shelf in my bedroom closet."

When Pagan and Henry eventually got to the buffet tables they each took up a drink and a paper plate. Over and over both set down their drinks to pick up something from one of the platters of sandwiches and finger food to add to their own plate. Both opted for the vegetarian options.

"Congratulations on your book," Henry said as they neared the end of the second table.

"Thank you. I thought that your introduction was … interesting. Everyone was enthused about their own book project and talking it up, and proud of it, except you. Are you really that negative about your own writing? It sounds like you're ready to give up."

"I'm on my way there. Frustrated, I guess. Maybe I just set my expectations too high."

"Well, I'm not posing as an expert but I think that writing's like almost every other skill. We stumble around at first before we walk. Anyway you're here, and you're learning, so you're still at it."

"Yeah, but at this point I suspect I'm writing solely for my own entertainment."

The pair were distracted enough by their brief conversation to have lost track of what they were doing. They had stopped at the end of the buffet table holding a drink in one hand and a full paper plate in the other.

Simultaneously, they became aware of being boulders in the stream of hungry writers.

In unison, they took a couple of steps sideways until bumping up against the stage. They set their plates on the stage and stood face to face, each holding a drink.

From a distance Henry would have said that Pagan's hair was brown, but now, up close, he saw shades of russet and auburn. Her eyes were green, and there was a pinkish shade to her cheeks with subtle flecks of faded freckles across her nose. Viking influence amid a darker Celtic inheritance, Henry guessed, based on her Irish surname: Egan.

"I don't see anything wrong with writing for yourself," Pagan said, "if that's what it comes to. Not everybody has to write to be published. I think, with myself, that sometimes writing is a form of therapy that helps me work out things in my life. I imagine that I'd write even if no one ever read any of it. ... But I wonder how you came to the conclusion that you can't write. Did someone trash your manuscript?"

"No. I don't know anyone who writes and if I did I don't know if I'm at the point where I'd let them read it. I'd be very self-conscious, I think, like I was showing off my dirty laundry. And I'd feel it was presumptuous to ask someone to read what I've written."

"I know those feelings. I wish I was a bit more like the people who are egotists, who think they're brilliant and want to show off. I spent two years writing my first novel and no one's read it."

"No one?"

"Well, maybe one person but I doubt it. I mustered up the courage to send a copy to an agent, back before I learned I should have just sent a query letter and an outline. I wish I'd known that beforehand because it cost me an arm and a leg to print and mail the stupid thing, even with my roommate's discount at the copy shop where she works."

"So it could be another *War and Peace* and you might never know."

"Oh, I'd know. It's a little bit bad, not dreadful, but it was a great learning experience."

"I've read about published authors who sent manuscripts to hundreds of agents and publishers before they were published. I doubt I'd have that sort of stubbornness to keep sending stuff out if I was them."

"You and me both."

Henry and Pagan fell silent and focused on their food. They'd run out of small talk, as strangers do.

Gradually, while they ate, they turned towards the room, shifting positions one notch at a time until their backs were against the stage.

They watched their fellow mystery writers, diverted by each staccato burst of laughter from an individual or group.

With their conversation at an end, Henry began to say that he was going to get a drink at the bar when Pagan said, "I noticed in the introductions that you're from Megumawaach, like me, but our paths have never crossed. Have you lived there long?"

"Only about four months. I moved here from Toronto."

"Oh, and how do you like New Brunswick?"

"I haven't seen much of it." That brought the conversation to a screeching halt, again. Henry silently chastised himself for having lost his conversational skills in four months.

Pagan resumed her interest in the people socializing on the ballroom floor. It was her turn to consider greener conversational pastures. As she was about to strike out, having spotted the man she'd sat beside at the presentations that morning, Henry asked, "Were you born in Megumawaach?"

"In the hospital there, so yes, but I never lived in the city growing up. My parents' house was near a small town a ways away."

"That's like me. I said I was from Megumawaach because it's easier than explaining where I really do live. I recently bought an old house that I'm renovating. It's on the side of a secondary highway. I call it a hobby farm although I don't know if it technically qualifies."

"That's quite a change from Toronto."

"It is. A big adjustment. I wanted to live more self-sufficiently, with some land and a large garden."

"So you're not just a writer but a farmer and builder too."

"No. I have about as much talent for farming and renovations as I do for writing. I'm trying to fix up the house myself but everything I do needs to be re-done. I learn how to do something by screwing it up on my first try. And I keep finding new ways to hurt myself. I smash my hands with the hammer on a regular basis. Actually, I can do some serious self-damage with almost every tool."

Pagan feigned a wince. "Ouch. It must give you a greater sense of satisfaction though, when you're finished a job."

"I suppose."

"And you're done with the renos?"

"Not by a long shot. Just the basics so far. I put in new windows, and solar panels, and did some insulation too, so I'm trying to do my bit for the environment. ... And that's also part of the reason that why I want to have a vegetable garden."

"Very good."

"It's not much but it's something tangible. I was active in an environmental group in Toronto but nothing here so far, so I'm more focused on living an eco-friendly life. I understand that environmental improvements require legislation but I've met people who think—because of that—they have no obligation to change anything in their own lives. I think individuals and communities can make a tremendous impact for the good so … Sorry. I'm preaching."

"No, not at all. Are you going to get involved with any environmental groups here?"

"In time … soon. I know there's a lot of great groups in New Brunswick focused on issues like spraying in forests and waterways, forestry practices and bird habitat, wetlands, energy, education … I just haven't joined any yet."

The couple had been gradually turning as they spoke so that they were once again facing each other, more relaxed than previously. If you were watching from across the room and trying to read them, the way you would a mime, you'd likely conclude that they were beginning to become friends.

"I bet Tolstoy couldn't install a solar panel," Pagan said.

"Oh, you're just saying that to make me feel better."

"True. He was probably a whiz at it. By the way, you didn't say where your hobby farm is."

"On Jersey Road. At the front of the property there's a concrete block building facing the road. The previous owners used it as a workshop to make wooden furniture."

"And before that there was a cheese maker. I know the place. And I know one of your neighbours. He's a … a family friend. In fact, I'll be seeing him next weekend at a wedding rehearsal at my mother's."

Pagan suddenly turned away, as if upset, and plunked her back once again against the stage.

Henry wondered if he'd said something wrong. He added hesitantly, "A wedding. That's exciting."

"Oh, yeah. Yeah. A family wedding too." Pagan's tone

couldn't have been flatter and less enthusiastic.

"I see you're pumped."

"Uh huh. Yeah, over the moon. I can't think of anything I'd rather be doing."

"You said 'family wedding'. Is it your sister getting married?"

Pagan twisted her head to look at Henry accusingly. "And I'm the jealous, wallflower sister? Please."

Her chin in the air, she turned her attention back to the other conventioneers.

Henry persevered. His social skills had grown numb but he felt certain that Pagan wanted her story to be sussed out; that they were now playing a guessing game. "No, no, I didn't mean it like that. Sorry, I'm being nosy but I assumed it would be someone around your age. ... Your brother maybe?"

Pagan lazily shook her head back and forth.

"Cousin?"

Another slow shake and, "No."

Henry was out of suspects but he was intrigued. "I don't know anything about your parents, if they're still together or not but you said the rehearsal lunch is going to be at your mother's so I'm wondering if she's the one getting married."

Pagan didn't answer which was answer enough.

"And you're not happy with it. Do you hate ... the groom?"

"Oh no, he's quite nice. But ..." Pagan turned sharply and was again face to face with Henry.

He interrupted, "But he's broke and after her money."

"No. He's doing quite well for himself plus he's too simple and direct to manage any kind of stratagem. And he's too upright to do something like that anyway."

"Okay, he hit on you and you don't trust him."

She laughed. "No and no! And he adores her."

Another pause in Henry's sleuthing while he considered other possibilities. "Okay. He's eighty and she's forty-five."

"Forty-seven and twenty."

"Your mother is twenty? Oh wait, stupid me. Oh geez. The

groom is twenty? That's younger than ..."

"Exactly! I don't know what she sees in him."

"Well, I wonder ...?" Henry pondered.

Pagan stared expectantly but Henry was stalled either by indecision or the lack of an alternative explanation. She eventually said, "Thank you for not echoing my friend Lindy's crude speculations about the reason, although I can see the physical part of things might be appealing after years with my drunken father who's best days are probably long past. But that hardly seems like enough reason to marry someone."

Henry, wishing to avoid a line of inquiry that might require some stick handling, said safely, "Empty nest syndrome maybe?"

"You mean, she wants to mother him?"

"It's a thought."

"Possibly. Likely, even."

"Although it could be he just makes her happy, I guess. Maybe they have shared interests."

"Well, they do to some extent, but is that enough? The thing is that I keep thinking, 'How long will it last?'. Jarrod's a simple guy. Inexperienced. I don't want my mother to get hurt. And what really freaks me out is that they're talking about having or adopting kids."

"Ah." Henry had no answer for that.

"Geez, listen to me. Do I sound like a kid upset that her mother's getting remarried; secretly wanting her parents to reconnect?"

"No, I ..."

"Because I'm not, not at all, I'd just rather he was a man nearer her age instead of a child from your neck of the woods."

"My neck ... where does this guy live?"

"He owns the farm directly east of you. He's your next door neighbour."

"... Next door? ... All the bee hives? Ah, okay, now I know who you're talking about. I think so anyway. There's a young guy. He came over to say hello when I moved in. Very friendly." With a shocked look spreading across his face, Henry added, "That's the groom? And it's his farm?"

"Yeah."

"Geez, I thought he was just a kid. A teenager living with his parents."

"Exactly."

"Oh my. I see a bit of what you mean. He may be twenty but he looks seventeen and he's marrying a woman near fifty, I can ..."

"I know looks shouldn't come into it but it creeps me out every time I see them together. The thought of them pushing a baby carriage. Eww. I just hope at the rehearsal I don't say anything."

"Really?"

"Not really, no."

The two of them were quiet for a moment.

Pagan reached out and clasped Henry's arm. "Listen, if you want someone to read your book and give you some feedback I'll be happy to. I know it's not finished but if it would be of any use to you I can look at it."

And that was how the plan was struck that Henry would courier Pagan his manuscript and she would come by his place in a week's time, at noon on the Saturday of the wedding rehearsal, and provide some comment.

If you were watching from across the room and trying to read Pagan and Henry, the way you would a mime, you'd likely conclude that they'd become friends.

8

Druids Bringing In The Mistletoe

On Wednesday morning, just before lunch break, Pagan sat at her desk in the Traffic Department.

She was examining a month of invoices from their primary freight carrier. Every shipment her company had made over the previous month was listed, with a charge beside it.

Pagan had to go through each invoice, line by line, comparing them to the daily manifests produced by her shipping department that gave details about every parcel that had been shipped. The two documents had to match.

It was detailed, slow work, and mind-numbingly dull. You could fall asleep. But it had to be done. In fact, it was Pagan who'd taken the lead in scrutinizing what her company was being charged. Before that, invoices had just been paid.

The new process had immediately shown it's worth when Pagan discovered that the freight carrier had significantly overcharged them every month of the previous year due to a computer error.

Her manager took credit for the discovery and the eighty thousand dollar rebate from the carrier, neglecting to mention Pagan's central role in the affair. The manager was a company hero after that.

Her manager's act wasn't surprising to Pagan. The woman spent her time schmoozing with the director, relying on chumminess rather than accomplishments to get ahead ... and by taking credit for the results achieved by others.

Pagan often thought about quitting her job. It was an idea driven by more than having a deceitful manager who was expert at office politics. It was also about escaping the close proximity to her ex who wasted no opportunity to express his jealousy and feelings of betrayal.

Pagan hoped that ultimately she would have her own business and be able to make her own decisions. In a perfect world, in addition to making some income from her writing, she would own her own bookstore or small press. But for now—since she didn't have the resources to start a business of her own—her only option was to find another job. And any job would do at the moment. It was just a matter of time until she handed in her notice.

At noon, Pagan made her way to the The Cafe. Calling the lunchroom a 'cafe' was an affectation of Blair, the company president who'd been parachuted in earlier in the year.

The expectation was that, like other young executives tabbed for advancement, he would come in and make some unsustainable change that his data would show to be earth-shattering, and he'd then be moved up the corporate ladder at another location. To date though, his main accomplishment had been to give the various meeting rooms grandiose names, like The Albert Einstein Room.

Pagan took a tray and placed it on the rails in front of the food counter. She nudged it along, waiting her turn for Dick, the attendant, to shovel out a plate of the daily special, which today was spaghetti.

Ahead of her, a nice looking man in a suit, who she'd never seen before, turned towards Pagan and said, "Nobody told me that the cafeteria prices were so low."

"Yes, the company subsidizes them. It's a nice perk," Pagan replied.

The man turned back towards the cashier, paid for his meal and, before beginning to walk away, glanced back at Pagan and smiled.

"Friend of yours?"

The speaker was the Ninja-quiet person who'd queued up behind her a moment before. Her eternally jealous ex, Patrick, whose eyes always seemed to be on her.

Pagan considered his jealousy to be Patrick's second most annoying quality, and it persisted no matter how many months had passed since their relationship ended. It felt like another passive-aggressive means of control, and she no longer played those games.

Pagan and Patrick were still friends at work, in a manner of speaking. The mature option. At times she could even recall why she'd liked him in the first place, but when his jealousy was in play she was convinced that it was imperative that she change her lunch time or make good on the promise she'd made to herself to find that other job. Maturity was over-rated.

Pagan didn't reply to Patrick's question and walked to their usual table where he soon joined her; the agreed upon post-break-up game plan of maintaining the habit they shared when they were together.

They were a group of four mid-level managers. Pagan was the Traffic Manager and Patrick was a supervisor in the IT department. Gary, who ran the Shipping Department, was already seated. He was a forty-something man who smoked heavily and laughed heartily. He was busily slurping spaghetti.

The group were soon accompanied by the last of their usual foursome, Cinders Cassidy, the Customer Service Manager, dressed to the nines as always. She'd recently graduated with an MBA so her days as a member of the foursome were numbered. Cinders had confided to the group that she was actively seeking other employment.

In Pagan's estimation, Cinders suffered from something that she called "toxic femininity." She wasn't a princess, since she liked to ski and go camping, but she played the delicate, helpless female around men. When Patrick wore tight t-shirts to show off his muscles, Cinders swooned over him. Men accordingly adored her.

"How was the date?" Pagan said to Cinders.

"Another date with some stud?" said Patrick, grinning.

"A hoity-toity dinner date with a doctor no less," Gary elaborated for Patrick's benefit and perhaps for a bit of gratuitous torture since he sensed that Patrick was in love with Cinders.

"An architect," Cinders corrected.

"Yet another guy?" Patrick said with mock surprise.

"What happened to the doctor?" asked Pagan.

"Nothing, I just like dating. If I could, I'd like to go on a date every night with a different guy."

"That'd be a lot of men to sleep with," said Patrick.

"What? Is that how men see dating?" Cinders was genuinely alarmed. "I only want to be a trophy date and a trophy wife," she added sweetly.

"With ten kids," added Gary.

"Ugh," said Cinders. Her typical response to any mention of children. They weren't part of her fairy tale ending.

"Don't listen to Patrick," said Pagan. Three months previously she'd come to the conclusion that Patrick was in love with Cinders but Cinders seemed to go back and forth about Patrick, at times talking to him like he was her boyfriend and at other times like they were only casual acquaintances. It had been Pagan's opinion that Cinders needed to make a decision about what she wanted with regard to Patrick, and now it seemed she had.

There were lingering smiles between Patrick and Cinders at every mention of one of her dates. Pagan guessed that the architect, doctor, dentist, and Cinders's other dates over the past weeks were all, in actuality, a cover for her and Patrick. Maybe they role-played, Pagan mused, then shook her head to get the creepy image out of it.

Pagan feigned confusion, pretending to look at Cinders's lap and feet. "I don't see the doggy bag. You did bring it didn't you?"

"Not a huge request," added Gary.

In the past, the group had playfully pushed Cinders, asking that when she was on one of her dates with a wealthy young man, that she order the most expensive food on the menu, and more of it than she could possibly eat. Then at the end of dinner she was to ask for a doggy bag and not tell her date that she was bringing the food to work for her friends.

"Damn! I have one but I forgot to bring it in. I'll have to give it to the dog." She was staring at Patrick when she said this, with a half smile on her face.

Pagan noticed. Did he now fancy himself a dog when it came to women? Maybe that would soothe his battered self-esteem; the result of being dumped. She stole a glance at Patrick. He was still locked in eye contact with Cinders, with a shared glimmer of a smile on his face.

"You gotta big date this weekend?" Gary asked Cinders, oblivious to the exchange between her and Patrick.

"Yes, Saturday night."

"Then you have a chance to redeem yourself about the food." Turning to Pagan, Gary said, "And what about you? You look happy today. You goin' on a big Saturday night date too?"

Patrick's head immediately swivelled in Pagan's direction. His face no longer bore any trace of a smile.

"No," said Pagan. "I have my mother's wedding rehearsal lunch on Saturday afternoon so I'll probably drink too much while trying to come to terms with it."

But Gary was right, she was happy today. She'd received Henry's manuscript the day before and was anxious to get back home and finish reading it.

Pagan noticed that Patrick was watching her intently.

She smiled sweetly at him. A smile like a knife.

It was just another day at what might more suitably have been named, The Heartbreak Hotel Cafe.

9

Set in the 1940s and clearly meant to be a revision of the Bonnie and Clyde saga, Pagan's recently published novel, *Jack and Jill Went Up To Sackville*, was ostensibly about a pair of lady bank robbers but it was also about their intense sexual relationship. Both the crimes and the sex were characterized by complete abandon; each reinforcing the other.

The notion behind the book, as far as Henry could make out, was that modern life destroyed passion, in part, because people who lived and loved with passion were a threat to power because they resisted being constrained into lives of passive, repressed obedience.

"Two lovers on the run. A sexy heist novel," according to the cover blurb, "where crime itself becomes an erotic thrill."

In the novel, a man and woman rob a bank. The woman is dressed as a man. After the robbery they stop the car at a prearranged stop to switch vehicles, and for the woman to lose her male disguise. It's a set up however. The woman's lesbian lover is hiding in the bush. The women force the man into the trunk of the robbery car and the two women drove away in the other one.

With Jillian driving the Chevy, the pair headed south, back towards Sackville.

Somewhere, not far behind, a police car, also driving southward, rounded a bend. It was visible in Jillian's rearview mirror, but she didn't notice.

The two officers inside the car had heard a radio report about the Sackville bank robbery. They were speeding to the bank and looking out for a late model red Ford. Two male suspects. Armed and dangerous.

The escalating wail of the siren soon caused both Jackie and Jillian to desperately search their side mirrors. A vehicle was rapidly approaching.

"Jesus!" said Jackie. "It's a police car. Bloody luck."

"What do I do now?" asked Jillian, her voice shaking from fear and excitement.

"They're not after us. Not to worry. Pull over and let them pass. We've got nothing to hide. Two women out driving."

With the cruiser getting closer, Officer Jobe cursed at the driver of the car ahead of them, poking along and not pulling over.

"Some old lady I bet," said his partner, head craned forward, peering intently.

Jackie took her eyes from the mirror to glance at her companion. What was she doing? The shoulder of the road was narrow but that was no reason not to slow down and move to the right as far as possible.

Ahead, on the right, was a gravel road.

"There! There!" Jackie pointed. "Turn off there and let them pass!"

Jillian made no movement. They were almost at the side road.

"Go! Go!" Jackie yelled, waving her hand toward the right. "Jillian! Right! Go! Go!"

Jillian, suddenly came to life. Abruptly, she jammed on the brakes and swung the steering wheel violently rightward.

The Chevy slewed around the corner in a shower of dust.

As soon as the car was on the sideroad, Jillian floored it, sending up a spray of gravel.

"What the fuck," said Officer Jobe, as the cruiser sailed past the sideroad. He slammed on his own brakes and the car fishtailed to a stop. He backed up to the sideroad and again changed gears. He wheeled the cruiser around the corner and set off in pursuit of the women.

"Whoa!" yelled Jillian in triumph, looking in the rearview mirror. "Here they come!"

Henry set the book down on his desk. Instead of taking up his pen and jotting down another note he just sat and wondered. Were there autobiographical elements in the novel? Did the plot reflect a pent up desire on Pagan's part for adventure and maybe even danger?

10

Robert walked down one of the small town's dusty perimeter streets until he discovered the gas station he was looking for.

Approaching the garage he saw a young man inside who he presumed was René.

The man saw Robert and said, "Hello. Can I help you?"

René wasn't a big guy like his old man, Robert noted. Not small like his mother either though.

Robert said hello and went into a story about how his car had broken down just outside of town.

"Uh huh, uh huh," René said, listening. He asked a few questions, then said, "Could be a few different things."

"Do you have a tow truck so we can get it?"

"Naw, but I got a pickup and some chains. Lemme get my keys."

Stepping inside the garage after René disappeared, Robert scanned the tools on a wooden workbench.

"Okay, let's get going," said René, coming up behind him, wiping his hands on a rag.

As he turned, Robert kept his hand low, down by his side. He was holding a ball peen hammer. With a vicious uppercut he drove the hammer into the guy's testicles.

René Gagnon fell to his knees clutching his groin and then onto his side with his knees drawn up in front of him in a fetal position.

"Fuck! Fuck! Fuck!" he screamed, gasping for breath.

Robert straddled him, grabbed the front collar of René's shirt, and shoved his fist upward, pushing the young man's mouth closed and his head back so he had no choice but to look him in the face.

"You don't look like your old man but you're stupid like

him. What did you think was gonna happen; that you'd get away with it?"

"What the fu ..." was the strangled response.

"I'm Rob MacQuigau. My wife was Madeleine MacQuigau, the woman you murdered." Rob was yelling now.

There was no attempted rejoinder. René stared back, wide-eyed.

"Yeah, you weaselly prick, I know what you did."

"The bitch ..."

Robert drove the hammer into the guy's mouth, smashing in most of his teeth.

René sobbed and struggled to breathe.

"You're only alive 'cus of the woman you killed. Your old man was this close to killing your mother and maybe you too. Do you remember the present of the broken arm he gave you? The rifle he was waving at you? Maddy acted for one reason, to save the two of you, and all she got was grief for it from your damn mother."

He didn't know whether the guy heard him through his pain or not.

He raised the hammer again.

Pagan wondered whether Henry's novel could be classed as gratuitously violent, like the movies Patrick loved. Why is it that men think that justice requires beating the crap out of someone, like life is a hockey game?

She'd have to wait till she'd finished the novel before deciding where Henry stood with regard to violence. She had no interest in a friendship with another man who was steeped in toxic masculinity.

On the other hand, Pagan reflected, Henry's plans for his life and house showed a rare personal concern with living an ethically responsible life. He seemed to be kind and conscientious.

She'd get to know him a little better on this coming Saturday which would help her to sort things out.

11

Helene Schlapp

The house that Grace and Calico Jack were heading for sat on a huge lot overlooking the Megumawaach River in the east end of the city. It was the home of Vera Gallant and her two young children, Hélène and Anthony.

Vera had moved to Megumawaach and bought the five bedroom house after her divorce from Grenville who, at that exact moment, was having brunch with his current lover Kulia at her condo in Saint John.

Vera worked as the manager of a downtown bank but it was Saturday morning so she was at home sitting on her livingroom couch, reading the *Globe and Mail* while Hélène, five, and Anthony, three, lay on the Chinese carpet at her feet, engrossed in an English language cartoon playing on television.

Calico Jack stopped the pirate's car, a black Honda Civic, on the shoulder of the road, a few hundred metres from the Gallant house. It was an empty stretch, devoid of houses, so there would be no one looking out a window and accidentally observing the two occupants slipping on their green cotton gloves and pirate masks.

"Do we go through with this?" Calico Jack asked Grace. "We're almost forty minutes behind schedule because of the accident on the highway."

"Some brave pirate you are. We have lots of time."

Grace O'Malley pulled enough of her black hair out from under the elastic attached to the back of her mask to drape it over the strap. Her hair effectively hid the elastic's presence.

Calico Jack slipped a balaclava over his head before donning his own mask.

"Ready Grace?" he said.

"Ready Calico Jack, Scourge of the Megumawaach River."

With a deep breath, Calico Jack put the car into gear.

Less than half a minute later the Civic turned onto the circular driveway of the Gallant home and stopped in front of the double garage doors.

After ascertaining there was no street traffic passing by, the pair climbed from the car and walked to the front door where Calico Jack positioned himself to one side.

Grace stood in front of the door but turned her back to it so that all Vera would see when she looked through the peephole would be the black hair of a woman. Vera might sigh about salespeople but she would still open the door.

Each of the masked pirates clasped a handgun, held low by their side.

As soon as the door began to open, the two pirates threw their weight at it. They knocked the uncomprehending Vera flat on her back as they burst into the foyer of the house.

A short time later, Hélène stood watching the pirate queen who was speaking to Vera. Her initial lack of comprehension about what was happening, after her mother suddenly screamed and was thrown to the floor, was immediately followed by intense fear. But the little girl had now settled to the point where she accepted standing a metre away from her mother, holding Calico Jack's hand, and watching the proceedings.

Vera stood with her back to the front door, facing Grace. She held Anthony in her arms. The boy had wet his pants during the initial terror and continued to cry while clinging to his mother for dear life.

"Okay. Now listen very closely to what I have to say," Grace said, "because your kids' lives depend on it. Understand?"

Vera said nothing.

Grace moved her face to a few centimetres from Vera's. "Understand?" she roared.

Knocked back on her heels, Vera said, "Yes."

"And I don't want to hear any more about what you can and can't do at the bank. You *will* make this happen and you *won't* go to the police. Remember, once you get the three million bucks together—and I don't care how you get it—you'll wire it to the account I gave you. Only after we see the money will we release your kids. Savvy? You have seventy-two hours. If you get smart you'll never see your kids again. Calico Jack here will cut their throats. Understand?"

Calico Jack's head jerked to take in Grace but he still said nothing. He'd been silent the whole time.

"Yes," said Vera in a half whisper.

"Understand?" a demanding Grace said loudly.

"Yes."

"There's no point in going to the cops anyway, since we won't be here."

Grace held out her arms to take Anthony.

Handing him over was the hardest thing that Vera had ever had to do, but she managed it.

She walked out of the front door, in tears, with Anthony's intense wailing in her ears, his arms reaching out for his mother as he writhed and kicked at Grace.

Vera drove away from the house but not before noting the licence plate of the black Civic parked in the driveway beside her car.

After rounding the first corner of the road, she stopped at a neighbour's house, ran to the front door, and pounded on it. Barely managing to control her emotions, Vera told the startled home owner who answered the door why she was there and added that unless the police got to her house immediately, before the kidnappers could leave, that she might never see her children again.

12

Grace O'Malley's castle

Looking through the peephole, Calico Jack watched Vera drive off.

He cracked open the front door, just wide enough to allow him to listen for street traffic. Hearing nothing, he scooped up Hélène and threw open the door.

Grace, holding Anthony, followed him outside.

As they ran towards the black car Calico Jack popped its trunk.

Both children began to struggle as they were shoved into the trunk. The last thing the kids heard as the lid slammed closed was Grace screaming at them, "Shut up!"

With Calico Jack behind the wheel, the car sped away from the house in the opposite direction to the one taken by Vera.

Only after there was no possibility of being observed by any security cameras outside the house, if indeed there were any, did the two kidnappers remove their masks.

Unbeknownst to them, the police were already en route to the Gallant house.

The kidnappers had prepared for the possibility.

Calico Jack's plan involved getting on to one of the back roads in the area as soon as possible. "The highway is where the coppers will focus their attention," he'd told Grace, during their planning session. "They don't have the manpower or cruisers to cover all the smaller roads."

Jack drove southeast but only for a brief stretch. His planned route involved him zigzagging along the secondary roads he knew so well, but staying close to the coast as they headed in the direction of Richibucto.

He kept well within the speed limit and managed to maintain some degree of calm in spite of Grace's anxious fidgeting and the hubbub emanating from the trunk.

Hélène was screaming and kicking the back of the car's rear seats. Anthony's crying was now a terrified howling.

"If they don't stop that shit I'm going to get you to pull over and I'll make them stop," Grace said.

There was no reply from Calico Jack.

Grace half climbed over the back of her seat and added her own yelling to the cacophony. "Shut the fuck up little girl and stop kicking the seat or I come back there and break your damn legs!"

The kicking intensified.

The car travelled southwest, then south along another road, this one running parallel to the highway.

Calico Jack had initially doubted his decision to take this route but soon convinced himself that it was a good one. He had a knack for choosing the right option in critical situations.

As a teenager, he, Grace, and her boyfriend, had once jumped the back fence of a scrap yard. Rumour had it that there were thousands of dollars in the office shack.

The teens unknowingly set off an alarm when they smashed a window to get into the office, and they were still there when a police car squealed up to the front of the business.

The three teens ran, booting it back over the fence and onto a narrow street. Grace and her friend ran up the street while Calico Jack went down it.

Having spotted the fleeing threesome, the cop driving the cruiser swung around the scrap yard and onto the street behind it. Grace and her boyfriend were immediately stopped and arrested.

Calico Jack, meanwhile, had come to a main road. Rather than hiding in the dark he crossed the road and went into a doughnut shop. As luck would have it, a family friend was on his way out the door at that exact moment. The guy drove Jack home.

A second policeman on the call, slowly driving by, saw the pair exiting the restaurant but did nothing; just a family outing apparently.

As further proof of his luck, Calico Jack's partners insisted that it had only been the two of them that did the break-in. They stuck to their story even at their court trials.

Their testimony was a blessing for Jack because a criminal conviction would have wrecked his future plans. He'd felt indebted to Grace ever since.

Calico Jack saw the flashing red light ahead moving speedily towards them long before he heard the siren. "Get down," he said.

Grace slid down in her seat. "Bitch called the cops already. Shit!"

"I told you she would. No problem."

Calico Jack maintained his speed and watched as the cruiser sailed past. He followed its progress in the rearview mirror as it disappeared from view. The cops were, without doubt, on their way to the Gallant house.

Calico Jack had meant to switch the Civic's license plate in case they encountered the police. He assumed that Vera would have noted the plate number as she left the house, and he'd hoped for it. Jack suddenly realized that in all the excitement he'd forgotten to change the plate.

The thought that he'd screwed up hit him like a blow.

Under his breath he cursed at himself for his own stupidity and felt a surge of panic.

If his lucky mojo held, Jack thought, the passing copper wouldn't have noted his license plate since it was on the rear of the car, but he knew that he was being unrealistic. That the cruiser would reverse it's course was inevitable. But when?

"One, two, three," Jack silently and slowly counted while glancing into the rearview mirror.

The police car didn't materialize.

"Five, six, seven." Still nothing.

And then Calico Jack heard the siren behind them. Faint at first but rapidly increasing in volume.

He repeatedly checked the rearview mirror as he drove, watching the approaching car. Grace did the same by twisting in her seat. They both put their masks back on.

Soon, the cruiser was almost at their rear bumper. And there it remained.

"Damn it!" said Grace. "That was fast."

"You know what to do."

Grace, reaching to the floor of the car, slid her hand under the seat and dug out the two loaded 9 mm semi-automatic handguns from where they'd been stashed. She handed one to Calico Jack, which he laid on his lap. She clasped the other in her right hand.

Calico Jack dutifully slowed the Civic, pulled it onto the shoulder of the road, and stopped.

The police car stopped well back of them.

"Okay?" said Grace.

"Yes."

"Now!"

The pair flung open their car doors.

Calico Jack followed the plan and dove to the pavement, shooting at the cruiser's tires. He hit one of them.

Grace, who was supposed to do the same thing, improvised. She dove on to the dirt shoulder of the road but aimed her gun upward. Her shots shattered the front window of the police car.

Within seconds the pair were back in their car.

Calico Jack gunned the Civic, sending up a shower of gravel.

The police officer in the cruiser slowly raised her head over the dash and watched the suspect vehicle drive off. She knew enough not to shoot at a car with children in it.

She urgently reached for the cruiser's radio.

Calico Jack's lucky mojo re-emerged, just when he needed it the most. The Civic raced along four different dirt roads for nearly twenty minutes without seeing another police car.

Arriving at their destination—a grey lakefront cottage on the shore of Faery Lake—Calico Jack turned the Civic onto the unpaved semi-circular drive and parked in the middle of it. A stand of trees blocked the car's visibility from the road.

"Remember to keep your mask on before we open the trunk," he said.

Smiling, Grace replied, "Aye aye Captain, Scourge of the Megumawaach."

The Scourge decided that the Pirate Queen didn't need to know that he'd forgotten to change the license plate on their car after leaving the Gallant house. In turn, he wouldn't mention that Grace's improvisation, in shooting not at the police cruiser's wheels but at the officer inside, meant that if they were ever arrested that, in addition to everything else, they'd be charged with attempted murder; to say nothing of the fact that the cops would now approach them with guns drawn, and likely shoot first and ask questions later.

13

The Masterpiece

Henry noticed that Pagan was flushed and anxious when she arrived at his house. He led her into the room that he referred to as his study. It was formerly the dining room.

They were soon drinking chamomile tea from an old teapot that had once belonged to Henry's grandmother.

Pagan, Henry observed, had noticeably relaxed.

"Your book is well written," Pagan said, after critiquing Henry's book. "I think you really underestimate your ability. Could I make a general suggestion though?"

"Of course."

"Try to think more about scene instead of spending so much time telling us about your characters. Readers want scene. You're a little wordy at times."

"It sounds like you're saying I should approach it as I would if I was writing a movie."

"Yes, exactly. Dialogue and movement, tension between characters."

"And what do you think about the Native character? I'm worried someone will say it's cultural appropriation."

"Well, I'm sympathetic when people speak about their culture being appropriated. White culture takes from every other one and commercializes it. But, on the other hand, unless you only write about white, heterosexual males, you're going to have to appropriate the identities of other people to some extent. It's what writers do and it actually forces us to see other people's points of view. For me, I focus on voice. I won't steal someone's story that would be more effectively and honestly told by a person with the same cultural background, but I do want to show society the way that it actually is, diverse, and so I try to reflect that by including diverse characters with diverse backgrounds."

Henry hadn't been asked to read or make notes on Pagan's published novel but he did both and Pagan was obviously pleased that he'd taken the time.

He went through his comments but hesitated before reading his final note. He finally blurted, "I could feel the eroticism. It was palpable at times and it pulls you in."

Pagan laughed, obviously pleased with the comment. "Bless you. That's exactly what I was going for."

Henry exhaled in relief.

They were sitting at each end of the study's overstuffed couch, across the room from the alcove where Henry had kept the old oak desk that he'd found upstairs, left by a previous tenant. Newly repaired and refinished it was almost invisible in the blinding sunshine enveloping it.

Although the time was close to noon there was no talk of lunch since Pagan was due at her mother's place for lunch at 1:00 PM.

"You've left the inside of the house intact I see," said Pagan.

"Yes, just some refinishing. Where things had to be replaced I managed to get my hands on discarded materials from similar houses and recycle them. It's part of the beauty of doing it yourself I guess, you have to learn skills instead of being helpless. The upstairs is empty. I won't have to keep it particularly warm in the winter. Just the bathroom at the top of the stairs."

"And you won't freeze in your sleep?"

"No. I recommissioned the old parlour on this floor as a bedroom."

"Well, it's a wonderful opportunity to exercise your creativity. I'm envious. I love this room." Pagan got to her feet and did a slow pirouette, taking in every corner. She approached the old desk and said, "May I?" pointing at the ancient desk chair.

"Of course."

Pagan sat down, took hold of the edge of the desk, and sent the chair spinning. "Whoa," she laughed. The chair rocked. "It's tipsy. Like its drunk." She gabbed the desk to stop herself in mid twirl to avoid falling backwards. "I'd enjoy writing here. It's the kind of room I could spend hours in. You're lucky." She leaned her head back and closed her eyes, basking in the warm sunshine.

Henry happily watched her disappear into the light. "Yes. I thought I was setting it up as a room where I'd spend a lot of time writing, possibly even for a living. That's not going so well, as you know, but I like sitting here so much it almost doesn't matter anymore if I'm typing words that no one will ever read. ... But I'm being positive now. I'm going to rework the book."

"That's good to hear, I think you were about to give up on yourself too soon. You have talent, I think. I'd never have been able to write my second book—the one that was published—if I hadn't struggled through the first one"

"Do you think you might go back to the first one and revise it?"

"No." Pagan paused and seemed hesitant to continue but eventually said, "It's not because of the quality of the writing because, yes, as you're getting at, things can be reworked. I don't want to touch the book again because it's morally repulsive. The story involves the kidnap of two small children. I wanted to create a successful, clever bank robbery. Kidnap a bank manager's kids and force her to rob her own bank. But as I got into it I realized how horrific the crime was. It wasn't until I finished it that I realized my antiheroes were just too despicable to sympathize with."

As Henry walked Pagan towards her car she asked him about his family background.

"Toronto on my mother's side. Ireland if you go way back. My father is from Nova Scotia but his family moved to Ontario when he was a kid. He's Acadian but the logic was that you were doing your kids a favour by never speaking French around them. My father dropped the accent on our surname for that reason. Anyway, I missed out on being around my extended family."

"So you're living out the quintessential Acadian story it seems—returning home."

"Yes." Henry laughed. "I never thought of it that way but I guess so. My father was happy when I said I wanted to move here and my parents gave me a chunk of my future inheritance to do it. So here I am, an outsider who fled Toronto looking for a better life."

"Welcome to New Brunswick. A lot of people are here because their ancestors came looking for something better. The Acadians returned here after their land was stolen, the United Empire Loyalists fled the American War of Independence, and escaping slaves came looking for freedom. And of course, lots of Irish and Scots came here during the famine. It's no wonder that so many people supported the Syrians who came here a few years back to escape the civil war in their country. I think a lot of people here know in their bones what it means to seek refuge and a better life. It's visceral."

Standing by Pagan's car, commenting on the bugs, Henry said, "At least the ever present wind here has some use. The mosquitoes aren't so bad today because of it."

"Don't speak ill of the wind, my mother says, or the spirit of the wind may punish you for it. It's always windy here so you need to get used to it. When I was a kid a Mi'kmaq elder spoke to our class and taught us a bit of his language. Useful phrases. I remember the first phrase he taught. 'Weju'sɨk'. It means, 'It's windy'. He told us a legend about a giant bird whose wings made the wind. Its lesson was that life needs the wind."

Shifting topics, Pagan said, I think you had the right idea when you bought land. Not only do you need it to be self-sufficient but—to paraphrase what my mother always says— it gives you more control over your life. She is big into gardening so she often talks about food. She says that with land she can not only control the food she eats but where and how it is grown. ... You'll have to meet her someday."

Henry was thrilled at the idea of being included in Pagan's

personal life. "I'll look forward to it."

Pagan looked to the sky and breathed deeply. "I love being in the country. It's my restorative and I've been missing it lately, since I began avoiding my mother's. It's not about getting out of the city so much—Megumawaach isn't Toronto by any means—but work is work and it makes all the difference in the world to be able to step away from the stress, frustrations, and boredom; to just be outside in the sun. Plus I love to listen to nature. It's never quiet and restful. It is vibrant and alive. Every part of it communicates. The trees groan and complain to each other about the wind. Animals scream warnings at all and sundry, grunt and lie, and birds make the most beautiful music. And what could be better than hiking through the bush? My mother taught me the names and properties of the wildflowers and all the edibles, and my father had a telescope to watch the stars. It's still at my mother's and I use it whenever I'm there. It helps me to remember how vast and amazing the world is and how unimportant a lot of what goes on in my life is. It puts all the negatives in perspective."

Pagan opened her car door, climbed inside, started the car and lowered her window.

She and Henry said their good-byes and Pagan backed the black Civic onto the road.

They waved good-bye as she drove off.

Looking in her rearview mirror, Pagan thought about how wonderful and fulfilling it would be to have a new place to live, new challenges, and an adventure in life to pursue.

Her attention then focused on Henry. It was such a pleasure to be around someone who admired her writing, respected her as a writer, and thought that it was something of value. Patrick had only seemed interested in the details of the crimes her characters committed. It was a chance to briefly offer his expertise before his eyes glazed over.

Pagan felt sorry to be heading back to her life.

14

Aisling Níc Aodhagáin was sprawled on her livingroom couch across from her daughter Pagan. They were sipping glasses of mead, made with Aisling's fiance Jarrod's honey.

"Do random words ever pop into your head?" Pagan asked.

"Random words? I don't know what you mean."

"Geez, it sounds psychotic when I say it out loud, like I'm hearing voices. It's not like that. Psychotic. It's an echo. Like I heard a TV announcer once say the word 'superficial' about something or other and I suddenly hear the word in that person's voice but it's months later and I'm just walking down the street when it's popped into my head for no apparent reason."

"It's not the game you play? The thesaurus game where you try to find the best adjective for something?"

"No. That's just adjectives. Trying to catch the nuance in words. That's an intentional exercise. What I'm talking about is unintentional."

"So a word summons itself?"

"Yes. I guess you could put it like that. Sometimes a phrase … more likely a phrase actually."

"Maybe it demands to be heard. Words have power. Words have spirits, like everything else. You were destined to be a bard, I've always known that, so it's not surprising that words will seek you out."

Pagan looked at her mother and then towards the ceiling. Did other people's mothers talk like this? Half mysticism, half poetry, half intriguing. Too many halves. Too much mead. If she wasn't careful her mother would return to her wedding plans.

"You know Mom," Pagan said, "it's not too late to change your mind about the marriage if you're apprehensive at all. Everyone would understand and no one would judge you."

Her mother, who'd been looking off into the distance, lost in contemplation of the mysteries of life, was suddenly cold sober.

And Pagan knew she'd said the wrong thing.

"Apprehensive? The only person who's apprehensive is you!" Aisling's voice was now raised. She never raised her voice. "What a horrible thing to say."

"I thought I was being supportive. Forget it."

"I won't. Even if you hadn't said what you did, your feelings about my marriage have been clear from the beginning. I can tell by the way you roll your eyes and shake your head whenever I talk about it that you don't approve. And I'm sick of it. It's none of your damn business."

Pagan was suddenly aware of movement at the doorway into the kitchen. Jarrod was standing there, checking out the fuss no doubt. She'd forgotten he was nearby. Jarrod's expression was muted; impossible to read, but he neither seemed to be angry nor supportive. Just curious perhaps. In any case, there was no ally at hand.

"Maybe I'd better leave," Pagan said getting unsteadily to her feet.

There was nothing from her mother. There was no, "You've had too much to drink to drive." And no, "I'd rather you stay." Nothing. It wasn't like her mother: anger, exasperation, and lack of concern. None of it.

15

Landscape at Night

It was almost midnight, when Henry got the phone call from Pagan.

She spoke in a tone of voice he recognized; that of someone mildly inebriated making an effort to speak clearly, which ironically makes it very clear that they're drunk.

"Henry, I know this is outrageously presumptuous but I was wondering if … hoping … that I could crash on your wonderful old couch tonight. My mother and I have had a bit of a falling out and I need to get out of here."

"Sure, I …"

"I know this is an awful imposition but I've had a little too much to drink to drive." Pagan's uncertain and slow cadence had suddenly quickened, perhaps from rehearsing her speech ahead of time.

"It's not putting me out. It's fine," Henry said, then hesitated. Pagan hadn't actually asked him to pick her up, although her intention seemed clear. "I'll leave right away."

"Oh, thank you, thank you."

Henry got directions and soon fired up the old pickup truck he'd bought to cart home materials for his renovations.

Driving through the dark, he worried about not being able to spot the house he was headed for. It was a cloudy, starless night. Mother Moon—as Pagan's mother sometimes calls her—was apparently on a girl's night out.

His destination was on the north side of the highway, just past the first town he came to after passing through McCann. A fifteen minute trip.

The house sat by its lonesome, well back off the road on a large lot. Its lights were the sole pinpoints against the black landscape.

Swinging onto the driveway of the house the beam of the

truck's headlights momentarily crossed over Pagan, sitting on the hood of her car, awaiting his arrival. She jumped up as the pickup approached, and waved.

As they set out on the drive back to Henry's, Pagan was clearly in a mood to talk, and less concerned with sounding sober than during her phone call. "When I told you I might say something to my mother about her marriage I was only joking. I never seriously entertained butting into her business no matter what I felt. She's my mother and I have to be supportive. At least that's what I thought I was doing when I reminded her she didn't have to go through with the wedding if she changed her mind ... a kind of inoffensive way of showing support ... but she was too angry to talk about it ... she said my attitude all along had been negative." Pagan turned her head away to stare into the night. "So I told her I was leaving and she didn't say not to."

Henry was at a loss as to how to respond, or whether to say anything at all.

"Do you think I was out of line saying what I did?" Pagan asked looking towards Henry.

"I don't know. On the face of it, it may be the sort of thing that friends say to each other, but only if the bride is having second thoughts. If she isn't it could ..."

Pagan, not appearing to be listening, interrupted, "And maybe the worst part is that Jarrod heard my mother yelling, so by now he knows what I said and will forever hate me. And I more or less made sure, by intervening, that my mother will definitely marry him. And now, it'll forever be awkward being around the guy."

Carefully measuring his words, Henry said, "I wonder. Can I say I think it might not play out like that since you didn't say anything about Jarrod to your mother, at least it doesn't sound to me like you did?"

"I didn't."

"So you weren't being critical of him, or your mother. You were just showing concern. I don't know your mother but she may calm down pretty quickly and understand you meant well."

"Should I apologize?"

"I suppose so, for ... I don't know ... speaking out of turn maybe. You didn't advise her not to get married or anything like that. Maybe you could tell her that you support her decision."

For the first half hour back at Henry's house Pagan continued to go over the events of the evening, with frequent pauses where she'd say, "What do you reckon?" or with words to prompt Henry's solidarity, to which he'd reply with something positive and optimistic.

Pagan then lapsed into a bout of self-criticism for drinking too much at her mother's; evidence perhaps of her sobering up or an omen of impending sentimentalism.

Henry was careful when being supportive for fear of saying something that Pagan might interpret later as criticism of her mother.

It was likely Pagan's repeated recitations, rather than Henry's consoling, which eventually eased the former's anxiety and sharp sense of humiliation.

Abruptly, Pagan finally said, "Okay! Enough of boring you with all that. Time to move on."

"I wasn't bored. And maybe you needed to talk things through."

The pair were ensconced in Henry's study rather than the living room, at Pagan's request, once again sitting at opposite ends of the overstuffed couch. Or at least Henry sat at his end of the couch. Pagan was facing him, laying on her back with her head resting on the wide arm of the couch, her legs bent in front of her. Her toes squeezed under Henry's leg.

Only one lamp illuminated the room. The serene atmosphere, the booze, and Pagan's ebbing anxiety was having a soporific effect on her.

Seizing his chance, during a long lull in the conversation, Henry shifted to a new topic.

"So, your mother's house. Is that where you grew up?"

"It is."

"It looks like a big spread."

"She just has an acre of land but there's bush behind it."

"I saw what looked like a chicken coop—hard to be sure in the dark."

"That's what it is. The chickens were my father's passion for awhile. He sold eggs as a sideline."

"At the farmer's market?"

"No, he had regular customers and a delivery route. On Wednesday and Saturday he'd drive all over and make his deliveries. I think it was a profitable sideline and he might still be at it if it wasn't for the divorce. After that he got a little apartment in the city."

"Are you close to him?"

"Kinda. I was when I was young. Those were the best years of my life. I helped him with his chickens. I fed them, cleaned the coop, and gave the chicks names. I got to know all about chicken feed, predators, diseases and how to spot them, and I could identify chickens by their breed. It didn't feel like work. You know what the best thing was when it came to my father? We'd go to the back of the property on weeknights and weekends, or into the bush to shoot targets with our .22s and a sort of skeet with shotguns. And sometimes we'd go to the shooting range with our handguns."

"I see why you know your way around firearms."

"Indeed. I'm a crack shot too. Be forewarned."

There was another lull and Henry soon noticed that, this time, Pagan had closed her eyes.

He collected the empty mugs and took them into the kitchen and then went to the bathroom.

When he returned to the study, with a blanket for Pagan, he saw that she had stretched out on the couch and was sound asleep.

16 Sunday

Henry was up before dawn.

He immediately headed to the river for his daily endorphin-releasing swim and now, with dawn breaking, he was on his way home.

The bush was thick with pine and balsam firs, their naked lower limbs allowing the occasional glimpse of the house some fifty metres away. The narrow and circuitous path worn through the trees had been flattened by thousands of trips made over the years by various kids who'd once lived on the property.

There was just enough early light to allow Henry to make out the smoothed earth of the path underfoot and the thick roots spanning it that needed to be stepped over.

It had rained during the night and the light was not that of a new day announcing itself with a spectacular sunrise, but the dull soggy murk of fatigued night. Wisps of clouds, the ominous colour of the deepest ocean, slid across the sky.

The bush had a slightly terrifying and Gothic feel with its deep shadows and depths. If a wild animal had appeared Henry's heart might have stopped.

The bugs were out in force and of course there was the omnipresent and malicious wind. A gust ruffled the leaves overhead and maliciously doused Henry with the raindrops that had been resting on them.

He looked ahead into a haze punctuated by darting specs of black. It was a world of mystery that held a certain degree of fascination for him, reminding him of his own ignorance. Even though blackfly season was done there were still mosquitoes, deerflies, mooseflies, tics, and hundreds of other bugs whose names he didn't know. All of whom wanted to feed on him. All of them supposed members of the 'brotherhood of the forest', as Aisling called them.

Henry quickened his step while swatting at the bugs in a game of whac-a-mole. There was always another bug who'd marked him out as breakfast or maybe as an interloper in one of nature's ongoing territorial wars.

Henry arrived back home earlier than usual. His timing was based on wanting to be home when Pagan got up.

After hanging his towel on the clothesline, he took a moment to smooth his still wet hair then gently opened the kitchen door and crept into the house as quietly as possible.

Pagan wasn't in the kitchen and obviously not still sleeping because the radio in the study could be heard. That's where Henry headed.

Peeking past the open study door he saw Pagan pacing back and forth in an obviously agitated manner.

"Hello," he said.

Pagan spun about on one foot then took a couple of quick breaths to compose herself before saying, "I just heard my name on the radio."

"That's great."

"No, no, no! That's not great."

Henry was about to console her, for what he thought must have been a bad book review, when Pagan added. "This wasn't about my book. It seems there was a kidnapping—part of a bank robbery scheme—and the police are looking for me in connection with it."

"You mean like, as a suspect?"

"I was referred to as a 'person of interest'," Pagan's voice rose as she elaborated, "but they said—the cops I mean—not to approach me as I may be armed. So yeah, I'm a suspect."

Henry had to take a moment to absorb what he'd been told. "When was this robb … I mean kidnapping?"

"It said it was yesterday morning."

"Well you were with me at …"

"Eleven-thirty."

"Exactly," said Henry, recalling that Pagan had texted him on Friday night asking for their get-together to be changed to 11:30 instead of noon because she'd made so many notes about his manuscript. "Was it then?"

"I don't know," said Pagan, resuming her pacing. "It could have been 5:00 in the morning."

"Do you know why the cops are looking for you?"

"No. Well, yes I do. I mean I think I can guess. It sounds like the kidnappers were following the plot of my first novel. They wore pirate masks."

"Pirate masks?"

"Like in my first novel."

"The unpublished book?"

"Yes!" Pagan said with annoyance as if she was speaking to an idiot. "The one I mentioned to you, where I sent the full manuscript to a literary agent instead of a synopsis."

"But that's just a coincidence."

"It sounds like it's more than that. Not only did the criminals wear pirate masks but they kidnapped the kids of a bank manager, like in the book."

Henry spoke slowly and deliberately, trying to be a calming influence, "It sounds like the cops think you would copy a crime from a book that you wrote and that other people could identify as your unpublished book. That's a crazy assumption."

"I don't know what they're thinking but yeah, it seems like that's it. Who'd be stupid enough to do something like that; to imitate a book they wrote when it's out there in public? Oh Henry! What's going on?" Pagan's tone was suddenly pleading.

"Maybe this can be sorted out. What about calling the cops and finding out what's going on?"

"I want to check on some things first." Pagan's tone of voice had taken on an incisive, back-to-business tone. "Can you take me to my mother's so I can get my car? Maybe the police spoke to her."

"Yeah, sure."

Pagan bustled past Henry, heading into the kitchen where her shoes were on a mat beside the back door.

Henry rushed along behind her. "It'll be okay."

"No! Don't say that. You don't know that." Then, in a gentler way, Pagan added, "Sorry about raising my voice."

"It's okay."

"Let's go," Pagan said, with urgency.

"Yes, yes."

As she strode towards Henry's pickup, Pagan appeared to be speaking to the wind, when she muttered, "They said not to approach me but to call 9-1-1. Jesus."

As Henry was pulling his truck onto the highway he said, "Since your novel is unpublished how would the police even know about it?"

"I don't know. Can I use your phone? Mine died during the night and I want to see if the cops went to my place."

Henry handed his phone over.

Pagan punched in a number and waited. "Darla, it's me. Are you home? ... Yes. ... Yes, I heard it on the radio. ... They what? Oh for god's sake!"

Henry glanced in Pagan's direction. There was a look of shock on her face which hardly changed as she listened to whatever it was that Darla was saying.

Henry looked back and forth between the road and Pagan.

She eventually turned her face towards him and shook her head to communicate that what she was hearing was unbelievable.

"Just a sec," she said into the phone. Taking it away from her ear, she brought Henry up to date. "The police were at my apartment first thing this morning. Darla said they tore apart my room and took some things. They asked her a ton of questions."

Pagan returned the phone to her ear and said, "Back again Darla. ... With Henry, driving back to my mother's. ... They should be there, on the shelf in the closet. ... Ah, I wondered. ... I'll think about it. I want to sort through this before I talk to Wolf. ... Now that can't be. My car was with me. ... Yeah, yeah. I don't care what they said they saw, it wasn't my car. ... Thanks, Darla. I'll keep in touch."

Pagan tapped the phone to end the call. She sighed with frustration, made a noise that sounded like a growl and vigorously plopped backwards in her seat, looking upwards.

Turning her head to look at Henry, she said, "Darla told me that she just got off the phone with her boyfriend Wolf. He told her what happened. Two people wearing cloth gloves and pirate masks broke into the house of a banker, took her kids, and told her to rob her own bank and wire them the money. It's my plot. The specific details match precisely so they obviously copied my novel. This makes no sense. ... And in answer to your question, apparently the kidnapping was all over the CBC news last night and the literary agent I sent the manuscript to saw it. She called the cops and gave them my name."

"And they think you're the kidnapper based on that?" Henry shook his head.

"And unfortunately there's more. It's not just the plot. Someone got a look at the kidnapper's car and wrote down the licence plate. It was my license plate and my car."

"The Civic?"

"Yeah. It makes no bloody sense." Pagan shook her head and sighed. "Oh, oh, and listen to this. My father's old handgun and mine that were on my closet shelf are gone. Darla didn't know where they were when the cops asked her but they didn't find them so apparently someone walked off with them." Pagan smiled and feigned a laugh so farcical had the story become.

"Do the cops know you were with me?"

"Yes. And they think you're the other kidnapper."

"For the love of ..."

"Oh, and this is something you'll want to know. The handguns they took—the kidnappers, bank robbers, whatever you want to call them—tried to shoot a police officer. So now we're both supposedly armed and dangerous, and on the run. There's no going to the police now. If they see us they might shoot first and ask questions later."

"Do they know where we are?"

"I don't see how anyone could. ... Darla said she'd call Wolf and tell him I had nothing to do with this."

Pagan clenched her fists and banged them off her knees. She half-screamed in frustration. "I don't understand this

Henry. How could this be happening? Help me understand." Tears welled.

Wolf was still sitting by his locker at the police station when his cell began to vibrate. He took it from his pocket and saw that the call was from Darla

"You got something babe?" he asked. He'd told Darla to call him if she heard from Pagan.

"Yes. I just got off the phone with Pagan. She said she heard on the radio that you—the police—are looking for her."

"Did she say where she is?"

"She's on her way to her mother's."

"She mention this boyfriend of hers? Did she say where he is?"

"I gather Henry's driving her."

"Good. Better go."

"Oh, and there's one more thing. I remembered that she got a courier package this week. She said it was from Henry. She put the packaging in the garbage. I just dug around in the cans downstairs and it was still there. The packaging I mean. I can give you Henry's last name and address."

"You're a dream. Go ahead."

After relaying the information to Wolf, Darla said, "I looked up the address on Google Maps. It's the old Todd house on Jersey Road ... you know, the father used to make furniture."

Wolf hesitated in thought. "Oh yeah, yeah, Debbie Todd, we ... I knew her well in high-school."

"I thought she was younger than you. More my age ... no matter."

Wolf was pleased, as usual, that Darla didn't jealously jump on stuff he said. She wasn't the jealous type at all it seemed. Or maybe she simply didn't pick up on things. In either case, it made his life easier.

"I gotta go," Wolf said. He signed off the call and looked down at Henry's address. Unlike the old lady's house, which was out of the force's jurisdiction, Henry's place was at the furthest edge of the westernmost parish that was the responsibility of the Megumawaach Police—and in the zone where he was about to go on patrol.

Henry navigated his truck around the final curve in the road ahead of their destination. Aisling's house was now visible, though still off in the distance. He leaned forward and squinted to take in the scene before him before loudly blurting, "Get down! Get down!"

Pagan responded by immediately sliding her knees forward till her head dropped below the level of the windows.

There were three police cruisers parked near the house, two in the driveway and one along the side of the road.

When he was almost at the driveway, Henry slowed the pickup to better take in the scene.

"What is it? What is it?" said Pagan.

"Shh," Henry said, without moving his lips. He'd noted a police officer observing him.

Henry did a lot of head-bobbing to give his best impression of a rubber-necking local. As an added touch he nodded to the officer as he passed and the man nodded back. Just some local presumably.

Once past the house, Henry relayed what was happening and added, "Stay low for a bit, until we're out of sight."

A half minute of silence ensued before Henry said, "Is there a road up here I can turn off on; one that leads to a road I can take back to my place?"

"Can I please sit up now?"

"Yes."

Pagan pushed herself backwards and upwards in her seat. "Turn right just up here and I can direct you after that."

After making the turn, Henry said, "I wonder if the cops will be checking traffic."

Pagan considered the thought. "This stuff went down at a house in Megumawaach and they said on the radio that the kidnappers went south. I don't see why they'd be looking around here."

Soon after, she directed Henry to turn right once again.

They drove through bush-covered land and past small

clusters of houses. Sightings of people were few and far between. Pagan stared straight ahead, oblivious.

Henry had to prod her when he spied a dirt road ahead, "Should I turn here?"

"What? Oh yes, yes, turn right."

The soon arrived back at Jersey Road and turned left.

They'd managed a complete loop and were now heading to Henry's without having had to pass Pagan's mother's house a second time.

17

In Fairyland

It didn't take many minutes before the pair were once again at Henry's.

He placed a mug of hot coffee in front of Pagan who was sitting at the kitchen table, absorbed in thought. He then sat down.

"God no," Pagan said eventually, awakening to the world around her, "my stomach is churning, but thanks." She shook her head. "Those poor kids. You know what the worst part of this whole thing is? It's that, since the police think that we kidnapped the kids—one of them is just a toddler—that they might be focusing all their attention on finding us, thinking that'll get the kids back. Meanwhile those kids are facing an ordeal and no one is actually looking for them."

"It's outrageous."

A long silence ensued.

"Is that a reason to turn ourselves in?" Henry said. "So the police will know we're innocent and can start looking for the real culprits."

"If I knew that's what they'd do then yeah, sure, it would be the ethical thing. But they might not believe us and if that was the case they might spend their time looking into every place we've ever been, and talking to every person we've ever known."

"And trying to force us to tell them where the kids are."

"And trying to force us to tell them where the kids are. And anyway, Darla said that she'd let the police know that we had nothing to do with anything, so we've sent that message already. I think that we have to find those kids ourselves."

"Even with the possibility that if the cops come across us they may shoot us?"

"Even then."

"So where do we start?"

"Well, I'm thinking that there's a couple of possible

reasons why someone would copy the crime in my book. The first is that—because it's unpublished—the kidnappers thought they could use the scheme and get away with it since no one would suspect them."

"They couldn't have known that the literary agent would call the cops and report the connection."

"Right, but I've told people about the novel so there's a few of them out there who know the plot even though they haven't read the book. Surely one of them would have tipped off the cops when the kidnapping hit the news."

"When kids go missing it's always all over the media."

"Exactly. I'd have called them myself as soon as I heard about the crime and anyone who is close enough to me to know the plot of the book would know that about me."

"So we rule out the possibility that the kidnappers thought that the cops wouldn't connect you to the crime. What's the second possibility?"

"The only thing that makes sense is that someone explicitly tried to point the finger at me. I mean they wanted money, I guess, and thought the scheme in the novel would work, but it sounds like they didn't change a single thing from the manuscript. They did the opposite. They copied every detail, even the pirate masks." Pagan suddenly looked at Henry with alarm. "You don't think I was involved in this do you?"

"No, of course not. ... So someone wanted to do the crime and have you blamed for it. It makes sense but—since a limited number of people know the plot of your book—wouldn't they also be making themselves suspects?"

"To you and me yes, but to the rest of the world it will only be us that's suspected. The car that was used had my license plate on it, and the guns used were probably mine. So it's us specifically who are being set up."

"Okay. So maybe we should figure out who knew the plot of your novel."

"Right."

"I guess at the top of the list is the literary agent."

"Right. Nobody else has read the manuscript, and maybe

not even her. I did send her the manuscript but her reply was just a generic one—'this book is not of interest to us' sort of thing—which I assumed meant she hadn't read it."

"She did though."

"Or maybe an employee of hers read it and reported back. But it makes no sense that someone in Toronto would be behind this. I mean, the kidnappers stole my car!"

"And you don't think that could be someone from Toronto?"

Pagan considered the remark. "Well … maybe, I guess … but the kidnappers also knew about my guns."

"So, who in New Brunswick knew both the plot and about your guns?"

"Well … I really don't know. I can't remember who I've told about the guns. … My former boyfriend Patrick definitely knew about them and where they might be. I always kept them on a shelf in our bedroom closet."

"And he knew the plot of the novel?"

"I don't know how much I told him but I do remember that he was interested in some details of the crime. Actually, the computer transactions that happened after the crooks got the money—to disappear it offshore—were a combination of Patrick's ideas and my research. He knows his IT stuff. You know, now that I think about it, Patrick would have been able to access my laptop if he really wanted to read the manuscript." Pagan paused before adding, "Oh, and my mother knew about both the book's plot and the guns."

"But we can eliminate her, I think."

"Yes."

"Would Patrick have set you up?"

"Whew, he's been really pissed off at me, but no, I can't see him doing something criminal for money or revenge. And I don't know who his accomplice would be."

"Did you tell Darla the plot?"

"No, no. I didn't live with Darla at the time I wrote the novel. … Correction, I did tell her about it after I moved in, when I was shopping my two novels around. I didn't give her much detail though. … I can't see Darla doing anything illegal. … Oh, but she would have had access to the guns … and my car keys too for that matter."

"Did you leave the manuscript around where she might have found it?"

"No. Actually, there's no physical manuscript. It exists only on the cloud and on a memory stick that's encrypted, that I keep in a safety deposit box at my bank. And even if there was a copy of the manuscript laying around I can't see Darla rummaging through my room, although … no, wait." Pagan stared intently at Henry and continued, but with slow deliberation. "After I sent the manuscript to the agent I belatedly discovered that the correct approach is to send a query letter and a synopsis. I wrote a pretty detailed plot synopsis after that in case I wanted to approach other agents. I wrote it in a notebook that I keep in my desk. Someone could have found the notebook and read the synopsis."

"So we're back to Darla then."

"Oh no, I don't think it was her. It's not just access that matters, it's also character. It was her boyfriend Wolf!" Pagan vigorously nodded her head in affirmation. "Think about it. He has a key to our apartment. He's pretty slimy, too. I could easily see him rooting around in my desk and dresser. And my closet. Plus he'd recognize a gun case when he saw one."

"He has a key to your apartment?"

"Yeah. Darla gave him one so he could get in to wait for her if we weren't at home when he got there to pick her up. And he could have taken my car on Saturday morning before I went out, if that's when the kidnapping happened. I leave my keys on a hook by the door and he stayed over on Friday night."

"But I thought it was a couple who committed the crime— a man and a woman."

"So you're saying that Darla might have helped? Shit. Hmm … it makes sense but still, I don't see Darla doing this. She and I have become good friends and I can't see her setting me up, even for a boyfriend."

"So it's Wolf and someone else."

"I think so. I wonder if he was waiting for the right

opportunity to do the kidnapping. I told Darla that I'd be here on Saturday around noon. Maybe Wolf thought that timing the kidnapping for the morning would put a man in the picture as my accomplice since I might have left home earlier than I did and picked you up."

"And someone seeing the car leave, with Wolf driving, might think it was you. Would Darla have seen Wolf leave?"

"No. The parking lot is at the back of the house and her room is at the front. Plus, she goes to work on Saturdays so Wolf could have even come back after the kidnapping and returned the keys … I mean, depending on the timing."

Henry got up, put his coffee cup in the sink then walked to the small window at the end of the kitchen which overlooked the front of the property and the driveway. Grasping one of the curtains, he was about to pull it back but instantly dropped it. "Pagan, the cops are here," he said.

"What?" She leapt out of her chair to join Henry at the window. He was still peeking through the curtains and she pushed her face up against his.

Three police vehicles—two cruisers and a mini-van—were slowly moving into the yard, apparently trying to take up positions by stealth. The vehicles stopped.

Two officers, after emerging from their cars, immediately withdrew their handguns.

Pagan recognized one of the policemen. "That's Wolf! We've got to get out of here," she whispered urgently.

"Right," Henry said. "The back door."

He scooted across the room. Gently opened the kitchen door using both hands. Silently made his way down two wooden steps. Crossed two metres of yard. At the bush trail he paused and confirmed that Pagan was behind him. "Watch your step," he whispered.

They began walking. As silently as possible. Being an obstacle course it was slow going. Ten metres along, the path joined the river trail. They continued in that direction.

The two armed police officers each took a door of the house.

Wolf, at the back door, spotted movement. "There! There!"

he yelled. "In the bush. Stop! Police!"

A second officer soon raced around the corner of the house.

Wolf pointed to where he'd seen movement.

The pair plunged into the bush in that direction.

The fugitives heard the cops crashing though the underbrush. They panicked. And ran.

There was a loud crack from a service revolver. In rapid succession, three more.

Henry and Pagan heard the whistling sounds of the bullets. They felt them pass by.

They ran faster. Obstacles be damned.

The spirits of the forest are either mischievous or malicious. Bushes grabbed at Pagan and Henry's clothes. Trees seemed to jump up, pinballing them around. Roots tripped them. As expertly as someone intentionally sticking out a foot.

Not on any path, Wolf and his partner stumbled and fell repeatedly. The underbrush was almost impenetrable.

Henry and Pagan reached the stream. Gasping for air. Suppressing the pain from new bruises.

Without stopping his momentum, Henry flipped his canoe over using only his right hand. A spectacularly deft move.

He grabbed the back of the boat, now in the water. He simultaneously snatched up the paddle with his free hand.

"Get in, get in," he loudly urged.

Pagan obeyed. She was barely seated in the front of the boat when Henry set them in motion with a mighty shove. He piled into the canoe. His paddle dove into the water with bold strokes. He dared not turn to see if their pursuers had reached the stream.

Pagan said over her shoulder, "Did you feel it? The bullets. That bastard Wolf tried to shoot us."

She glanced back at the spot they'd shoved off from. No one had yet arrived.

The canoe rounded the first bend in the stream and the site was lost from view.

Pagan swung around in her seat to face Henry.

In the distance came the first sounds of barking.

"A dog!" said Pagan. "A bloody dog!"

Henry tried to intensify his paddling as the volume of the barking increased but to little effect. He was already struggling to breathe.

The dog had picked up the scent of the fugitives and led his handler along the path to the river. It hadn't taken long before they reached the water's edge. The dog was now pacing back and forth, sniffing the ground and the air before committing to the direction that Pagan and Henry had gone.

"Whoa! Whoa Sally!" the dog's handler called out to no avail as the animal plunged into the thick bushes along the water's edge. The officer stumbled to his knees and was dragged a metre or two before he slowed the trajectory of the dog enough to get back on his feet.

Wolf and his fellow officer had eventually found the path, but even so, they were just then reaching the stream, soaking wet and sporting several significant scratches.

Wolf looked out at the stream and then the dog. He shook his head in frustration.

He took a formal tone of superiority with Constable Woods, who was standing beside him—although as a member of the Criminal Investigation Unit, Woods was technically in charge—saying, "Let's go back to the house and check for the kids. If they're not there we can drive up the road to the next house along the river. Cut these guys off. There's a little farm about a kilometre away."

18

The Dryad

The King of the Waters was kinder than the fairies of the forest.

Henry's muscles were burning and cramping. He took three-second breaks. The canoe glided as he shook life back into his arms.

There was no sign of the police behind them.

They neared a small farm, perched on the right bank of the river.

"I'm going to pull in there," Henry called, pointing at the property.

Looking over her shoulder, Pagan replied with alarm, "But that's Jarrod's farm!"

"Maybe he can help us. I can't keep paddling like this. My arms will fall off."

Henry nosed the canoe up to the bank.

As the boat touched shore, Pagan leaned over the side and grabbed the branches of a bush overhanging the bank.

Henry swung the rear of the canoe towards the shore. He also took hold of some greenery.

One by one the pair climbed out of the boat and onto dry land. Henry reached own and pulled the canoe out of the water.

"What about the dog?" said Pagan.

"We'll have to chance it. I can't hear it anymore."

As luck would have it the dog had stopped its pursuit of the fugitives, apparently losing the scent. She returned to the spot where the canoe entered the water and sniffed the ground, going back and forth. If there was a scent to follow it had been dispersed by the wind.

The handler was now taking Sally back to the minivan.

Henry took Pagan's hand and they ran to the farmhouse where she rapped sharply on the back door.

Jarrod Augustine soon appeared. Pulling aside the curtain on the door's window he brightened on seeing Pagan and swung open the door.

"Jarrod," Pagan said breathlessly, "I'm really sorry to ask this but we need to get away from here as quickly as possible. The police are looking for us, *for something we didn't do*. Could you give us a lift somewhere? This is Henry by the way."

Jarrod didn't seem phased by the strange outburst. He nodded to Henry. Smiled. And, as if they had all the time in the world, held out his hand.

Henry shook the hand and looked at Pagan.

They shared the same thought: that it had been a mistake to seek help here. The guy seemed to be clued out to the urgency of their predicament.

Languidly, Jarrod said, "Let me get the car keys." He disappeared into the house but soon returned. Still the definition of unfazed yokel, he said, "You better come inside. A couple of cruisers just pulled into the driveway."

Pagan slid inside, squeezing past Jarrod, with Henry close behind.

"Go upstairs," Jarrod directed them.

"They may have a police dog," said Henry. Hesitating, he added, "My canoe's on the bank though they may not know we have a boat."

"Just go," said Jarrod calmly.

Pagan and Henry fled upstairs while Jarrod went to the half bathroom inside the back door and snatched up an aerosol can of room deodorizer. He sprayed it around the entrance way then returned the can and went out onto a small deck.

Ahead of him was thirty metres of lawn. He spotted Henry's canoe laying on the riverbank. Off to his left were dozens of beehives and beyond that a field of clover surrounded by an assortment of wildflowers.

A second after he'd turned to his right, two police officers rounded the corner of the house in front of him. Each held a drawn firearm. They reacted to Jarrod's presence by swinging their guns upwards to point at him.

"Wolf!" Jarrod said, with a tone of happy surprise, as if he hadn't seen the guns. "Hi. How's it going."

Wolf immediately lowered his handgun. His anxious rigidity lessened markedly and he waved at his partner to also lower his firearm. "Jarrod! This is your place?"

"Yes. My grandparent's old farm." Jarrod, as always, spoke in a drawl that caused people who didn't know him to describe him as slow or dim.

"The honey farm. Right, right," Wolf nodded, remembering. He holstered his handgun and his companion followed suit. "Grant Augustine's brother," he said to Constable Woods.

Jarrod advanced down the three steps of the deck, stopping at the bottom and sticking out his hand in the second officer's direction.

The man shook it. "Darren Woods."

Jarrod detected a grimace of dislike on Woods' face and wondered if it reflected his attitude to Grant in particular or to Natives in general.

"Listen Jarrod," Wolf said, "have you seen anything in the last, say fifteen minutes?" He swept his hand back and forth in the direction of the creek. "We're looking for a couple from the place just down the road."

"And they were on the river?" Jarrod appeared to be puzzled and then deep in thought as he gave the matter grave consideration. "Nooo. I've been out and around back here for awhile. Haven't seen anything at all."

"That canoe down there; that yours?"

"Yeah. Go for a paddle every morning, rain or shine. Best exercise in the world. Just got back fifteen minutes ago or so."

"Upstream or down."

"Up … oh wait, I see what you're asking. Upstream, and no, I didn't see anybody along the bank."

"You see the officer with the dog?"

"Nooo, sorry," Jarrod said, again appearing to strain his brain. "Maybe a matter of timing."

"And I don't hear the damn animal," Constable Woods said in an aside to Wolf. "They musta given up."

Wolf thanked Jarrod for his help.

Woods, speaking gently in the manner he might use if speaking to a slightly dim-witted child, said, "Call 9-1-1 if you see anything. And be careful, those two are armed and dangerous."

"You know," Jarrod said, "the bush is really thick along the edge of this creek. It's a helluva slog to walk it. If I was trying to get away from the police, and a police dog, I'd have swum across the creek. It's no wider than twenty feet anywhere upstream, at most. There's farm fields and roads on the other side, all the way to the u in the river. The river's easily crossable there too, even if you're not much of a swimmer. There's an island right in the middle to break up the swim."

Wolf and Woods looked at each other. It was a reasonable idea but not one that either had considered because the sniffer dog had wanted to set off downstream.

Wolf again thanked Jarrod and added that the people they were searching for were his neighbour, Henry Hebert, and Pagan Egan.

"Oh yeah, heard on the radio you were looking for Pagan. Didn't know about Henry."

"If you see them, don't approach them. Call me instead. You got my number."

As they were walking back to their cars, Constable Woods said to Wolf, "Do you believe him, that he hasn't seen anything?"

"Sure. Why would he lie?"

"I don't know. I guess he wouldn't, plus he seems a bit simple. Not likely he could convincingly play act."

"Actually, he's not simple by any means. When he was in high school a teacher told his parents that he and his twin sister had the two highest IQ's of all the kids in the school."

"What happened to Grant?" Woods said, laughing. "I gotta admit, it's not a bad idea that Egan and Hebert maybe went across the river."

"I'm gonna mention it when I call in. I told you. He's no dummy."

As soon as the officers headed for their cars Jarrod had set to work in his yard. He kept an unobtrusive eye on the departing officers. When the cruisers drove away he went into the house and called for Henry and Pagan to come downstairs. There was no response. He called again and immediately heard the sound of footsteps along the upstairs hallway.

Standing in the kitchen, Jarrod told Pagan and Henry about his visit with the two police officers.

"Was Wolf Byron one of them?" Pagan asked.

"Yes. How did you know?"

"He was just at Henry's house."

"Of course. Well fortunately he doesn't seem to know about me and Aisling; that I might have a reason to cover for you. Told me to call him if I saw you and to run for my life." He smiled mischievously.

"Aisling's my mother," Pagan explained for Henry's sake.

Turning to Jarrod she said, "Thank you so much and ... and I'm so sorry about last night."

"Not a problem. You obviously meant well. I don't think your mother was upset for long. She figures she over-reacted. I think she was only upset because she wants your blessing. Happy family relations sort of thing. Right now she's just worried about you."

"Yes, damn. I must call her. Do you have a phone I can use? Ours are probably in Henry's kitchen." She glanced at Henry who nodded confirmation.

Jarrod picked up his cell from the kitchen counter, handed it to Pagan, and she stepped out of the room.

"Please sit down," Jarrod said, waving Henry to the kitchen table. "Can I get you some sage tea with honey?"

Henry saw a cup of the tea sitting on the table. "No thanks. I'm fine."

"It's my own honey," Jarrod said with a shy half-smile as he sat down.

It struck Henry that Jarrod not only looked young but his manner was almost childlike.

For a couple of minutes the pair sat in silence, waiting for

Pagan, whose muffled voice could be heard coming from another room.

"How do you know Wolf?" Henry asked eventually.

"He's a friend of my brother Grant's so he was around my parents' place a lot. The two of them joined the force at the same time. Sounds like you know him too."

"No. Pagan does. He goes out with her roommate Darla."

"Really? Her roommate. For how long?"

"Seven months," said Pagan on entering the room. She returned the gazes of both men with a forced half smile on her face. The relief of being back on good terms with her mother wasn't enough to erase the stress of the situation she was now caught up in.

"Do you want some sage tea with honey?" Jarrod said.

"No, no thanks," said Pagan, pulling out a chair.

"He produces the honey here," explained Henry.

Jarrod blushed.

"Do you know why the cops are looking for us?" Pagan asked him.

"Just what I heard on the radio. There was a kidnapping apparently; the kids of a local bank manager."

"Yes, to force the manager to rob her own bank. The reason that they suspect me of being involved in this is because the kidnapping was staged in an identical manner to the kidnapping and robbery in an unpublished novel of mine. It's a stupid assumption to think I'd do that. We think that someone is trying to point the finger at me."

"To send the police off in the wrong direction. Makes sense. Who knew the details of the book?"

"Well that's what we've been trying to figure out. So far as I know only one person has actually read the manuscript; a literary agent in Ontario who called the police. My ex-boyfriend would recognize the plot and there's a synopsis in a notebook in my desk. Only Wolf and Darla had access to that —when I wasn't home—but I don't see Darla doing anything to hurt me. My money's on Wolf."

"Really! But ... Wolf being involved is hard to believe. He's no angel, and he thinks he's God's gift to women, but I don't see him as a criminal. Couldn't there be others who know the novel's plot? Your mother knows, at least the gist of it. She told me about it so maybe the word's been passed around."

"It's possible," said Pagan. Word of mouth wasn't an idea she'd yet considered. It broadened the list of possible suspects considerably. "But ... I don't know ... this wasn't just about the book. Whoever did it had access to my flat. They took my handguns and, I assume, took my car yesterday morning before I got up. That all points to Wolf and no one else."

"He knew where the guns were kept," Henry added.

"Right," Pagan echoed.

Jarrod stood, picked up his tea mug and put it in the sink.

Pagan noted that there were no other dirty dishes. She looked about the room; it was spotless. The rest of the house was the same. Like a woman lived there instead of a man barely out of his teens. Was this her mother's doing? The two were soon going to live here after all. The thought revived Pagan's feeling of resentment that her childhood home would be sold. Her refuge. Her continuity. The place she often dreamed she was in. The location telling her she was home.

"And there's something else," Henry said for Jarrod's benefit. "Wolf shot at us when they raided my house."

"What? God! I suppose he was scared. They keep saying on the radio that you're armed and dangerous."

"We were running away," said Pagan, "unarmed. We posed no danger."

Jarrod, who'd remained standing, his back leaning against the counter, said, "That makes no sense—sorry. He had no reason to shoot you. You don't have any evidence that he's guilty of the robbery so far as I can tell. Plus—if he set this up so he could rob a bank and make the police think you did it—he'd want you to stay alive and free. I'd think so anyway. If he captures the two of you, nobody's gonna pay out any ransom. So why would he shoot you?"

Henry and Pagan were slow to answer. There was no obvious reason why Wolf should want them dead.

"Well, technically we don't know that Wolf was the one who fired the shot," Henry said. He didn't look at Pagan. He felt like he was betraying her, although he was giving her a way out if she was wrong.

"No," Pagan agreed. "It could have been the other cop."

Jarrod said, "Okay. Can I stop you for a moment? I can understand the argument that Wolf might be behind this but I think the rest—that he's trying to kill you—is … I don't know … a little much. I think it's more likely, I mean if you're right and he's one of the kidnappers, that he would have missed you on purpose. He'd just want to make you afraid to turn yourself in 'cus you'll think you'll get shot."

"To make us keep running. That would explain it," Pagan said.

"A big question mark," said Henry, "is who is Wolf's partner—I mean if he did the abduction. Apparently there was also a woman kidnapper and Pagan's convinced it isn't Darla."

"Darla wouldn't do such a thing," said Pagan. "Whoever did this—is doing this—is trying to set me up. Darla's my friend."

"I might be able to suggest a name," said Jarrod. "I was surprised when Henry said that Wolf was dating your roommate because he's had the same girlfriend for years—Morgan Macrae. She's a police officer too. She took a job in Moncton several months ago with the RCMP. Grant told me that Wolf was going to Moncton a couple of days a week, to Morgan's place, and he was trying to get a job there too."

"Poor Darla," said Pagan. "Wolf told her that he's taking advanced courses in Moncton to get a promotion, and that he stays at his cousin's place when he's there."

"So you think that Morgan could be in on this with Wolf?" Henry asked Jarrod.

"I don't have an opinion one way or the other. I don't really know Morgan. She's a cop, but then so is Wolf. She obviously knows how to use a handgun. … Don't you think you should call the police, maybe through Darla, and let them know what you suspect? As long as you're free the cops will be looking for you."

"No," said Pagan. "Darla would probably just get pissed off and defensive, and the cops, well Wolf's one of their own, so they're going to take his side. Plus we don't have any confidence that if we were in custody that the cops wouldn't spend their time investigating us, hoping to find the kids in that way. I think we need to look for them ourselves."

Jarrod, suddenly straightening up, signalling it was time for action, said, "That ride you wanted. We should go. We can talk about this later. Wolf didn't know the canoe was yours so I told him and Darren that any smart person would swim across the creek and then head for the river. They seemed to buy it. I don't know anything about the police but I'd guess, at this moment, that they're swarming along the edge of the river, on both sides, near Henry's place. And will be, for awhile. Once they don't find any tracks they'll start blocking the roads and then you'll never get out of here. They may even be doing that as we speak. I think that now is your best chance of getting away. I mean immediately. I can put you in the trunk of my car and head east. It's a big car. You won't suffocate. We could get you a long way from here in half an hour, to somewhere they won't expect you to be."

"Where would you take us?" said Pagan. "We can't go to my apartment."

"They'll never look for you at the place I have in mind: my parents' house. They're away visiting family in Dartmouth so they won't be popping in. And their place is just up the road from Wolf's."

"Where the kids might be," said Pagan. "Let's go."

19

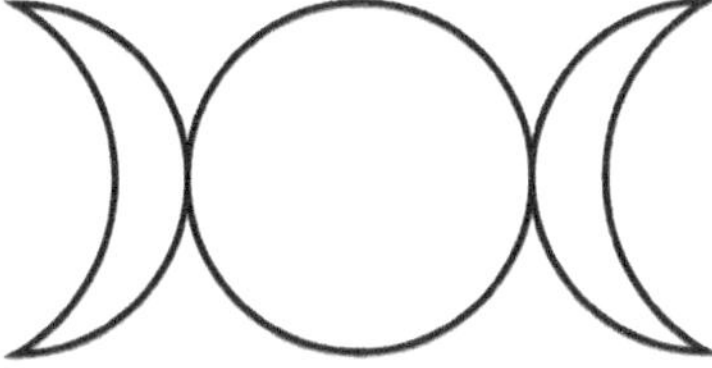 Jarrod emptied the trunk of his car, moving his emergency tool box and first-aid kit to the floor of the back seat.

On Jarrod's cue, Pagan and Henry, who'd been watching from behind a curtain, scuttled from the house to the car. Each carried a pillow.

With a sense of impending doom because of mild claustrophobia, Henry put on a brave face and climbed into the trunk, where he lay in a fetal position. Pagan followed suit, spooning in front of him.

In spite of the discomfort of being in the trunk, the bumpy movement of the car on Jarrod's driveway as they left the farm, acted to ease the tension that both Pagan and Henry felt. They were moving away from the police search, cocooned in secret.

Jarrod drove east along the secondary highway towards Megumawaach. He reasoned that if the police were to begin blocking roads that they'd start with the highway so he turned south at the first road they came to.

Pagan modulated the volume of her voice, hoping it would be just loud enough to be heard over the noise of the car but not so loud that Jarrod would hear it. "Can you hear me okay?"

"Yes."

"It's a relief to be escaping Wolf."

"Yes."

"I know that Jarrod's dismissive of the possibility that Wolf tried to kill us but I'm still not convinced. I think it might be a thing he's capable of. There's something sinister and phony about the guy."

"Jarrod did raise some good objections."

"Sure, but I think he just assumes I'm some melodramatic mystery writer who thinks life is like my books."

"Well, he didn't say ... Does it matter what he thinks?"

"No. Even if Wolf didn't try to kill us in the bush it doesn't mean that he won't try sometime if we get close to the kids. He went to all this trouble to make us look guilty, the way he staged the robbery and all that, so he wouldn't want that perception to be changed. The surest way to do that will be to kill us. Probably after the ransom is paid."

"But that would mean ... the kids ... when they're rescued will know that we weren't their kidnappers, so ..."

"But I thought of that when I wrote my damn novel. The kidnappers never let the kids see their faces. Hopefully they copied that part of the book like they copied everything else in it. ... I don't want to think about ... Maybe Jarrod's right and my imagination is just getting the better of me and Wolf's not involved."

One of Henry's arms was pinned between him and Pagan, but his other arm rested along her side with his hand on her shoulder.

In the dark of the trunk both were suddenly aware of the proximity of the other and they fell silent.

Henry's face was against Pagan's hair. It smelled like heaven. "Sorry," he said eventually. "I must smell like sweat from all that rowing."

"Not to worry, I hadn't noticed. ... You know what's funny?"

"There's something funny?"

"Well no. Ironic. A couple of weeks ago I was talking to Darla about how bored I was and how I could use a little excitement in my life."

"Are you having fun yet?"

"Not only is this too much excitement for anybody, and the wrong sort, but I'm thinking about those two small kids. What must they be thinking? How terrified must they be? They're in mortal danger. I want to go to Wolf's house as soon as we get to Jarrod's parent's."

At that moment the car stopped. The conversation between the passengers in the trunk ceased as well. Their hearts beat quicker until the car resumed its movement.

Soon, Pagan and Henry were both sweating and concentrating on slowly breathing the stifling air.

Pagan tried to calm herself with her mental game she called, 'Name the best adjectives to capture this moment'. She thought, 'cramped' but then checked herself. That wasn't what she felt. It made a lot of difference to know you weren't alone when going through something this awful. 'Companionable', 'supportive', 'comforting', 'intimate'.

The Augustine house was fifteen minutes south of Megumawaach on a paved road. It overlooked an ocean bay.

Jarrod pulled his car into the double garage and closed the door behind them. He popped the trunk.

His prisoners seemed dazed as they raised their heads. After climbing from the trunk they flexed cramped muscles back to life and sucked in huge breaths of fresh air infused with the smell of salt water.

Once inside the house, Jarrod led Pagan and Henry into the kitchen. The room was much more than that. There were cupboards at one end with an island in front of them, and a large oak table and chairs on the other side of that.

But that was only one half of the space. In the other half was a love seat, rocking chair, and wardrobe. And a stone fireplace. Along the entire east side of the room were floor to ceiling windows that faced the bay.

Pagan looked about. Through a doorway she could see enough of the livingroom to note the cathedral ceiling and massive stone fireplace. The house was what she'd call a mansion. "This is a beautiful place. Is Wolf's as opulent?"

"I wouldn't say so, no, but it's a nice house."

"Did it once belong to his parents?"

"No, he grew up downtown. His folks may have helped him buy the house but he has three sisters so I doubt they could have given him much money, or loaned it to him. I mean, parents do try to treat their kids equally—at least in my experience they do. Wolf always talked about wanting to have a house around here since his first visit with my brother Grant."

"How can he afford it on a cop's salary?"

"Well, it's on the other side of the road which makes a big difference. But ... I don't know."

"This is a big house for just two people," said Henry, standing in the middle of the kitchen. "There must be like ... how many bedrooms?"

"Six. I think my parents are counting on us all—the kids, I mean—having big families and coming here for Sundays and holidays."

At the mention of Jarrod having children, Pagan turned towards the windows, apparently just then noticing the stunning ocean view.

"How many kids do your parents have?" asked Henry.

"Four. The oldest is Grant, then Beth, and lastly me and my twin sister Ellie. I don't know where my manners are. Guys, please sit down."

Henry, who'd been standing beside the loveseat, sat down at one end. Pagan crossed the room and sat beside him.

Jarrod took the rocking chair after turning it to face the loveseat. Looking at the pair in front of him he said, with a business-like attitude, "So, what are you going to do now? Wait ... before you say anything, I had a thought. You said you aren't going to the police but if you want I could call my brother Grant, who's a cop, and informally ..."

"No, not when they think we're guilty," Pagan blurted forcefully. "I think, as a first order of business, that we need to find the kids and get them out of danger."

Jarrod cast a questioning look at Henry.

"Yes," Henry said with an affirmative nod.

"Okay," Jarrod said, "and how are we going to find them?"

"Well, first, we check Wolf's house," Pagan said. "That's the simplest step and hopefully all it takes. How far away is his place?"

"About a kilometre up the road."

"Can you drive us?" Henry asked.

"Now?"

"Yes. Pagan wants to do this ASAP and I agree."

Jarrod considered the request before saying, "We know

that Wolf won't be home so if the kids are there the woman will be with them..." He shook his head. "Sorry, I'm still trying to get my head around the idea that Wolf's a kidnapper ... but whatever ..." He cleared his throat and resumed. "It might be a fair assumption to think that, if the kids are there, the woman who's with them will keep them inside. That means you'll either have to barge your way in or spy through the windows ..."

"Spy through the windows," Pagan interjected, anxious to speed up the conversation. Jarrod's laborious cadence was proving excruciating."We don't want to panic the woman holding the kids. Once we're sure the kids are there, we'll call the cops."

"Or Grant," said Henry, "so Wolf won't know we're on to him and interfere in the arrest."

"Right," Pagan confirmed.

Jarrod, having subtly brought the couple round to his view, said, "Given all that, that we want to secretly spy on the house and call ... whoever, if we confirm the kids are there, I think it would be best to wait until tonight. We can park a ways off and you can walk to the house in the dark. And you can look in the windows without being seen."

After further discussion, a plan was developed.

Concluding the session, Jarrod said, "If there's no one home when you get to the house, and you want to look around inside for any reason, I know where Wolf hides his back door key. I had to drop off some moose meat for my brother a couple of years ago when Wolf was away and he told me where it's kept."

20

A more detailed plan was developed, of the sort you might expect from a group that included two mystery writers. It combined deduction with needless complication.

It was still early in the day, not yet 10:00 AM, when Step One was initiated.

Henry was far from being convinced that Jarrod could pull off the tasks that the plan demanded since their success might require a facility for quick ad-libbing. But he wanted to believe things would turn out well—for Pagan's sake—so he didn't share his doubts with her.

Jarrod phoned his brother Grant Augustine's cell. Receiving no answer he left a message, asking for a call back.

On hearing the message, a short time later, Grant felt sure that Jarrod wanted to know what was happening in the search for Pagan Egan. It was understandable, Jarrod was engaged to her mother.

"You're not calling because something's come up are you?" Grant said when Jarrod answered the phone.

"No, no. Just wondering how things are going."

"Going how? With the search for Pagan I presume. There's nothing to report. I can't really talk about it anyway."

"No I know, but her mother's worried. I promised I'd ask."

"Not surprising. Tell her that, for Pagan's sake, if she hears from her daughter, to tell her to turn herself in. This is strictly unofficial but I'll try to let you know when anything happens, and something should happen soon. There's a major search going on and if Pagan and her friend steal a car there's roadblocks everywhere—well on the highway anyway. They won't get far."

"I'll pass it on," Jarrod said earnestly. This was all bonus information since the real reason for his call was still to come. "Oh, while I have you, there's something I've been wanting to ask you about. It's not related to what's going on with Pagan but with something else. At the wedding rehearsal, Pagan told me that her roommate—a Darla something or other—is dating Wolf Byron. That surprised me. When did he break up with Morgan?"

"Ahh … never." Grant chuckled. "Wolf's a dog. Always has been. I know he's still seeing Morgan during the week, in Moncton, because last week he was complaining that she'd be on vacation at her parent's cottage this week and he couldn't get the time off to be there."

Once he was off the phone, Jarrod relayed his conversation to Henry and Pagan, who continued to share the loveseat.

"Sounds like you're right about Darla not being involved," Henry said to Pagan. "If this crime is Wolf's doing, Morgan is the more likely partner. She's off work this week and staying at her parent's cottage. That's not too coincidental now is it?"

Pagan nodded vigorously. "If the kids aren't at Wolf's place then they're likely to be at that cottage."

The second Step in the master plan was to definitively eliminate Darla as Wolf's accomplice and, again, the task fell to Jarrod.

Darla doesn't work on Sundays, Pagan had explained. "Between 11:00 and noon she always walks to Sobeys for her groceries."

Wolf was working—they'd just seen him—so he wasn't with the kidnapped children. Pagan and Jarrod had agreed with Henry's thought that someone had to be with the kids, so if Darla was at home and following her usual routine then she could be eliminated as a suspect. Wolf's partner in crime would have to be someone else; Morgan in all likelihood.

Jarrod drove west, leaving the bay behind him, and turned north onto the highway heading to Megumawaach. He soon came to a police stop. It struck him as an odd place for a roadblock until he remembered that the Megumawaach airport was just ahead, so a possible destination for escaping criminals.

He didn't recognize the policewoman who approached the driver's side window. She glanced past him, checking out the interior of the car, and asked Jarrod whether he'd seen the two suspects that the police were looking for, or anything out of the ordinary.

"No officer," Jarrod said wide-eyed.

"Pop your trunk please sir."

A second officer—a man that Jarrod recognized as a friend of his brother's—did a quick scan of the trunk, shut it, and waved to the officer waiting by Jarrod's window.

"Have a nice day sir," the first constable said, stepping away from the car.

Jarrod drove into downtown Megumawaach. He parked in a spot where he could watch the front entrance of the converted house where Darla and Pagan shared a flat. When a woman matching the person in the Facebook photo provided by Pagan, emerged from the house, Jarrod raised his phone and took a snap.

He watched Darla interacting with an old man on the sidewalk who was walking towards her.

Jarrod kept Darla in his sights on her route to Sobeys.

He eventually followed her back home.

Back at his parent's place, a short time later, Jarrod stood in the middle of the kitchen with Pagan and Henry on either side of him, showing them the photos he'd taken. The woman was definitely Darla, Pagan confirmed.

"Stop at that one," she said and Jarrod halted the photographic slideshow. "The old man in that picture is Barney, our neighbour. He's a hoot. And look, Darla's smiling. It's not the expression of someone in the middle of a major crime."

"So confirmation that Darla's not involved," Henry said.

Step Three commenced.

Jarrod phoned his friend and neighbour Todd Melanson

who owned a garage situated on a road near his farm. Most of Todd's business involved repairing farm equipment and small engines, but he also did some towing.

Shortly after the call, Todd left in his tow truck and headed for Jarrod's. There, he hooked up the pickup—the door of which was always left open—and towed it to the home of Jarrod's parents on the other side of Megumawaach.

The story that Jarrod had given Todd was that his parent's car was in the shop for repairs. He'd loaned them his car after they got an urgent phone call about a family crisis because they had to leave immediately. He was now stuck at his parent's place and wanted his other vehicle towed there.

Todd thought that it might have been a lot cheaper for Jarrod to find a way home rather than to have his truck towed to where he was, but it wasn't for him to say.

Since no one answered when he knocked on the front door, Todd left the pickup in the driveway as per his instructions and headed home.

21

The Goose Girl

Five-year-old Hélène lay on the double bed, her right arm draped over little brother Anthony who'd finally fallen asleep. She was the big sister and the little boy's protector.

The lights were out in the bedroom but the door was half open.

Pirate Grace O'Malley could see the two children from her perch at the end of the couch in the livingroom of the cottage. The open door wasn't a concession to the kidnapped children, to ease their fear of the dark, but to allow Grace to keep them in her sights and to have them remember they were being watched.

Calico Jack was on the phone and Grace was keeping her voice at a low volume.

"I've been thinking," Grace said. "When that bitch's seventy-two hours are up, if we don't have the money, we'll have to lose these kids."

The issue of what to do should the children's parents not meet the pirate's ransom demand had never been discussed as a possibility.

"Don't worry, the money will come in," said Calico Jack. "We agreed to be patient. She can't rob the bank because she called the cops. They'll be watching her now. So she needs to work with the ex-husband. It takes time to get that kind of cash together."

"Psh. That's all you can say? I'll believe it when I see it."

"No mother's going to jeopardize the possibility of ever seeing her kids again because of money."

"Well, the bitch went to the cops and she was told not to!" Grace slowly inhaled to calm herself. "That should be punished," she added with conviction. "We'd be in our rights to not even wait around for the seventy-two hours. Send the bitch a message. Show her what fucking with us does."

"Please be patient."

"I'm sick of wearing this bloody mask. My face sweats and it smells. I'm taking it off."

"Don't …"

"The little fucks are sleeping. If they keep pissing me off I'm going to tie them to the bed."

Never certain whether Grace would carry out one of her threats or not, but always assuming it was likely just talk, Calico Jack said soothingly, "It won't be for much longer and you won't have to worry about them."

"Yeah. One way or another." The statement was clearly a warning. Grace wasn't about to listen to Calico Jack for much longer.

22

The Huntress

Step Four. It was after 10:00 PM when Jarrod drove his car up the road to Wolf's house. Henry and Pagan were in the back seat, dressed in their borrowed dark clothes.

There were no lights on inside the house. A single bulb shone above the front door of what would likely, in a realtor listing, be referred to as a comfortable, two-storey family home.

There were no vehicles in the driveway.

Jarrod knew that beside Wolf's driveway was another one. It led to the house next door, sitting fifty metres or so off the road. He backed his car onto that second drive. A thick swathe of bush between the driveways hid any view of the car from Wolf's house.

The fact that no one appeared to be in the house called for Step Four, Plan B.

Plan A would have consisted of playing Peeping Tom and looking through the house's windows into illuminated rooms.

Plan B involved Pagan and Henry going into the house, armed with flashlights, and having a look around for either the missing children or any tell-tale signs that they'd been there.

"The back door key is under the 'third rock from the sun'," Jarrod explained. "Wolf's idea of a joke. One of the stones surrounding the garden bed, the one right beside the door, has a large sun painted on it."

Pagan and Henry climbed from Jarrod's car, gently shutting their doors behind them before heading for the road.

They stayed close beside each other as they walked up Wolf's driveway, hugging the bush side in case they suddenly needed a hiding spot.

They scanned the house and the road for any movement.

Their potential nervousness was mitigated by the fact that they were invisible in the shadows. Both had agreed to only use their flashlights inside. Once past the house they crossed to the back door.

There was a sudden burst of laughter from some teenagers next door, a long way away, but their voices were amplified in the night. Henry and Pagan momentarily froze but quickly recovered and returned to the task at hand.

The door key was where Jarrod said it would be and the house apparently had no security system. At least there was no alarm when the rear door was opened.

Pagan immediately went to work in the kitchen. The first order of business was to look for a landline telephone. She ran her flashlight beam up and down the wall and along the cupboards, hoping to get lucky. Nothing.

Henry, meanwhile, went through the upstairs bedrooms and then headed for the basement.

Seeing nothing in the kitchen, Pagan moved to the livingroom. She soon spotted a telephone on the small side table beside an easy chair.

Pagan snatched up the receiver and punched in several numbers.

"Hello babe," said Darla at the other end.

"Listen Darla, it's me, Pagan, I have to talk fast so please listen."

"What's going on? Why does Wolf's name come up on my phone?" Darla sounded annoyed.

"We're at his house. Henry and I. We're looking for the kidnapped kids. You have to listen to me. You have to call the police and tell them to confront Wolf because he's the kidnapper."

The headlights from the pickup pulling into the driveway played across the inside wall of the room.

Pagan dropped the receiver and ducked low. Her flashlight inadvertently turning towards the ceiling.

Wolf was still in the moving vehicle when he spotted a bobbing light through the picture window.

"It's Wolf! It's Wolf!" Pagan called out to Henry. She

sprinted for the back door.

Wolf jumped from his truck. He ran to the front door. Fumbled with his key in the lock. Flung open the door. Stepped into the house. There was a shape, a man he would have said, exiting through the kitchen door directly ahead.

Wolf flicked on a light. Grabbed his .308 rifle from the closet.

He strode into the kitchen. Wrenched open a cupboard drawer. Removed a box of shells. He efficiently loaded bullets into a clip. Inserted it into his rifle. Ran back to the front door.

He saw no one. The robber, or robbers could have fled anywhere. The sound of a revving car came from the driveway next door. Wolf ran towards the road.

A dark coloured sedan, engine roaring, squealed out of the next door drive. It zoomed past him.

Wolf took quick aim and fired off a shot. He heard the ping of the bullet bouncing off the car's body.

He sprinted to his truck. Tossing his rifle onto the passenger seat, he got in.

Wolf turned the ignition. Put the car in gear. But he immediately realized that he wasn't going anywhere. He shook his head in frustration.

In the distance Wolf heard the diminishing sound of the fleeing car. The laughter of the teens next door had been silenced by the rifle shot.

An inspection of the passenger side rear tire would show that it had been slashed with a knife.

Darla stood silently, phone in hand, considering what Pagan had said to her. It was horrifying that her roommate suspected Wolf of being involved in the current kidnapping. She dialed Wolf's cell. She knew he'd laugh when she told him about her conversation with Pagan. It wouldn't phase him at all.

Kneeling on the back seat of Jarrod's car and watching the road behind them, Pagan and Henry expected to see Wolf's pickup come roaring after them.

"Stop worrying," said Jarrod looking in the rearview mirror at his two passengers. "One of Wolf's tires may have had a little accident."

Henry and Pagan looked at each other, turned, and plunked themselves down onto the seat.

Pagan felt a rush of relief and took Henry's hand.

Back at Jarrod's, his car safely stowed in the garage, the three newly minted criminals discussed their next move: the yet to be devised Step Five.

"It's imperative that we make a plan tonight," Pagan said, "and put it into play first thing in the morning. Who knows how much danger those kids are in?"

Henry, sitting beside her on the loveseat once again, their default setting, asked, "How did Darla take what you were saying about Wolf?"

"I only got to tell her that Wolf was behind the kidnappings before he showed up. I have no idea what she'll think. Probably be pissed off by it, I guess. She's pretty infatuated with the guy."

23 Monday

At four in the morning, Jarrod, who was cursed with being a light sleeper, became aware that someone was stirring.

Following the complaining squeaks of the floorboards, he listened. The person walked down the bedroom hallway and into the kitchen.

The back door opened and closed.

Jarrod debated whether to get up to see if the person was okay but hesitated since he wasn't their guardian—or jailer. They were entitled to come and go as they pleased.

Two minutes passed before he heard the back door open and close, and the deadbolt slide shut. The person retraced their steps along the hallway and back to their room.

Jarrod was up at 6:00 AM, an hour before the time the others had set their alarms for. He filled the coffee-maker and turned it on.

His noticed his phone sitting on the kitchen table. He knew it had been used in the night because he was absolutely certain he'd left it on the counter, as always. Looking at the call record he saw that only one call had been made, but he didn't recognize the number.

Jarrod wasn't sure exactly where he'd heard it, but he knew that Jessica Macrae's family owned a landscaping supply yard near Moncton. Using his parent's computer in the study, he made a list of the possible Macrae businesses and looked each of them up.

One of the company Facebook pages not only had a post announcing they'd be open on the Monday of this long weekend, today, but it listed the owners' names as Scotty and Anna Macrae. Lady Luck was smiling.

In further searches, Jarrod found an address for the Macrae home in Riverview, but nothing on their cottage.

Turning to the CBC News website, he read an article about the kidnapping. It was the top story of the day, not surprisingly. The police were revealing little except that the two kidnapped children were still being searched for, as were Pagan and Henry. The reporter mentioned that the area behind Henry's property, around the stream and river, had been searched.

What gave Jarrod pause was seeing the photo of Pagan that accompanied the piece. It occurred to him that since the photo was likely on all the news sites, and in all the newspapers, that most adults in the province had likely seen it. That would make it exceedingly difficult for Pagan to avoid recognition as she and Henry went driving about, searching for the Gallant children. And it now seemed certain that they would have to drive to Moncton in the hope of getting the address of the Macrae cottage from Morgan's parents.

Subsequent internet searches of the CTV News, Global News, and the local newspaper websites, confirmed Jarrod's suspicion about the ubiquity of Pagan's photo.

There were no photos of Henry, not yet, but that could change at any time. There was however, on all sites, a description of him provided by the police in their press conference. It included the phrase 'long dark hair and short dark beard'.

After Henry and Pagan came out for breakfast, Jarrod told them where things stood with respect to tracking down the location of the Macrae cottage, and what he'd seen online.

Using an electric set of hair clippers owned by Jarrod's father—who liked to keep his hair cropped military short— Henry went to work. First, he shortened his beard to stubble, then he trimmed a considerable amount off his hair.

Pagan had spent the night in the bedroom of Jarrod's twin sister Ellie where she'd spotted a box of black hair dye on the dresser. She retrieved it and dyed her hair.

Later, following Jarrod's invitation, she went through Ellie's closet and dresser and picked out a suitable outfit.

Pagan and Henry got their first post-makeover look at each other a short time later.

Pagan, instead of being the naturalistic, make-up free woman in loose hemp clothing, now had dyed hair. She wore ruby red lipstick, jeans, and a sleeveless top that revealed a large tattoo on each of her shoulders. A sunflower on one and a spiral goddess on the other.

Henry meanwhile, sported a white shirt and dress pants. With his short hair and fashionable stubble he was no longer the mountain man but looked more like a model in a men's fashion magazine.

Henry and Pagan both felt self-conscious about their transformations as they entered the kitchen, and even more so as they were being scrutinized by the other.

They were both shyly thrilled as they observed the exotic person they now confronted.

On Pagan and Henry's way out the door, Jarrod handed them the keys to his pickup. He also gave them his cell phone, a credit card, and a piece of paper. On one side of it was a map of Moncton and Riverview showing the locations of the home and business owned by Morgan's parents. On the flip side of the page was a map of the roads to take to get well south of their current location before turning onto the highway.

"You shouldn't run into any police if you follow the route I've given you," Jarrod said. "It will keep you off the highway as long as possible. I can't imagine the cops setting up roadblocks too far from Megumawaach, on lightly used roads, and the further south you get the likelihood decreases."

"Thank you," Pagan said, "… again."

"You're a lifesaver," echoed Henry. "How do we look?"

"Transformed. Attractive. You don't look like yourselves at all."

Normally such a comment wouldn't be seen as much of a compliment but today it was taken as high praise.

The pair climbed into Jarrod's pickup.

Henry snuck his tenth covert glance at the tattoo on Pagan's right shoulder. It was a silhouette of a woman, broad hipped with hands raised openly, unafraid, and there was a spiral on the figure's stomach.

As she started the truck, Pagan glanced at Henry and saw him looking. "Do you know what that is?"

"A fertility symbol maybe."

"I suppose it could be. It's a Neo-pagan icon—a goddess —so like any icon it's meaning isn't fixed. It opens up like a good poem. To me it stands for powerful women. Most people would see the spiral as being about birth, death, and renewal. I don't disagree but I see it mainly as being about personal growth. Going outward, the spiral expands, grows, and encompasses the world. Reverse it, and the spiral takes the outside world into the heart of us, changing us."

"And is that a sun on your other shoulder?"

"A sunflower. Symbol of veganism. I got the tattoo in my teens when I was a vegan. I backed off of that somewhat because of my father's egg business—I didn't want to hurt his feelings and make him feel like I was being judgmental about him. I now eat eggs and cheese, but still not meat."

24

Force and Reason

At the Megumawaach Police Headquarters, Sergeant Robert Landry, was placed in charge of the investigation into the kidnapping of the two Gallant children,

He had put together an ad hoc incident team made up of members of the Criminal Investigation Division.

One of those in his group was Constable Darren Woods, whom he was addressing: "I told you and Byron from the beginning that I was highly doubtful that the river search would turn up anything. We wasted a whole goddamn day beating the bushes around Hebert's property. These people are mobile. ... You said at yesterday's meeting that there was a canoe at the farm next to Hebert's house at the ... the ..." He snapped his fingers—with rapid multiple clicks—to prompt Woods.

"At the Jarrod Augustine place. And sir, the idea about the suspects crossing the river came from Augustine. I didn't agree with Wolf that it was a good suggestion. I don't trust Augustine."

Landry ignored the comment. "So, okay, we're talking about Grant's brother. Pay Jarrod another visit. See if the canoe is still there. And if Augustine's there too for that matter."

"Gladly."

"Oh, and check to see if the two vehicles are in the driveway. Both of them. You said there were two."

"Right, a pickup and a sedan."

Woods turned and began to leave but paused at the open door after Landry called his name.

"And if Augustine isn't there," said Landry, "speak to Grant and see if you can get a lead on where he might be."

"I will. … Sir, could I ask something?"

"Go ahead."

"I wondered why we're focused on finding Egan and Hebert instead of the kids?"

"Where would we look for the kids?"

"I don't know."

"Exactly. They could be anywhere. It's not uncommon for kidnappers to keep children shut up somewhere while they go on with their lives so as not to arouse any suspicion of their involvement. All we can do is to pursue those we think are responsible for the kidnapping and hope it will lead us to the kids."

After Woods had left, Landry sat down and stared up at the whiteboard in the incident room. He rubbed his nose as if relieving some discomfort where a pair of glasses had been.

He was thinking about what he would say to Philpott.

Deputy Police Chief Bryce Philpott had left the investigation to Landry and the sergeant hoped it would stay that way. It was always harder to operate when someone questioned your every move. And it was a constant headache to have to report to Philpott about the state of an investigation when there was no progress. He could sense the deputy chief's negative judgment, even if nothing of that nature was being stated.

Landry was more worried about the crime his team was investigating than he was about Philpott however, and he returned to that. They were down to only twenty-four hours remaining until the deadline given by the kidnappers to meet the ransom demand, and they were still no closer to finding Pagan Egan and her boyfriend.

And no ransom payment had been made. Not that the police were urging the thing be paid but, given the state of the investigation, Landry had reached the point of secretly praying that the parents coughed up. It's what he'd do if these were his kids.

His understanding was that it was Grenville Gallant, the father of the missing kids, that was the holdup. The guy had first insisted that nothing be done until he was back in

Megumawaach so he could negotiate a deal. Negotiate! The useless son-of-a-bitch sounded like a greedy prick who was trying to get out of paying anything.

Landry focused on the face of Henry Hebert in an image newly added to the whiteboard. Until an hour ago they'd had nothing, but a group photograph from his last workplace in Toronto had been emailed to them. The photo, cropped to include only Henry, was just now being released to the media.

"Excuse me sir," said Corporal Leslie Carruthers, her face suddenly appearing in the doorway.

"Yes," said Landry, "Come in."

After stepping into the room, Carruthers said, "There's a funny thing. I had a second look at the email from …" she looked down at her notes, "from Corporal Childers in Toronto who sent us the photo of Hebert. In the email he included the names of the three other people in the picture. It suddenly occurred to me that I recognized one of the names: Gillian Morris. She's the literary agent in Toronto who tipped us about Pagan Egan."

Landry, who'd thus far been looking back over his shoulder, spun in his chair to face Carruthers. "We thought that Morris had been eliminated from all consideration as someone involved; that she was just a concerned citizen. Have you spoken to her?"

"No. I just now looked at the email."

"Well follow up with her please, right away, and see what she has to say. And find out where she is … I mean is she here or in Ontario. Then get back to me immediately. Oh, and good work."

When he was once again alone, Landry considered this latest news. Was Morris in on the kidnapping along with Pagan Egan and Henry Hebert? It seemed unlikely since it was Morris who'd tipped off the police.

But what about Morris and Hebert—the Toronto connection? Was it possible that Pagan Egan was being set up by the two of them? He'd assumed that Egan was guilty because she'd run from the police and hadn't turned herself in but maybe that was Henry Hebert's doing. If he was setting

Egan up it would explain why they'd been tipped off that the kidnapping followed her unpublished novel. And it would explain why Egan and Hebert were together without the kids. It would be Hebert's real partner who was with them.

Landry got on the phone to Carruthers. "When you speak to Gillian Morris, please ask if anyone else in her office read Egan's manuscript. And I want to know where the thing is now and everywhere it's been since Morris received it."

25

The Kelpie

With Pagan driving and Henry navigating, the fugitives headed south, following Jarrod's map.

It eventually led them west and then south on the highway.

For Henry, the stress of being wanted by the police had eased when he and Pagan escaped the area of Jarrod's home. But here on the highway was the first time he actually felt calm. He could see all around, and for a considerable distance, and felt assured that there was no one nearby who would be shooting at them.

Pagan focused on her driving. She remained wary of her surroundings, frequently checking behind them.

She was mostly silent until suddenly saying, "I wish I'd never written that damn book for all the trouble it's caused. A miserable failure of a novel for my not grasping the full odiousness of kidnapping, like it was just a cozy subject for mystery stories."

Henry glanced over and said, "I think you're being too hard on yourself. You didn't cause what's happening."

"No, but I failed to grasp just how traumatic a kidnapping is. I treated it like an armchair diversion."

"Well, aren't all mysteries like that? It's a strange genre. People get murdered and we see it as the basis for an entertainment. We all do it, although, of course, the real thing is horrifying."

"Except I thought that I could make the perpetrators my heroines."

They fell silent again. A full two minutes of reflection passed before Henry, attempting to lighten Pagan's mood, said, "How do you know when to stop; when a book you're writing is finished?"

"When I'm sick of the damn thing."

"Sounds like a good rule of thumb for me to keep in mind."

After glancing once again in the rearview mirror and then up ahead, Pagan said, "It's just as Jarrod said, no roadblocks."

"He's clever in a way," Henry replied. "You know, my impression of him, at first, was that he's a little on the simple side. But he's not that at all, is he? The way he insisted we get out of the area around your place. The planning ideas he came up with and the way he carried them out …"

"Yeah. He doesn't strike me as slow either. He's on the ball. He misdirected Wolf about which way we went so he must have played it up believably. And then there's the fact that he's built up his own farm and he's barely out of his teens."

"And, it looks prosperous; well run."

"It's like he cultivates the bumpkin persona for some reason. … Would you say that Jarrod is 'enigmatic'?"

"Hmm," Henry said, furrowing his brow while giving the idea it's due.

Pagan was happy to wait for Henry's opinion.

After some consideration, Henry said, "I suppose 'enigmatic' works. 'Puzzling' perhaps? 'Inscrutable' maybe? What about 'delusive'?"

"Oh no. That implies 'phony', in the insincere sense, and I don't think he's that."

"No, and I've seen no evidence that he has ill motives."

"Nor I. How about 'mysterious'?"

"'Sophistical' perhaps."

"Which means what?"

"I think it means 'believable but misleading'. But maybe that suggests dark, self-serving motives."

"Sounds like the qualities of a good mystery story, 'believable but mysterious'. Maybe I'm more like my mother in my fascinations than I thought."

Henry noticed that Pagan was beginning to relax. Engaging in conversation was providing a necessary distraction. "Will you tell me a bit about your mother?"

"Ah, where do I start? … Well, naming her Aisling was

somewhat of an inspired choice by her parents. It means 'dream' or 'vision'. I've read that Aisling was even a genre of poetry a few centuries ago. Anyway, when she was young my mother became very interested in Neo-Paganism and Celtic history. She began to celebrate festivals, like those around the spring equinox and the winter solstice. She and her best friend Kate—who discovered her inner witch—set out to learn as much as they could about ancient practices and spirituality from the old legends."

Henry smiled.

"No," said Pagan, "one shouldn't be flippant. I don't mean to sound like I'm making light of it. I'm not. Not at all. Some people believe that an old man parted a sea, that their god impregnated a virgin, and his son walked on water and turned water into wine. And yet those same people think my mother's views are far-fetched. But they're not. She's interesting ... Do you know much about her sort of spirituality?"

"I don't know. I don't think so."

"The Celtic world-view, or at least the Celtic world-view as my mother describes it, is animist. Everything has a spirit. Everything. Which makes everyone and all parts of nature connected. There's reverence for the natural world. My mother first and foremost sees herself as a spiritual being. She tries to integrate the old practices into her life, but adapted to the modern world. There's much more to it than that, of course." Pagan paused in thought before adding, "You know, my mother mentioned last night that Jarrod was interested in the integration between the spiritual and the science with respect to the natural ..."

"Sacred ecology?"

"You know about it, I see."

"Yes. Some. I've read some books by David Suzuki."

"My mother said that Jarrod shares a number of her views because of his Mi'kmaq roots."

"Which I definitely know nothing about."

"Nor I, but I have a book called *Mi'kmaq Landscapes* by Anne-Christine Hornborg. Mi'kmaq is another culture that began as animist. Their modern spiritual beliefs around nature have become integrated with scientific knowledge to arrive at something akin to sacred ecology. Hornborg says you can't understand the traditional Mi'kmaq view of the world using our terms. They had a biocentric world view of things rather than a human centred view. It means that all animals and humans were seen as connected. It wasn't an absolutist moral position, that animals should be treated like humans and not killed—they recognized that animals killed and ate each other for survival—but they felt that animals understood this. The thing then was to seek forgiveness of the animals you killed, thank them, and show them respect. When you killed an animal you were enacting a pact and had to live up to your part of the bargain. ... Don't take my memories of what she said as exact. It's been awhile since I read the book. Anyway, now that I think about it more, and put my queasiness aside, I guess my mother and Jarrod do have a shared temperament and set of interests. Maybe that's the connection between them. I suppose I should be glad if she's found a kindred spirit."

"Will that thought make their marriage easier to accept?"

"Ah ... I still have to find a way to do that."

"And what about you? Do you have a spiritual view of the earth?"

"No, but I'm sympathetic to my mother's views and I appreciate that one can experience nature in a spiritual way. There are rhythms and cycles to life. It's like I told you back at your place, I always go to my mother's when I need calm in my life or to heal. It's like everything becomes unbalanced and I lose my way when I'm out of nature. Being in nature is how I return to a state of peace. It bothers me that she'll be selling her place. ... Anyway, what about you? Are you spiritual?"

"Well I've always dwelt in the limited world in front of me and saw it as a world of facts. But living here, and being in the country, I realize that no matter what you know about nature, that experiencing its power is a whole different thing. Its mysteries ..."

Henry left the thought dangling until Pagan asked him to explain.

"That's the thing. It's hard to explain. I wonder if that's why people look to the spiritual to explain it. It's that ... It's that there's forces at work that are way beyond my understanding."

"Now you sound like my mother. She would say that what you are experiencing demands a belief in magic and even reverence in the face of it. Anyway—putting all that aside—I suppose that whatever our differences—you, me, and my mother—that we're all on the side of nature."

"Yes. Taking responsibility for now we treat it"

A short time later, after some consideration of an idea but not the ramifications of saying it out loud, Henry said, "You don't suppose ... no never mind."

"What?"

"Nothing."

"No, what was it?"

"Well ..." Henry was hesitant, but continued because of the urging. "Jarrod checks all the suspect boxes, doesn't he? It sounds like he knew the plot of your book. He knew that you'd be at my place on the morning ..."

"No, stop! Don't even say it," interjected Pagan forcefully. "Not everyone of my acquaintance is a possible suspect."

"Aren't they though? Can any of them be ruled out?" Henry immediately felt a sense of dread but it was too late. He was insisting that they couldn't exclude anyone close to Pagan of involvement in the kidnapping. What an awful thought that must be for her to consider. Was that why she was focused on Wolf? Wolf wasn't a friend so he wasn't betraying their friendship. Henry realized this was the end of the period of perfect harmony with Pagan. He'd said too much.

"If Jarrod set us up it would mean my mother ... no, don't go there."

"I didn't mean that she ... Jarrod has sisters ..."

It not only became quiet inside the car, but unlike the

previous breaks in the conversation this one was also accompanied by a tense atmosphere.

Damn, Henry thought, with his lack of social skills, he was probably doomed to live alone in the bush for the rest of his life.

Pagan slowed the pickup as they passed through a small town.

Just as they were getting back up to speed, having passed the last building, two patrol cars arrived behind them to set up a roadblock to check cars heading south.

"I'm sorry for getting you into this," Pagan said eventually.

"I don't think you got me into this. We're being set up."

"But without me, you wouldn't be in this situation. I appreciate how much you've helped me. And that whether or not we go to the police has been left up to me. You could have turned yourself in and insisted the police make a case against you, and I don't see how they could. With me, they can point to my novel and say it incriminates me. But there's nothing to suggest that you had anything to do with the kidnapping."

"I'll still have to clear my name at some point."

"So, what's our plan to wheedle the address of their cottage out of Morgan's unsuspecting parents?" Pagan said brusquely in a back to business tone. "You do have one don't you?"

"I was hoping you did. I guess it's a bridge we'll have to cross when we come to it, as they say."

During the ensuing silence, Pagan and Henry both refocused their attention, contemplating the countryside they drove through; rolling hills of heavily forested landscapes with beckoning deeps broken by the occasional, stunning vista of a body of water.

Pagan found it hard to look away. 'Stunning'. 'Complex'. 'Miraculous'. 'Staggering'.

She agreed with her mother that it was impossible not to be in awe of nature and to be aware of its power.

Her mother's lessons stayed with her. In the night she had dreamed of walking to the stream behind Henry's house. She came upon a beautiful woman sitting on a huge boulder by the shore. The woman lured her towards the water then grabbed her and dragged her in; trying to drown her. Pagan had flailed about in her sleep struggling for her life.

On waking, she realized that the woman was a kelpie: a shape-shifter in Scottish legend. Kelpies primarily appeared in the form of a black horse, but they could also take human form, usually that of a beautiful man, but sometimes that of a beautiful woman.

Years before, Aisling had told Pagan that the legend may have been a way to encourage girls to avoid water because it's the entrance to the Otherworld. Or to warn them of being seduced by a beautiful man who may not be what he seems to be—that he might be deadly.

Pagan had awakened with trepidation and the phrase, "one can be two" running through her thoughts.

She glanced over at Henry and felt a stab of guilt about hiding things from him.

"You said at the writers convention that you haven't seen much of New Brunswick beyond the Megumawaach area," she said.

"No. I plan to though. I'd really like to visit some of the sites where the original Acadians lived."

"Search your roots."

"It's not just that. I'm interested in the society they built."

"We studied them in school. A bit anyway. Grade eleven I think it was. I can see how that sort of culture would appeal to you. They had remarkable farms with abundant crops. They integrated with the Native population and lived in peace in democratic groups."

"I wish that I spoke French. Most academic writing on Acadian issues is in French so I don't know what sort of views are out there. I gather that a lot of modern Acadian political thought has focused on French language rights and Acadian political power—and I can understand why—but it would be interesting to see if any Acadian activists look to their past for a model of how the future might look, not just for contemporary Acadians but for everyone. There seems to be much in historic Acadian society that could help us to build a greener and more humane future—inclusive and without bigotry—and for a more democratic model of society based on a network of self-sufficient local communities; including Native communities if they wish. My sense—after reading some Acadian history—is that they had no interest in being part of any governing state. Not British. Not French. They wanted to lived outside of that. They wanted to live in their small farming communities of mutual support, at peace, and in harmony with their neighbours."

"Maybe it's in your blood to want to look closely at their culture—which is your history too—and to want to emulate it."

"I credit that with my feeling that I need some land of my own if I'm ever to feel in control of my life and have some independence."

"My mother is like that too. She says that if you don't own your own land you can only eat what others decide to produce, and how it is grown. ... So any plans to work on your French?"

"Absolutely. And what about you? Do you feel an affinity with the Irish here?"

"No. My family are outsiders. At the Frye Festival in Moncton I saw a quote from Northrup Frye. He said that Moncton was a suburb of Boston and I imagine that much of the province still is—for some people at least. I see an awful lot of Bruins and Red Sox bumper stickers, and team sweaters. We get a lot of Boston television. I think that many people here have strong connections to New England, historically and currently; family ones. And, of course, the roots of those people often go back to Ireland. It's what drew my mother here when she became a hippie. Megumawaach bills itself as 'Canada's Irish Capital'."

26

Fortunately, the Macraes of Greater Moncton owned one of the few local businesses that was open on Monday of the long weekend.

Pagan drove Jarrod's pickup past the chain length fence surrounding Macrae's landscaping business and into the yard. She parked in front of a trailer that served as the office.

It had been decided that Pagan's black hair and sunglasses were an adequate disguise as long as she was in the cab of the pickup or somewhere at a distance from other people. Up close however, anyone who'd seen one of the photos of her plastered all over the internet and the news, would likely identify her. So it was only Henry who entered the trailer office.

Several groups were wandering about the property, comparing and discussing piles of stone and tailings, but the only people in the office were a middle-aged couple. The woman was busy at a desk and the man stood behind the counter. Having seen the business's Facebook page, Henry was certain these were Morgan's parents: Scotty and Anna.

"How can I help you?" asked Scotty, smiling.

Henry launched into a story about needing an estimate on some crushed stone.

After getting the dimensions of the area to be covered, and the depth, Scotty set about calculating the volume of stone that would be needed for the job.

Henry made a show of a getting a good look at both of the Macraes. "The two of you look very familiar," he said. "I don't live in Moncton so I wonder if I've seen you around the cottage where I live. Do you have a cottage or a trailer?" The fact that it might appear odd to the Macraes that he seemed to know that they were a couple didn't occur to him

Anna looked Henry over carefully. "We do but I don't

recall ... Where's your cottage?"

"It's east of here. Near Grand-Dique." Henry instantly knew that he shouldn't have said that. He had only a vague idea of where Grand-Digue was. Hopefully there were cottages somewhere near it.

Anna looked blankly back at Henry, waiting for him to elaborate. She soon said, "No. It wouldn't be us."

"And I get into Shediac for groceries," Henry said hoping it was near Grand-Digue.

"No, it's not us you're thinking of. We're up north."

"You're probably thinking of a couple of movie stars," said Scotty with a smile. "One of the beautiful people who come here for the summer."

"Undoubtedly," Henry said, smiling back.

Pagan looked expectantly at Henry as he climbed back into the truck.

He shook his head and quickly relayed what had transpired in the office.

"I haven't a bloody clue about how to get information," he concluded. "Talk about detective amateur hour."

"So I guess we head north then. I'll call Jarrod and give him a progress report. Pass me the phone please."

Speaking on his parent's landline phone after listening to Pagan's news, Jarrod said, "I thought that Henry might pose as a friend of their daughter Morgan and ask how to get hold of her."

"The idea did occur to me," said Pagan, "but I assumed they'd call Morgan before giving out any personal information, especially to a man."

"True enough. That you didn't find out where Morgan or the cottage are might not be what we hoped for, but we're still a step forward. We now know that the cottage Morgan is staying at might be near here. I'll do a search and see if I come up with anything. So you're headed for the Macrae house in Riverview?"

"Why would we do that?"

"On the off chance you might find something. If you can't

get inside you could look in the mailbox. Maybe there's a repair bill in there or something with a northern address on it. Finding anything would be a long shot I suppose, and you might be seen, so be careful if you check it out."

"Okay, we'll head over there."

Pagan hung up, looked at Henry and laughed. "Jarrod wants us to nose around the Macrae place in Riverview and see if we can find out anything. He mentioned breaking in."

"What?"

"Yeah, I guess after breaking in to Wolf's place he thinks that's our style."

"Maybe he is an idiot after all," said Henry, shaking his head.

27

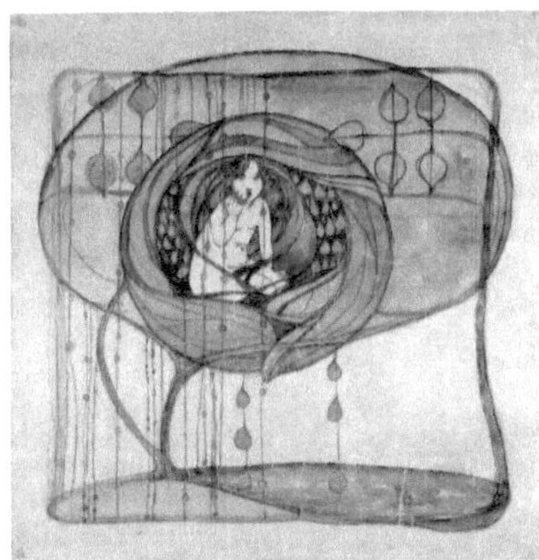
Girl in a Tree

Grenville Gallant was pissed. That was clearly evident. And the object of his ire was his ex-wife Vera.

"There has to be a way of negotiating with these people. The amount they want is ridiculous. And what about simply dangling the money? Make it contingent on us first getting the kids back then once that happens we can pull back the cash. There has to be a better way of handling this than just wiring money we don't have." Grenville was pacing the conference room in the office of Vera's lawyer, Charles Luks. He again turned his ire on Vera. "If you'd come to see me instead of the police we wouldn't be facing this problem."

"I can't believe this," Vera said. "How can you get so worked up over anything to do with money when your kids' lives are at stake?"

"Because if you'd come to me instead of the police we'd be in a lot better shape right now."

"You'd have had me steal the money from the bank."

"Borrow it—of necessity. I don't have any money. Spent it all on a divorce."

"I'm not sure this is helping," lawyer Luks said.

He was cut off by Grenville who spun around to face him. "And I ended up paying your fee too; enormous no doubt. Everybody made out like bandits at my expense."

"Do we have to go over this now?" said Vera in exasperation.

"You said I was worked up," her ex-husband said, "and I'm telling you why. If you'd come to me in the first place instead of the cops I'd have told you: Take the money you need and worry about the consequences later. It's the only way we're going to get enough to pay the ransom you insist on paying. I certainly don't have it. If you'd kept your mouth shut ..."

"Take the bank loan you're being offered," Vera interjected forcefully. "I've already taken out a second mortgage on my house and cashed in all my investments, and my RRSP. There's nothing left I can do. What about your condo? Or is this about something else? Do you think she'd dump you if you were broke?"

"Here we go again," Grenville said, throwing up his hands in mock exasperation. "I have nothing. The condo's not even mine. Just let it go."

"Why? You're angry with me and saying everything's my fault. You make zero effort to keep a lid on your feelings but then bitch at me when I say the slightest thing."

"You were supposed to be looking after those kids!" The volume of Grenville's voice had been steadily rising and he was now yelling.

"Wait, wait, wait, Mr. Gallant," interjected Charles Luks, as loud as he could without yelling himself. "And you too Vera," he added, more softly. "Please. We need to focus on getting the ransom money in place and then getting it transferred. We need to treat this simply as a logistical challenge and not re-litigate your divorce or renew hostilities. It's imperative for the next, what, twenty-four hours or so, that the two of you make every effort to get along." Luks' frustration at Grenville was compounded by the fact that, at the time of the divorce, Mr. Gallant's assets had been estimated to be three times the amount of the ransom demand. His claims of penury were based on pure stinginess.

28

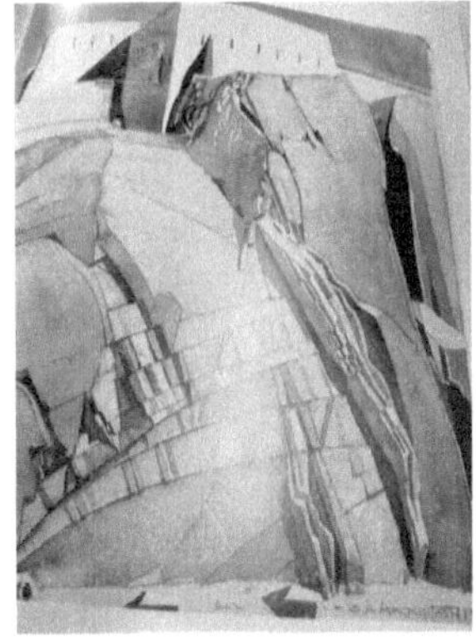

Landscape

Henry couldn't stop himself from stealing looks at Pagan as they drove. He was thrilled by her bad ass appearance.

It pleased him each time he noticed that Pagan kept glancing at him as well, and on the one occasion when instead of pretending he didn't notice he'd looked back at her, she was embarrassed.

The Macrae house in Riverview sat on a crescent in the middle of a suburban subdivision so there was no way for Henry and Pagan to check it out clandestinely.

"If the people in Riverview are anything like people in Megumawaach then there's probably someone in every nearby house who's constantly checking up on the neighbours," said Pagan, hunched over the steering wheel, looking down the street.

She slowed the pickup as they neared the Macrae house.

Henry said, "I don't see any way of checking the mailbox little own breaking in without being visible to the next door neighbours and the ones across the road."

Craning her neck to look up the Macrae driveway as they passed, Pagan said, "Yes, and the neighbours in the houses behind theirs can see everything."

"Maybe we should have dressed like religious canvassers. People would be hiding themselves."

After passing the house, they continued along the crescent.

"Remind me," said Pagan, "to write a book sometime about a helpless looking old couple who are crooks. If we looked to be ninety years old we could pull up to a house and no one would assume we were up to no good. ... Wait! Let me circle the block and come back to the house. Is there any paper in here?"

Henry began looking all around the cab. Not surprisingly, given what he'd seen of Jarrod so far, the interior was spotless. He opened the glove box and rifled through it. As luck would have it, the vehicle registration and insurance documents were together in a plain envelope. He took the documents out of the envelope and put them back into the compartment. He grabbed a pen that he saw before snapping the lid closed.

"Do you need me to write something down Pagan?"

"No. This time, when we get to the house, I'll turn into the driveway and pull up right beside the mailbox. The truck will block the view from the neighbour on the other side of the driveway. My body and the open truck door will stop people, ahead and behind, from seeing the box."

Taking the envelope from Henry, Pagan added, "I'll put this envelope in the mailbox and when I do I'll feel for other mail. Maybe there's a bill that covers payments on the cottage, like a tax or power bill. It's a long shot but …"

Henry wanted to counter that mail theft was a pretty serious offence—at least it always said as much in old American movies—but he kept quiet.

Pagan pulled the truck onto the driveway and followed the steps she'd outlined to shield what she was doing from the potentially prying eyes of the neighbours.

"It's empty," she said as she climbed back into the truck. "Exactly what you'd expect on the Monday of a long weekend. This was a stupid idea."

Five minutes into the drive north, Jarrod's cellphone rang and Henry answered it.

"I had some good luck," said Jarrod. "I just put the Macrae name into the search option on a site where people rent New Brunswick cottages. I found what we're looking for! The Macrae cottage is listed—it's on the Richibucto River—and the website even gives their names as contacts. There's a map at the listing that shows the street name and a street view. Plus there's a photo of the cottage. I'll give you the URL if you have a pen. If not, there's one in the glove compartment."

"That's great!" said Henry. "And I see an envelope there I can write on. ... It's a good thing you found the place because we had no luck in Riverview. Pagan had a look in the mailbox and there was nothing. And there's too many potentially prying eyes around to break in."

"I thought as much. Anyway, this place should be a lot easier to get at. Henry, you could even get out of the truck and look around. Knock on the door. Tell them you're a potential renter. You could say you saw the cottage listing online and wanted to have a quick look before renting it."

Henry jotted down the URL for the Macrae cottage and ended the call.

"So we're getting somewhere at last," Pagan said after Henry relayed what Jarrod had told him. "I wish I knew how long we had. I mean how long the kids will be held hostage before there's a problem. In my novel the crooks gave the bank manager seventy-two hours to wire the money."

"Sounds like the kidnappers are following your plot line so maybe we should assume that they've given the mother the same amount of time. That means she has until tomorrow morning. Is it safe to assume the family will get the money together, do you think?"

"God, I hope so. I don't even want to consider the alternative. In my book, the kidnapping was the means to force the bank manager to secretly rob her own bank of three million dollars. Since this has blown up all over the media she won't be able to do that—I wouldn't think—which means she'll have to find another way of getting together a hell of a lot of money."

"Then we better get going. The kids should still be at the cottage when we get there."

"It won't be long now."

29

Soul of the Blasted Pine

Henry and Pagan were both in pensive moods as they drove north. The cottage had to be where the children were being held but neither of them approached the subject, not wanting to deal with the possibility that their search might be futile.

"Are you going to write me as a character in one of your books?" Pagan said, apropos of nothing. "The poor damsel in distress."

"Ah ... yes to the first question, properly disguised, unless you don't want me to, but no to the second question. It isn't like that."

"How will you write me?"

"I don't know. With some metaphor I suppose."

"How about a nature metaphor."

"Is that what you'd like?"

"Yes."

"Any preferences?"

"Well, not a sheet of ice or field of snow. How about: 'A woman with the deep and dark shadows of a Gothic forest. The suggestion of hidden depths that would lure the unsuspecting into her world. He knew that he better leave a trail of breadcrumbs to find his way home if he succumbed to his impulses and wandered into her world'."

Henry smiled. "Sounds like you don't need anyone else to write you; you got it under control."

"Oh, no, you can't get out of it that easy. It's your character in the end, so you have to decide how you would write me."

"Well, I guess it depends on the scene and what fits. The metaphor could change though. If I come up with something good I could change your character to suit my needs."

"I don't like men trying to change me."

"Point taken." Henry smiled and asked, "Do you think you'll be able to quit your job and make a living as an author now that you're published?"

"Oh no. I wouldn't think so. I assume I'll be stuck for life working in logistics. My book is with a regional publisher, after all. It's not like it'll have national and international exposure. And even if I was with one of the large presses they're becoming so monopolistic that it's a buyer's market and they're not in the business of paying authors a cent more than they need to—or so I've heard."

"Won't they advertise your book?"

"My publisher you mean? No, nothing that costs money. Even the big presses don't spend advertising money on most of their authors."

"Really? That makes no sense, putting money into publishing a book and then not promoting it?"

"It makes sense from their near monopolistic position. Why compete against yourself and take away business from your blockbuster? You focus on your big names. That's where the money is. It's like the movie business, I suppose. The small film about family dynamics will get no advertising. Its potential fans will find it. All the ads are for the big superhero blockbusters and the like. They cost big bucks and they need to return even bigger bucks."

Henry stopped himself from pointing out to Pagan that, at that moment, she might be the most famous author in the country. That would surely be distressing.

After a long period of silence, Pagan again broke the silence, saying, "You've never told me what you did for a living before you came to New Brunswick."

"I worked for an environmental charity. I managed the bookstore they own. It sells science related books and educational material. Even clothes."

"Nice. I loved all that science stuff growing up: microscopes, globes, and cool gadgets."

"Me too. The charity was a good place to work, for the

most part, but even there you still got personality conflicts and ... office politics, I guess you could call it. But it's no reason to give up on the causes. There were a lot of good people there willing to work for little because they supported the charity. A lot of environmental activists."

They were nearing Richibucto River.

Pagan said, "So you're living by yourself now. Is anyone coming to from Toronto to join you?"

"You mean am I in a relationship? No. I was living with someone but she got a good job offer in the States. I knew it was what she wanted to do and I encouraged her to go. I didn't want to live there."

"And you didn't want to stay in Toronto."

"No. I couldn't justify paying an enormous rent for the luxury of living somewhere because of all its amenities. Toronto has lots of theatre, lectures, music venues, art, and so on, but I'd stopped using them. It was too much of an ordeal. Too time consuming. Too stressful. Everything is jammed into the downtown core. And the situation has gotten worse. Massive condo after massive condo is being built downtown. ... Anyway, I'm blathering on. If I can ask, do you live with ... someone?"

"No, I lived with Patrick for a couple of years but there's been nobody since we broke up several months ago."

"Do I say sorry, or was breaking up a good thing? Or maybe it's sorry either way. Of course it is."

"It was necessary. We're still friends at work. It can be hard work. Patrick's something of a machismo neanderthal, and possessive to boot. Not sure why we were ever a couple." Pagan's voice had tailed off as she recollected how wrong she'd been at the time—after she and Patrick had broken up —thinking that stepping back into a friendship would be easy, like it was with Lindy. She added, "Maybe my awful choices in men is another way I'm a bit like my mother ... I meant my father ..." She bit off her words. She'd just told a potential boyfriend that she had terrible taste in men.

It was perhaps fortunate that Henry's thoughts had drifted

to another subject. "I was thinking," he said, "about my idea that we can't eliminate any of your friends as suspects. Thinking about it now, I think that's wrong. Whoever did this did their best to implicate us—as you said—but they must have known that eventually the police will look at all your friends to exclude the possibility that we were set up. That alone tells me that in all likelihood the kidnappers aren't among your friends. People don't make themselves potential suspects in serious crimes."

Pagan reached out her hand and squeezed Henry's.

30

Sergeant Landry stood in front of the whiteboard in the incident room, addressing his team.

The stress he'd been under for the last forty-eight hours was evident from the puffy shadows below his blue eyes.

"The parents want to pay the ransom—that's their business—but I understand they're having trouble raising the money. In any case, it's up to us to find their kids before the payment deadline. And as the clock winds down it gets even more urgent. I don't need to tell you that. ... Ah, what else? The bank account. Still no luck on getting the name and personal info on the owner of the off-shore bank account the ransom money is to be sent to. I think that's all I have so let's get updates from everyone else."

Landry looked around the table in front of him where the team was gathered, settling on the woman immediately to his right. "Corporal Carruthers," he said before sitting down and taking up his can of cola. He was already one over his self-imposed daily limit and it wasn't even lunchtime.

"Thank you," began Carruthers. She cleared her throat and glanced at her notes. "I spoke to Gillian Morris." She nodded towards Landry, who'd already been brought up to date. "She's the literary agent in Toronto who tipped us about Pagan Egan. To our surprise she was in the group photo we got that included Henry Hebert. When we saw it, it suggested that Morris and Hebert—who seems to be Egan's boyfriend —could be setting her up."

Constable Roger Flynn, sitting across the table from Carruthers, interrupted. "Is he really her boyfriend?"

"Well, they spent the night together the day of the kidnapping so I assume so, but no, we don't know that for certain. Anyway, Ms Morris—and we've confirmed this—was in Toronto when I spoke to her so she's not directly involved in the kidnapping. She told me that she doesn't know Henry Hebert and that the photo was taken when she was at the bookstore for the launch of a book by a novelist she's the agent for. The book's plot involves a climate disaster and the bookstore specializes in books and stuff on the environment. She and Henry Hebert just happened to to be in the store at the same time."

"Is there any evidence she's lying?" Flynn said.

"No. At least none of the other people in the store who I spoke to has ever seen them together. … I asked her about the manuscript. She says that her assistant read it because the book sounded promising. Gillian only read the assistant's report. After that, the thing was destroyed. That's the policy apparently. Sounds pretty cutthroat. I spoke to the assistant. She's been in Toronto this whole time so she's not directly involved either."

Landry interjected, "By 'directly involved' we mean they're not holding the kids and we've no evidence that either person was in the province on the weekend."

There was silence. The promising lead had fallen dead in its tracks.

"Alright," said the sergeant, "lets leave that line of inquiry for now. We've also been looking into the background of Henry Hebert." He nodded at Flynn.

"Yes. Turns out Hebert has an arrest record for trespassing and resisting arrest," the constable said. "He was part of a group blocking logging trucks trying to access a Native reserve."

"When?" asked Landry.

"Four years ago. He was fined, as were several others, for the trespass, and the second charge was dropped …"

"Bloody woke attorneys!"interjected Darren Woods,

"… because the video evidence didn't support the resisting arrest charge."

"So nothing in his past to suggest that he could do this kind of crime," Landry said, intentionally challenging Woods' view of Crown bias. "Could money have been a motivator for him to turn to kidnapping?"

"Not according to his parents. They said they gave him the bulk of his inheritance and that's what he used to buy his place in New Brunswick."

"Whew," said Carruthers under her breath, "we should all be so lucky."

Landry said, "So there's nothing to tie him directly to this crime other than the fact that he's with Egan and could have, time-wise, been with her during the kidnapping—or done it with someone else."

He pushed his chair back and stood up. He waved in the direction of the whiteboard and all eyes went to what was written on it.

"Here's the timeline that I've worked out based on what we know so far."

Landry went through the notations, one by one, pointing to each line as he read them aloud.

- *7:00 a.m. Constable Byron leaves the Egan and Abbott apartment*
- *8:15 a.m. Darla Abbott exits apartment. Cannot say whether Egan was at home since her bedroom door was closed but her car was in the car park behind their house*
- *8:45 a.m. Abbott begins work shift (confirmed)*
- *10:30 a.m. Vera Gallant leaves her residence*
- *10:45 a.m. shots fired on Dube Creek Road from Egan's car*
- *11:30 a.m. Egan's supposed departure for scheduled noon meeting between her and Henry Hebert at his home (according to Egan's mother)*
- *1:00 p.m. Egan arrives at the home of her mother Aisling Níc Aodhagáin for the mother's wedding rehearsal and lunch (according to mother)*

"It's a plausible timeline except the sixth line. We don't know when Egan actually left for Hebert's. ... Let's turn to Pagan Egan. If Egan was involved in the kidnapping she obviously left home much earlier than the 11:30 her mother mentioned." Looking at Constable Woods he said, "Please interview the neighbours. See if there are any witnesses who saw her leave—at any time. If someone says they saw her leave at 11:30, ask if they also saw her leave earlier. She could have gone out early, did the kidnapping, and returned. And of course, if Hebert was her partner she'd have gone to his place and picked him up. I think it's safe to say that a conviction in this case will depend on timing." He caught sight of a raised arm. "Corporal Carruthers, you have something to add?"

"Yes. I spoke to Egan's old boyfriend—Patrick McSheehy —focusing particularly on where Egan might be keeping the children. He mentioned an old flame of hers—name of Lindy —who she seems to have remained close to."

Landry interjected, "Sorry to interrupt, but for everyone's benefit …" He looked at Woods who he'd spoken to earlier about the location of the kidnapped children. "We're assuming that the two suspects are working together and have stashed the victims somewhere. But we're also considering the possibility that only one of them may be involved and in that case they would have a partner who's holding the children. The possibility that Hebert may have been working with one of the literary agents from Toronto seems to have been disproved. That Egan could be acting in league with this Lindy woman is now our best hope for locating the missing kids."

Carruthers picked up the thread of her earlier remarks. "McSheehy doesn't know of anywhere that Egan has access to where the kids might be, but, as I said, he mentioned that before her relationship with him she'd been romantically involved with a woman who lives out in the country. He doesn't know the location or the woman's surname, only that her first name is Lindy. McSheehy says that he was driving downtown three weeks ago and saw Lindy and Egan walking together. In his words they looked, 'thick as thieves'. I don't know what that means. And McSheehy couldn't say what it means exactly. He seems angry and spiteful so I wouldn't take his characterization to the bank."

"That's two women," interjected Constable Woods. "I thought we were looking for a man and a woman."

"Remember, only one of the kidnappers spoke and both wore masks so it could have been two women."

"So we have a possible suspect and a possible location," said Landry, speaking to Carruthers. "Where do we stand on locating her?"

"I have Constable Clark following up with the people whose names we got from McSheehy—female friends of Egan—who might also know Lindy."

"Widen that," said the sergeant impatiently. "Get everyone you can working on this. And get some more from McSheehy. Find out what sorts of things Egan is into—hobbies and such—and anywhere she likes to go. Have people check out those places and ask around. I want the name and address of this Lindy woman!"

"Moving on," said Landry, after taking a moment to look at his notes. "As you may know Henry Hebert's next door neighbour—Jarrod Augustine, Grant Augustine's brother—owns two vehicles: a Nissan Altima and a Ford Ranger pickup. Since we found no sign that Egan and Hebert fled across the river behind Hebert's property, our attention has turned to Augustine's farm. The officers who checked in on the place, immediately after Egan and Hebert fled—Constable Woods here and Wolf Byron—noted a canoe on the property. They took Augustine's word for it that the canoe is his but we've subsequently learned that it belongs to Hebert. We also found out that Jarrod Augustine is engaged to Pagan Egan's mother, so there's a strong connection there. Our assumption is that Egan and Hebert escaped the area in one of Augustine's vehicles since neither is at his farm.

"There's nothing yet on the pickup but Grant Augustine took it upon himself to check his parent's property, south of the city. His parents are away. He told me that neither the Altima nor the pickup is on the property but he had a look inside the house and he thinks that his brother and the two fugitives might have spent last night there. But there was no sign of the kids having been there too. Um … I told Grant to hang around in case any of the three show up. As I'm sure you're all aware, first thing this morning—after Grant went to his parents' house—we put out a call to the public to be on the lookout for the two vehicles. It's only a matter of time till someone spots them … but it has to be today."

31

The White Rose And The Red Rose

Turning into the driveway of the isolated building, the driver of the car donned a balaclava and then a pirate mask to transform into Calico Jack.

He walked into the house through the front door and stopped cold.

Everything was silent and Grace was nowhere to be seen.

With a sense of foreboding sweeping over him, he walked apprehensively through the empty livingroom towards the bedroom, stopping at the slightly open door before gently pushing it open, clearly afraid of what might be revealed.

He immediately sprang forward and in three steps was across the room at the double bed where the two children were tied to the bed frame. They had gags in their mouths.

Anthony was untied first. He was wheezing and struggling to breathe. He was a terrifying shade of blue. Jack picked him up.

The sleeve covering the arm that held Anthony was immediately soaked from the boy's urine drenched pants.

Meanwhile, with his free arm, Jack freed Hélène from her gag.

Anthony continued to gasp but his struggle for air soon began to ease. Calico Jack laid him on the bed. "Sh, sh," he said while stroking the boy's cheek.

Turning to Hélène, Jack untied the ropes that held her. In doing so he noted the welts on her face. Grace had acted on her threats.

With surprising calm, Hélène rubbed her wrists where the ropes had squeezed into them and said, "He couldn't breathe because he has a cold and is all stuffed up."

Jack nodded. He pointed at her and then towards the floor as a way of telling her to stay put.

He went on a hunt for Grace.

Not finding her in the livingroom or the other bedrooms, Calico Jack went into the kitchen. It was empty too, but looking through the screen on the back door he spotted his quarry, not wearing her pirate's mask, sitting on the patio in a deck chair. She was holding a handgun and aiming at some invisible prey out on the lake. Music loudly emanated from a portable CD player resting on the patio, beside her chair.

Pushing open the door and stepping onto the patio, Calico Jack said with undisguised anger, "What the hell are you doing?"

Grace twisted her head and pointed the gun at her partner. "I told you I was going to tie the little fuckers up. They won't listen, especially the girl. She's in-cor-ri-gi-ble," Grace said, imitating a voice of authority from her her past. She laughed.

Closing one eye, pantomiming taking aim at Calico Jack, she said, "Bang," in unison with the click from the empty gun as she pulled the trigger. She laughed again.

"The little boy is blue and can hardly breathe. The girl is covered in welts."

Suddenly angry, Grace said sharply, "It's their own fault."

Calico Jack shook his head and knelt down beside Grace. He held out his hand. "The gun."

Grace laughed, took aim at something in the trees behind Jack. "Bang," she said and laughed again. "Now go and leave this to me," she added. She handed over the gun and reached down to crank the volume on the CD player to its maximum.

Calico Jack rose to his feet and returned to the house. Enough was enough. There was no way he could leave the children another night with Grace. Their great plan had spiralled out of control and was on the cusp of becoming deadly.

In the livingroom, he set down the handgun on the coffee table beside a matching gun.

He went into the bedroom, scooped up a child in each arm and walked to the front door. He shifted both children to one arm in order to free up a hand and managed to silently open the front door and then the back door of the car.

With both children inside the car, Calico Jack closed the door as gently and quietly as he could.

He went into the house to retrieve the two handguns, returned to the car, started it, and drove away.

Behind the house, Grace had laid her head back onto the deck chair. The volume of the music was too loud for her to hear the car leaving. She took aim at her right temple, with a finger and thumb mimicking a gun, and whispered, "Bang." She threw her open left hand out beside her other temple mimicking the spray of brains exiting her skull. And she laughed.

32

Flag of Calico Jack Rackham

Anthony lay curled up on the back seat of the car, his head resting in Hélène's lap.

As he drove, Calico Jack frequently glanced at the children in the rearview mirror.

He had no plan except to get away from Grace, but he was heading in the direction of Megumawaach.

Jack touched his pirate mask. He wanted to remove it and his balaclava too, but left them in place.

Seeing an approaching car, he removed the green glove on his left hand. He kept his head low and did his best to shield the mask from view with his bare hand.

They were nearing a police stop on the secondary road that he'd passed, not twenty minutes earlier. A decision about what to do next had to be made immediately.

Turning the car around was out of the question. Grace was unhinged and dangerous. He'd been mistaken in believing she could hold it together for three days, sequestered with two small children. Grace loathed children. It had been a mistake from the start to trust in her.

Turning off the road was an option but what then? Where to take the kids? Maybe it wasn't a realistic option at all.

On the right hand side of the road, just ahead, was a house sitting a dozen metres back from the road. An SUV and a pickup were parked in the long driveway.

Jack slowed his vehicle and pulled it onto the shoulder, perhaps fifty metres past the house.

He looked behind him and up ahead. Seeing no traffic he jumped from the car, walked to the passenger-side rear door and opened it.

He scooped up Hélène, and carried her several feet along the dirt shoulder of the road—behind the car—where he set her down on her feet.

In the distance, behind the house, a dog, constrained by a chain, began barking.

Calico Jack returned to the car and picked up Anthony, who'd been quiet and possibly sleeping. The little boy opened his eyes. Alarmed, he reached out his arms for his absent sister and howled.

Jack carried Anthony to the spot where Hélène stood watching. He tried to stand Anthony beside his sister but the boy promptly sat down on the gravel shoulder.

Calico Jack looked at Hélène, pointed emphatically at her, then at Anthony and then at the house jabbing his finger to indicate to her that she was to take her brother and head for the house with the barking dog.

Hélène turned her head to look at the house. She turned back to nod her understanding but by then Calico Jack was walking towards the car.

She watched until he drove away.

Behind him, in the rearview mirror, Jack saw Hélène, holding her brother's hand, trying to get him up on his feet.

33

"What's the mark on the back of your car?" asked Grant Augustine. "It looks like it came from a bullet."

"It did. Courtesy of your comrade, Wolf Byron."

Grant momentarily took his eyes off the highway to look incredulously at his brother. "You're telling me that Wolf shot at you?"

"Yes."

"When was that?"

"Last night."

"And why was that?"

"I was driving away from his house after picking up Pagan and Henry. Wolf got home and they left, and I drove off with them."

"And Wolf took a shot at your car. Why were Pagan and Henry at his house?"

"They were looking for the kidnapped kids."

"And they thought they were there?"

"Obviously."

"And you're an accessory to break and enter."

"Legally, yes. Morally though I feel okay. It was justified in the belief that a crime was occurring inside the house. While the police are focused on finding Pagan she's focused on finding the missing children. We were doing what we felt needed to be done."

"So, you've been helping those two."

"Yes."

"Since when?"

"Sunday morning. They were unarmed and running from the police who were shooting at them."

"Did you loan them your pickup or did they steal it?"

"I told them to take it. Gave them a map too."

"Jesus." Grant shook his head in disbelief.

The brothers fell silent, their eyes on the road ahead.

Grant had waited at his parent's house for an hour before Jarrod returned in his car. The two were now en route to the police station.

Jarrod looked sanguine while Grant was pale and worried.

"Why do you think that Wolf is involved?" Grant said eventually.

Jarrod shifted in his seat and stared at his older brother. "It's Pagan's assumption and it's a reasonable one. He likely knew about the plot of her unpublished book. He had access to her apartment and her bedroom where she had a detailed outline of the book's plot in her desk. He'd have known what the gun cases were when he saw them and how to use the guns. Plus, he likely knew about Pagan's Saturday plans and when her car would be free. And then there's the fact that he owns a house that looks to be beyond his financial means, so he must have a second income from other sources."

"Jesus. Who's his partner. That Darla woman can't have helped him. She has a solid alibi. We have CCTV of her at work on Saturday."

Jarrod smiled. The video confirmed their conclusion. "But Morgan wasn't at work. She's on holidays with access to a cottage. You told me so yourself."

"And Wolf was on duty."

"Easy enough to create a false record of what he was up to I should think."

"… I've known Wolf all my life …"

"And he was always in trouble growing up. He ran with the kids who were getting busted for one thing or another. It's amazing he never ended up in jail. … Did you know someone had broken into his house last night? Did he report it?"

"Ah … I don't know. I'd have to check."

"Okay. If he didn't report it you should ask yourself why."

"Maybe he did, or forgot to."

"Or maybe he didn't because the reason for the break-in will bring him under suspicion."

"But that's not the same thing as something coming up that

actually incriminates him."

"True, but it raises the question of why someone would be interested in his house. And you should ask why Pagan keeps getting shot at when Wolf's around."

"Jarrod, Jarrod ... so we come to the sixty-four thousand dollar question: Where is Pagan Egan now?"

"I don't know other than that she and Henry are trying to find the missing kids."

Grant focused on driving. He'd said too much. Asked too much. He should shut up. They were brothers so the nature of their conversation might come under scrutiny, and if it did it could be asked if their conversation involved Grant offering guidance on what to say to the police.

In spite of that, he was reluctant about stopping. "Were either of them, Pagan or Henry, on the phone with anyone at any time?"

"I don't know," Jarrod said.

Finally, Grant stopped the interrogation.

34

"I give up," said Pagan, laughing at the irony. "Whew," she added with an exhalation of breath. "It's almost too absurd. Black hair! The woman kidnapper has black hair and I dyed my hair black to disguise myself. They could have mentioned her hair colour earlier."

She and Henry had been listening to the truck's radio for any updates on the kidnapping and had just heard that, when last seen, the woman the police were seeking had black hair.

Henry switched off the radio.

Pagan shook her head in resignation then returned to the task at hand. She suddenly slowed the pickup and leaned forward over the steering wheel to better observe a cottage they were about to pass.

"Is that it?" she said, pointing off to her right, at a place on the river side of the road.

Henry glanced down at the image of the Macrae cottage displayed on Jarrod's cell phone that he held in his hand, then took a look back at the cottage. "No. Sorry."

Pagan sat back upright and resumed the truck's speed. "The black hair dye has got me thinking about Jarrod's twin sister. It was her dye that I used. She's at uni..."

"Ellie, I think Jarrod called her—so I guess her name might be Elizabeth."

"Really? The older sister is named Beth. I thought that she might be an Elizabeth."

"Ha. Either name could be a diminutive of Elizabeth. Funny eh? Anyway, Ellie's working on a Masters. So further evidence that Jarrod may have inherited some brains."

"Yes. It's not what I was thinking but it's worth keeping in mind, I guess. No, what I was thinking was that the hair dye tells me that Ellie dyes her hair black. As in, if Jarrod is involved in the kidnapping then Ellie could be his partner."

Henry was surprised at the change in tone; that Pagan was now the one suggesting that Jarrod was involved. "Don't a lot of people dye their hair?"

"Of course."

"Do you think she's capable of doing something like this?"

"I don't know. I don't know her. Jarrod doesn't come across as someone who'd do anything illegal. He seems squeaky clean but …"

"… But we've seen that he play acts."

"And does it well. So you never know."

"But then there's the question of where the kids are stashed," said Henry thoughtfully.

"We only have Jarrod's word that Ellie's in Nova Scotia at the moment. She could be in Timbuktu for all we know."

"Do you think that Jarrod was sending us astray with the Macrae stuff?"

"No. He didn't invent the Macraes. Pursuing Wolf was all my doing and the Macraes emerged from that line of reasoning; even though we only know about them because of Jarrod. Anyway, I'm being crazy. It's paranoia developing because of my situation; from not knowing I mean, and being increasingly frustrated about it. … I know what you said, that the kidnappers probably aren't my friends, but the fact remains, I think, that, in all likelihood, at least one of them has to be someone close to me … I hate suspecting everyone I know of being a criminal out to hurt me. It's corrosive to all my relationships and it increases my feelings of vulnerability."

"Yeah, we trust those close to us …"

"If I'm going to see every person I know as a possible suspect then it's just as likely to be Patrick."

"Does he have a partner?"

"I think he's in a relationship with Cinders. A money-obsessed woman from work who hates kids."

"You don't know?" said Henry.

"No."

"And you're not wondering about this because of ..." Henry bit off his words thinking, here I go again putting my foot in it.

"Of jealousy?" Pagan was nonplussed. "No. I genuinely couldn't care less. Actually, it would be great if he was with someone. Maybe then he'd stop fixating on me. I wonder though about why, if he and Cinders are together, they'd hide it. Not being suspected of the kidnapping would be a reason."

"Where I used to work there were people who got involved with each other and kept it secret. There's lots of reasons why that makes sense."

"I can understand people doing that, I guess." Pagan sounded reluctant about making the concession.

"Did Patrick know you'd be at my place on Saturday morning?"

"Ah ... no. I never mentioned you. But would he have had to know?" Pagan sat more upright and said, "Now that I think about it, I did say to the group at work that I'd be at my mother's house for lunch on Saturday so Patrick could have inferred when I'd be leaving home."

"You said before that you can't see him setting you up or doing something illegal. Are you having second thoughts about that?"

"I don't know." Pagan again sounded resigned to hopelessness when she continued, "Doing this crime and trying to set me up for it are evil and cruel, and I don't think he's like that. His feelings are hurt and his ego is damaged, and he seems to feel humiliated, so he's angry, but vengeance? I guess I still don't see Patrick stooping to that. Plus, until we know if he and Cinders were around town on the weekend it's just idle speculation."

"But it sounds like you're beginning to think that Wolf might not be the person behind this?"

"No. I'm just trying to keep an open mind. When I go over this I think more and more that it has to be Wolf ... and Morgan by extension. There's something else but I can't put my finger on what it is exactly. I just know."

"And ... There! There!" Henry said excitedly, sitting up

and pointing at the cottage they were passing.

Pagan stopped the car, then did a three-point turn. She drove back to the place and stopped the car on the shoulder of the road opposite the cottage.

Henry held the cellphone up so Pagan could see the picture of the Macrae cottage posted online.

"That's it," Pagan said.

"Shall we pull into the driveway? It doesn't look like anyone's home. No car anyway."

"Yes. Driving right up to the house like we own the place was the plan. And then going to the door. I'll stay here looking down at the phone, hiding my face in case someone's inside and they see me in the truck."

"And if anyone's inside I can tell them I'm looking for a place for my visiting parents."

Henry reached out. He and Pagan clasped hands. They were both clearly nervous.

"You'll do great," Pagan said reassuringly.

35

From *Irish Fairy Tales*

The dog behind the house only let up its barking after a man's voice boomed from the back door, "Shut up Sally!"

Twice, Anthony sat down on the gravel, insisting he was tired. Both times, after no amount of coaxing got the desired result, Hélène picked him up and carried him. But those episodes were brief. Anthony was too heavy and he made himself harder to carry by hanging limp like a rag doll.

Hélène eventually convinced her brother to continue walking by promising that when they reached the house ahead that whoever lived there would phone their mother so she could come and get them.

The children still had to go fifteen metres to reach the driveway when, in the distance, Hélène spotted a car approaching. She felt a surge of hope that it would stop.

"C'mon Anthony," she said, and took his hand.

"I'm tired," he whined, sounding like he was about to plop himself down again.

As the car drew nearer, Hélène's hope evaporated.

She squeezed Anthony's hand so firmly that he yelped in pain. She knew this car!

The vehicle slowed as it passed them, pulled onto the shoulder, and stopped.

"Anthony!" Hélène yelled. "It's the bad lady pirate's car. Run!"

Anthony gasped in fright.

Hélène ran for the ditch. She pulled Anthony behind her. He stumbled trying to keep up. They slid down the embankment. Hélène hoisted her brother to his feet. She yelled, "We gotta run!"

They started across a corn field.

Grace scrambled from her car. She ran to the spot where she'd seen the children.

"Fuck!" she cursed, looking out. The small children were invisible amidst the corn. "Little girl," she yelled, "wait!"

Grace stepped over the edge of the ditch. Tentatively. Edged her way down. Pitched forward and landed face down in the muck.

"Fuck! Fuck! Fuck!" she screamed. And got to her feet.

There was no sign of the kids. Just corn stalks. "I'm gonna kill you little fuckers when I find you!" She plunged ahead.

Hélène turned right. She led Anthony across the rows. Squeezing between the stalks.

A roof peak was now visible above the corn. "C'mon Anthony," she implored.

The dog behind the house was barking frantically.

Grace spotted the children. Off to her right.

The children broke clear of the field. They ran across a slim strip of grass.

The dog was in near hysterics.

"Doggy," gasped Anthony with alarm.

"It's a good doggy," Hélène said.

They reached the driveway just as Grace emerged from the corn. She sprinted towards the children. Reached out for Anthony.

The screen door at the back of the house slammed open.

The man who stepped outside held a shotgun. There had to be a reason for such barking. A bear? A coyote? A deer?

Grace braked. She stepped around the corner of the house; out of sight.

"What the hell?" the farmer said. Two small children—breathless—were at his feet.

The man caught a glimpse of Grace's movement but he was preoccupied with the kids now clasping his legs.

"What's going on?" demanded a woman appearing at the door behind him. She caught sight of the children and looked from one to the other.

"Oh my God!" she said to her confused husband, "This is the kidnapped kids everyone's looking for."

36

The Bubble

Henry felt nervous as he walked to the door of the Macrae cottage.

He feigned an air of naturalness to mask his apprehension because Pagan was watching. Maybe someone from inside the cottage too. Someone who was armed.

He knocked on the side door. No answer. He knocked again. Same lack of response.

Turning towards Pagan, sitting in the pickup, Henry shrugged in resignation.

He walked to the end of the driveway which afforded him a view of the river and the patch of overgrown lawn behind the cottage. There was nothing in the scrub to indicate that any children had been there lately. Nothing to indicate it had been walked on in weeks, by anyone. It wasn't surprising, Henry thought. Of course kidnappers would keep their prisoners out of sight.

Looking at the cottage, he observed a large picture window at the nearest end. He glanced back at the pickup and the road. Took a moment to listen for traffic. Heard nothing. Summoned up his courage and walked to the window. The livingroom was modestly and sparsely furnished. There was no evidence that now, or in the recent past, two small children had been present.

Henry made a quick retreat back to the truck.

He stopped beside Pagan's open window. She looked at him expectantly.

"There's a livingroom window on the river side of the house," Henry said. "I don't see any evidence, inside or out, that anyone's here or that there's been any kids around."

"Dammit!" Pagan's face fell. "Where else could they be?"

"Maybe Morgan and Wolf aren't responsible."

"Or maybe there's more to see. Watch out." Pagan purposefully opened the truck door, nudging Henry back.

She climbed out of the cab and strode briskly across the lawn towards the two bedroom windows on the side of the house that faced the road. Henry tailed behind, taking courage from Pagan's boldness.

The smallish windows were positioned too high up to allow anyone to look inside but not so high that Pagan couldn't get a brief glimpse with a small jump. After seeing enough in the rooms to ascertain they were empty of people, she circled the cottage and had a look for herself through the livingroom window.

She again swore in frustration before walking slowly back to the pickup. Henry continued to follow.

On reaching the truck, Pagan turned. Henry could read the disappointment on her face and felt deeply sorry for her. She'd been under an unbearable amount of stress from being hunted and from worrying about the kidnapped children. This cottage had been their last best hope of ending all that and they had come up empty. He reached out his arms to hug her.

"No, no," Pagan said, pushing him away. "I'll start crying and it's not the time. ... Let's get out of here."

Henry stepped out of Pagan's way as she opened the door of the truck. As she climbed inside, he walked around the back of the vehicle, heading for the passenger door.

Just then a black sedan appeared, coming up the road from the direction of Richibucto.

The driver slowed the car. She saw the pickup in the driveway so drove beyond it, pulled over to the right, and parked in front of the cottage.

Henry stopped walking. He watched a woman get out of the car. She was tall. Striking looking. Somewhere in her early thirties.

He waited as she approached. When she was near enough for her to hear him speak, he smiled broadly and called out "Hi."

The woman responded in kind, friendly but perhaps with some apprehension.

Henry said, again affecting an air of nonchalance, "We were hoping to catch you in. We saw your ad online for a cottage rental and wanted to have a quick look before booking it."

"Ah," Morgan said, smiling genuinely this time. She stopped in front of Henry. "It's really my parents you want to talk to but I can give you a quick tour if you like."

"Sure."

"You're lucky to catch me. I was just heading for town but remembered I forgot to bring that garbage bag sitting at the end of the driveway. It's full of old clothes that I want to donate to charity. I came back to pick it up."

Morgan walked past Henry.

She spotted the figure in the driver's seat of the truck. A woman staring down at her phone.

Morgan momentarily paused beside the woman, ducked her head and said through the open window, "Come on in and look around,"

This is insanity, Pagan thought, as she watched Morgan continue on her way. She was a fugitive and this woman was a police officer.

Seeing no alternative though, she stepped from the truck, emboldened by the thought that since Morgan was on vacation she may not have been following the news. She caught up with her and Henry.

The tour was non-existent. Morgan opened the front door of the cottage and told the pair to wander about wherever they chose.

"I'm just going to put my stuff in the car and when I get back I can answer any questions."

Henry and Pagan conducted a superficial survey of the cottage.

"Let's get out of here okay?" said Henry.

"Sure," Pagan said, obviously just as anxious to leave.

"Looks great," Henry yelled to Morgan when he got to the truck. "Thanks."

Morgan was at her car, standing beside an open rear door. She kept the hand holding her cell phone low. She smiled and waved with her other hand.

"Where to now?" Henry asked Pagan once they were seated inside the pickup.

"Anywhere. Just so long as we get out of here."

The pair were soon heading further along the riverside road—in the opposite direction to the highway.

Pagan had chosen this way impulsively but Henry assumed that her purpose had been to avoid admitting defeat by heading back to base camp at Jarrod's parents' house. It suited him. There were likely roadblocks along the way and he had no taste for being in police custody.

"Where are we going?" he eventually asked.

"I don't know. I have no plan and I'm out of ideas."

"Me too."

"Maybe we'll get lucky and spot a black Civic."

They drove in silence, turning here, turning there. Getting lost along the winding roads. They scrutinized every house they passed. A pointless exercise but one that allowed them to feel they were still engaged in the hunt for the kidnapped children.

"I wonder about these narrow dirt roads," Henry said, pointing to a trail the width of a lane as they drove by it. "We've seen a bunch. Where do they lead? To houses?"

"I'm not sure but Patrick's family had a cabin up a road like that. They called it 'the hunting camp'. In their case they owned the land and the lane was plastered with 'No trespassing' and 'Do not enter signs'."

"I haven't seen any signs on these roads."

"No. But I'm guessing that they still may be spots for hunters and maybe fishermen to park."

"The river … damn, we've made so many turns that I've totally lost track of where we are."

"This takes me back. My father knew where the creeks were. He would often stop and fish. Sometimes I went with him. He was expert at judging which pools to stop at and would haul out fish left and right. I was useless at fishing. I was just bug food and I hated it. I'd no sooner get my line in the water when Dad would be up and heading for another spot, jumping rock to rock."

They were on a road that wasn't much wider than a single lane. Pagan edged the truck to the right when they came upon a small, older model sports car of some sort. A little red thing. Unnecessarily loud Pagan thought. Imitating the power of a car in a street racing movie.

As the two vehicles squeezed by each other the driver looked up and made eye contact with Pagan. He was young. A teenager maybe.

The pickup continued on its way but when Pagan happened to glance in the rearview mirror she noticed that the sports car had stopped. Its brake lights were on. Then off as the car crept forward. The lights went on again. Hesitancy gave way to decision. The car did a three-point turn.

Pagan continued to watch.

"That red sports car that we just passed is now following us," she said. "It looks like a teenage boy is driving."

Henry twisted to look behind them. The trailing vehicle was a long way off. "Could have nothing to do with us."

"True."

Pagan and Henry both continued to keep an eye on the vehicle. It drew nearer until eventually settling several car lengths back.

"I can't tell if it's following us," Henry said, "or wanting to pass."

"I'll turn off at the next road we come to."

Henry could hear a note of concern in Pagan's voice.

She turned right a minute or so later.

The car followed suit.

"Should I stop on the side of the road and see if he goes by?" she asked.

Henry's calm was also deserting him. "No, no. If this guy's following us he could have a gun. Remember we're supposedly armed and dangerous."

"Maybe I could turn into the driveway of one of these houses. Like we belong there."

"I'd rather you didn't."

"This isn't the States where everyone is carrying guns."

"No, it's true, but if we pull into a driveway the guy could block us in with his car and then we're stuck. We'd have to wait for the cops or take to the bush and I'm not doing that again."

"There's a road up ahead, on the left. I'm gonna turn." Pagan slowed and the truck rounded the corner.

And the car followed.

"Shit," Pagan muttered under her breath. "Screw off!" she said loudly.

She jammed her foot down on the gas pedal. The truck sagged, then surged, and the engine roared in response.

A gap between them and the trailing car immediately developed.

Pagan and Henry watched as the little red car followed suit and was soon, again, perched on their tail.

On a straight section of the road, Pagan said, "Should I slam on the brakes? Let him pile into the back of us?"

"Well, we do have a truck and that's a little shitbox … I don't know."

Pagan slowed the truck dramatically. The car followed suit. Then she accelerated again.

She felt—or imagined she felt—the truck tip onto two wheels as they raced around a sharp corner. "I hate this thing!" she called out. "It's too light. I feel like we're in a bloody tin can."

The truck went off the ground racing over a small rise.

Pagan remembered her just published novel. The intense excitement of her protagonist as the woman's car flew down a highway. Pursued by the cops. A woman who longed for adventure. Like her. But all she now felt was a sense of impending doom.

Henry was half-turned in the direction of Pagan. His eyes fixed on the road behind. His right hand braced against the dash. His left arm hooked over the back of the seat.

"He's slowing down!" he announced loudly.

Pagan managed a quick glance. It was all she dared. But it was true. The red car was dropping well back.

"I think you can ease up," Henry said. "He may have stopped altogether. I don't even see him now."

Pagan slowed but only slightly. "I wish I knew where these bloody dirt trails lead. There's another. Next one I see I'm going to go up it."

When a dirt trail—in reality, two ruts through the bush—eventually appeared, Pagan slowed the truck and turned. The bush path ran straight for perhaps fifty feet and then ended. But there was a clearing on the left where vehicles could turn around. Pagan pulled into the space and put the pickup in park. "Do you think we can be seen from the road?"

"I don't think so. Is this one of those spots for hunters and fishermen?"

"I think so. Hikers too maybe. I don't know and I don't care. I need to take a break."

"Maybe you should shut the engine off," Henry said. We could give it a couple of hours. Maybe even wait for dark."

Pagan closed her window then turned off the motor. "We'll hear someone if they drive by. What do you think happened? You think the kid ran out of gas?"

"Maybe he was on the phone to the cops. Maybe they told him to stop."

"Well, if that's true we may find the road blocked up ahead when we do leave. I guess it'll only be a matter of time till they find us."

Twenty minutes later—after Pagan and Henry had used the time to relieve themselves in the bush and to discover that the mosquitoes here were unrelenting—they found themselves back in the truck.

"It's time for the news," Pagan said, turning on the truck's radio.

The lead story was the kidnapping. "In breaking news," the newsreader said, "the Megumawaach Police have just announced that the two children who were kidnapped Saturday morning in Megumawaach have been recovered."

"Finally!" said Pagan, clapping her hands together.

The only further detail given about the children was that they'd been taken to hospital for observation. A promise of updates, later in the day, followed.

"That's it?" said Pagan in disbelief. "Nothing about who was responsible and whether they've caught them. Nothing about whether the cops are still looking for us or not."

"And they didn't mention whether the kids were found or released after the ransom was paid," added Henry.

"And whether they're okay?" Pagan looked at Henry and clutched his arm. "I'll never be able to live with myself if they're not."

Henry cupped his hand over Pagan's. "You did everything you could to help them."

"But it got us nowhere. Anyway, this is a relief. The parents must have come through. Good for them."

The pair of fugitives were soon feeling restless and began debating their next move. Were they still being sought by the police? What had the children told them? Was it safe to turn themselves in? Would they be able to get back to their lives?

"So what do you want to do now then?" Henry asked. "I mean, right now?"

"I'd say get back on the road. It looks to be the one that leads to the highway. If it was blocked before maybe the cops have left."

"Then we can get back to Jarrod's and make a plan."

"Yeah. Negotiate turning ourselves in."

"He could call his brother again."

Pagan started the truck and was soon driving in the direction they'd been going.

They rounded a corner a few kilometres along and Pagan's foot went to the brake pedal. A police cruiser was parked cross-ways across the road.

She glanced in the rearview mirror and watched a second cruiser swing out of a lane or a driveway; its lights flashing.

"Well I guess this is it," Pagan said, stopping the truck. She reached out for Henry's hand, squeezed it then let go. "I think that when we get out of the truck we should keep our hands held high."

"Agreed."

37 Tuesday

Summer Time

First thing Tuesday morning Corporal Carruthers spoke to Sergeant Landry. "I just wanted to let you know," she said, "that we checked the phone calls made using Jarrod Augustine's cellphone. There's nothing to contradict anything we've heard but there is an oddity. A phone call was made at 4:12 AM yesterday morning to a woman named Lindy Thatcher; the person that Egan's ex told us about. Jarrod said that he didn't make the call."

"I was just about to follow up with you on that. To see where we were at on getting her surname and finding out if she was involved. We learned yesterday that the children were always accompanied by ..."

"Grace."

"Right, Grace. And the only possibility we have so far—as to who Grace might be—is this Lindy woman."

"Yes. We're still interviewing her friends. I was planning to make a complete presentation at the team meeting this afternoon. I figured that since the kids have been found that there may not be the same urgency ..." Carruthers broke off the statement. Landry's stern look told her that her assumption about urgency had been an incorrect one as far as he was concerned.

She resumed. "And it appears that Lindy couldn't have been involved. She's with another partner who says that they were together all weekend—plus she's pregnant. ..."

"So was the call significant?"

"I thought it might be but I'm now inclined to think not. I just spoke to Thatcher and she said that she and Egan are still friends. Egan left a voicemail to tell her that she was okay."

"The timing of the call is odd."

"I thought so too but Thatcher said that, in her message, Egan said that she was calling at such an odd time because she didn't think she would have access to a cell phone during the day so wanted to send the message when she could."

The Gallant children were interviewed at the hospital in a playroom filled with stuffed animals and toys.

Four people sat in chairs, encircling a round table. The little girl, Hélène, sat on a chair by herself. Anthony, was to one side of her, sitting on his mother's knee, and on her other side was Sergeant Isabelle Robichaud who would lead the interview.

Sergeant Robert Landry watched unobtrusively from a chair in a corner of the room. While he was hopeful of finding out something about where the kids had been held, his expectation was that the two abducted children would be unable to provide them with any more information about their captors than they already had. The little boy was mute, his head pressed against his mother. And could one expect to get anything from the little girl—even though she was the talkative sort—that they hadn't already heard?

"You said that the lady with the black hair stayed with you the whole time. Did she ever remove her mask?" the Sergeant Robichaud asked Hélène.

"Grace O'Malley. No," said Hélène.

"Is there anything you can tell us that we might not know?"

"Grace was mean and she hates kids. She told Anthony she was going to drown him."

Anthony picked up his head and looked at his sister, aware that he'd become the subject of the interview.

"I'm sorry to ask you this, but remember that she can't hurt you," the sergeant said, looking from one child to the other, "but did Grace say where she would drown him?"

"In the ocean," said Hélène.

"In the 'bloody ocean'," Anthony elaborated.

"Did either of you see the ocean when you were with

161

Grace? Through a window maybe?"

"No," said Hélène.

"No," Anthony quickly echoed.

"We were in the trunk of the car when we got to the house so we didn't see anything but the grey house," said Hélène.

"Yes. I'm wondering about when they took you out of the car's trunk and into the house. Did you see other houses or water; like the ocean, or a lake, or a river?"

"Just trees."

"And what about through the windows?"

"The curtains were always closed."

"Did you ever see the other person ..."

"Calico Jack, Scourge of the Megumawaach," interjected Hélène.

The sergeant suppressed a smile. "Yes, Calico Jack. Did you ever see Calico Jack without a mask?"

"No."

"And Calico Jack was only at the cottage twice; on the day you arrived and on the day you were released?"

"Yes."

"Do you know why Calico Jack let you go?"

"Because Grace was mean. She hit me, and tied us up, and put facecloths in our mouths."

"I couldn't breathe," said Anthony.

"He was gasping," said his sister. "Grace went nuts and was pointing a gun at us before she left."

Vera gasped.

Landry glanced up at the large clock on the wall. It was going on noon and he had a lot to do.

Sergeant Robichaud looked his way and saw his nod to her. "Maybe we should call it a day," she said to everyone around the table.

"Right, right," said Landry, standing up. "Hélène, Anthony, thank you for all you've told us. You are very brave and an awful lot of people are very happy to know you're safe."

Looking at Vera, he added, "If your children mention anything else about their experiences, anything at all, even if it seems insignificant, can you call and let me know?”

"Yes, of course,” Vera replied. “And thank you for all that everyone has done.”

38

At 1:30 PM Sergeant Landry conducted his first in-depth interview of Pagan Egan.

Landry outlined the events surrounding the kidnapping of Hélène and Anthony Gallant and the planned extortion. He cited the similarities between those events and the plot details in Egan's synopsis of her mystery novel, *The Pirate Robbers.*

SERGEANT LANDRY: Do you agree that the kidnappers based their plan on your book?

PAGAN EGAN: I'd think so. The likelihood of so many similarities—of so many coincidences—would be slim to impossible.

SERGEANT LANDRY: Do you hate kids?

PAGAN EGAN: What? No, why?

SERGEANT LANDRY: Are you guilty of kidnapping the Gallant children, and of extortion?

PAGAN EGAN: No.

SERGEANT LANDRY: What time did you leave your apartment last Saturday morning—the first time?

PAGAN EGAN: Around 11:00.

SERGEANT LANDRY: ... To confirm your version of events, are you positive you left at 11:00 AM for a noon hour meeting?

PAGAN EGAN: Sorta. I left at 11:00 for an 11:30 meeting. I made a lot of notes about Henry's book so I changed the planned meeting time.

Landry was thrown off guard. The timing didn't work if Egan left home at 11:00 AM rather than 11:30 AM as her mother had said. 11:00 AM would mean that Egan was in two places at the same time. Her stated departure time must be a lie. She was almost certainly making up the time she left home to alibi herself.

> **SERGEANT LANDRY**: And where did you go?
> **PAGAN EGAN**: I drove to the house of Henry Hebert.
> **SERGEANT LANDRY**: And your route?
> **PAGAN EGAN**: I took Ballantrae and then Jersey Road.
> **SERGEANT LANDRY**: Your car was captured on CCTV at the home of Vera Gallant at 10:30 AM. Were you one of the two occupants?
> **PAGAN EGAN**: No.
> **SERGEANT LANDRY**: Do you have any idea of how your car came to be in Megumawaach at that time?
> **PAGAN EGAN**: No. I wasn't there.
> **SERGEANT LANDRY**: Does anyone else have the keys to your car?
> **PAGAN EGAN**: No.
> **SERGEANT LANDRY**: How many sets do you have?
> **PAGAN EGAN**: One. I lost one during my last move.
> **SERGEANT LANDRY**: Your car was pulled over on Dube Creek Road by a police officer at 10:45 AM that same morning. The two occupants of the vehicle fired upon the officer. Were you one of the two occupants?
> **PAGAN EGAN**: Definitely not. It was someone else.
> **SERGEANT LANDRY**: At 10:45 AM your car was on Dube Creek Road but you say you left home at 11:00 AM. If someone took your car for the kidnapping it's impossible to believe they could have taken the kidnapped children to the place where they were being held, dropped them off, and then gotten back to your house by 11:00 AM, fifteen minutes later. Dube Creek Road is twenty minutes from your apartment.

PAGAN EGAN: Exactly. It proves my innocence.

SERGEANT LANDRY: That's only true if you left at 11:00.

PAGAN EGAN: It is. There has to have been another black Civic on Dube Creek Road. It's one of the most common cars out there.

SERGEANT LANDRY: But both cars bore the same license plate and those are unique.

PAGAN EGAN: Unless they're copied. Unless the kidnappers made a fake plate. ... You know, something just occurred to me. I bought the car used and it still had the plate on the front from before the law was changed. I removed the front plate and put it in the trunk. Maybe someone stole it.

SERGEANT LANDRY: Did you see any of your neighbours when you left home? Or, more accurately, did anyone see you?

PAGAN EGAN: I don't recall seeing anyone I know so I can't say if anyone I know saw me.

Landry made a note to check whether Egan's second license plate was in the trunk of the Civic. But whether it was or not, he immediately realized, it didn't matter. There was no way of proving or disproving that someone had used it.

Landry confirmed with Pagan that she owned two handguns, and that they used the same calibre bullets as those fired at the police officer on Dube Creek Road. But Pagan stated that she had no idea if those were the guns used during the confrontation with the police. Only the recovery of the weapons could confirm a match.

SERGEANT LANDRY: Do you know where your handguns are now?

PAGAN EGAN: No. If they aren't in my bedroom closet then someone stole them.

SERGEANT LANDRY: Have there been any break-ins at your apartment in recent weeks, or at any time?

Pagan Egan: Not so far as I know.

Sergeant Landry: Does anyone have access to your apartment besides you and your roommate, Darla Abbott?

Pagan Egan: Yes, Wolf Byron. Darla gave him a key so he could get inside to wait if we weren't at home when he came to pick her up for a date. Have you looked into him?

Landry wondered about the emphasis that Egan had put on Wolf's name. Did this woman suspect that a police officer had committed the kidnapping? It seemed so. But more importantly, was he willing to consider the idea?

Landry wasn't surprised about Byron seeing Darla Abbott. He knew of Wolf's longstanding and on-going relationship with Morgan Macrae but it was no secret around the detachment that Wolf was a serial philanderer. One of the more erudite members of the force had dubbed him 'Lord Byron'. In this case however, Byron had already informed Landry of his relationship with Abbott. He'd said nothing about having a key to the apartment though and Landry made a note to that effect.

Sergeant Landry: Were there any parties or get-togethers at your apartment when someone other than a key holder might have entered your room and stolen your guns?

Pagan Egan: There's been no guests for awhile. I'm sure if the guns were missing for more than a few days before the crime I'd have noticed.

Sergeant Landry: Okay. Let's return to your novel. So we have this book you wrote about two bank robbers who wear pirate masks and green gloves. They kidnap the children of a bank manager in an attempt to compel her to amass a great deal of money, mostly by robbing her own bank, which she then wires to an off-shore account. You've agreed that the details of the plan carried out this past weekend were too much like the plot of your novel for it to be a coincidence. Can we also agree that it must be the case that whoever kidnapped the Gallant children was familiar with the plot of your book?

Pagan hesitated. There was something in what Landry had said that wasn't right. Maybe it was just in the way he'd expressed himself. The interview was moving too fast to consider the question at the moment.

PAGAN EGAN: Agreed.

SERGEANT LANDRY: How many copies of the manuscript are out there?

PAGAN EGAN: One. The one I sent to a literary agent in Toronto. I had it printed at a copy shop and it was so expensive—even with Darla's staff discount—that I didn't print any more.

SERGEANT LANDRY: And the computer file of the book is saved where?

PAGAN EGAN: Just on the cloud—and no one has my password. Only me.

SERGEANT LANDRY: Anywhere else?

PAGAN EGAN: No.

SERGEANT LANDRY: Will you please tell me the names of all of the people who might have known the plot of your novel, *The Pirate Robbers*?

PAGAN EGAN: Well, to varying degrees, my mother and my former boyfriend Patrick McSheehy. I told Darla about it in broad strokes only. I don't know who they might have told. Their boyfriends and girlfriends, I guess. Darla may have told Wolf who may have told Morgan Macrae. It's also possible that Wolf stumbled on the outline of the novel in a notebook I keep in my desk. He did have access to my room.

SERGEANT LANDRY: Why did Morgan Macrae find you at her parent's cottage?

Pagan Egan: We were looking for the kidnapped children. I know Darla had nothing to do with this crime but I suspect that Wolf did and since he had to have a partner it must have been Morgan.

Sergeant Landry: You weren't planning to plant any evidence there?

Pagan Egan: Of course not. We had nothing to plant. You know that.

Sergeant Landry: You could have disposed of it … In any case, we discovered damage to Jarrod Augustine's sedan which he told us was caused by a bullet from a rifle fired by Wolf Byron after Wolf found you and Henry Hebert in his home. Do you deny that?

Pagan Egan: No. We were looking for the kids there too. The fact that we were out looking for the kids should speak for itself. It's not something we'd have been doing if we knew where they were. And doesn't the fact that Wolf fired a rifle at us say an awful lot?

Sergeant Landry: About what?

Pagan Egan: That he wanted to silence us. You don't fire a rifle at someone for breaking and entering.

Sergeant Landry: That strikes me as a pretty dubious assertion. He said he fired at the car tire of a fleeing housebreaker, to stop them.

Pagan Egan: It wasn't the first time he tried to kill us.

Sergeant Landry: What? When was this other time?

Pagan Egan: He shot at us multiple times when we ran from him at Henry's house. It's a wonder we weren't killed.

Sergeant Landry: I know about that incident. It was the other officer present who discharged his firearm—and they were warning shots.

Pagan Egan: The bullets went right by our heads.

Sᴇʀɢᴇᴀɴᴛ Lᴀɴᴅʀʏ: Why did you run away?

Pᴀɢᴀɴ Eɢᴀɴ: Because the radio news said that we were armed and dangerous and there are too many stories out there of cops shooting first and asking questions later. In any case, Wolf ticks all the boxes of who committed this crime, and only Wolf.

Sᴇʀɢᴇᴀɴᴛ Lᴀɴᴅʀʏ: Can you explain?

Pᴀɢᴀɴ Eɢᴀɴ: He had access to the synopsis of my story and to my guns. And he knew how to use them. Plus, he also knew that I was at home during the kidnapping so I would have no alibi.

Sᴇʀɢᴇᴀɴᴛ Lᴀɴᴅʀʏ: You also check all the boxes.

Pᴀɢᴀɴ Eɢᴀɴ: Me? Why would I implicate myself by copying a crime I wrote about in a book?

Sᴇʀɢᴇᴀɴᴛ Lᴀɴᴅʀʏ: That's what I'm hoping you'll tell me. Or did you think the connection with you wouldn't come out because so few people knew about your first novel?

Pᴀɢᴀɴ Eɢᴀɴ: Enough did that only a crazy person —or a very stupid one—would think that no one would turn them in. And there were people who knew the plot that aren't my friends and those guys would have had no reason to cover for me: the agent in Toronto for one. It was bound to come out. I'd have reported it myself when I heard the news of the crime. It's obvious. Whoever did this wanted it to seem to be me. Wanted to appear to use my car.

Sᴇʀɢᴇᴀɴᴛ Lᴀɴᴅʀʏ: Was Henry Hebert involved in the kidnapping?

Pᴀɢᴀɴ Eɢᴀɴ: No. He was with me and I wasn't involved.

Sᴇʀɢᴇᴀɴᴛ Lᴀɴᴅʀʏ: He could have done it with someone else before you arrived at his place. He may have used a Civic like yours. He would have been able to do the kidnapping and be home by the time you arrived.

Pagan Egan: Not Henry.

Sergeant Landry: How well do you know him?

Pagan Egan: Enough to be certain of him.

Landry picked up an 8 x10 photo of Henry Hebert that was taken at a book launch in Toronto. He slid it across the table so that Pagan could see it.

Landry knew that even though Gillian Morris and Henry Hebert were both in the photo together that there was likely no connection between them. But Pagan Egan wouldn't know that. If he could undermine her confidence in Hebert she might start talking and state some detail that would make a case against him. If they weren't working together that is.

> **Sergeant Landry:** This photograph was taken at a book launch in Toronto five months ago. A month before Henry Hebert moved to New Brunswick. You see the woman immediately to Hebert's right? That's Gillian Morris, the literary agent you sent your manuscript to. What's the connection between Hebert and Morris?
>
> **Pagan Egan:** … You'd have to ask him. Does he know her?
>
> **Sergeant Landry:** He says he doesn't.
>
> **Pagan Egan:** Well then, that's good enough for me. He managed a store that sold books, she's a literary agent, so I imagine their paths crossed. The sign behind them says, 'Book Launch'.
>
> **Sergeant Landry:** Do you know that he has an arrest record?
>
> **Pagan Egan:** No, for what?
>
> **Sergeant Landry:** He can be violent. Did you ever mention to him that you owned guns?
>
> **Pagan Egan:** Um … I think so. Yes.
>
> **Sergeant Landry:** Did he know where you lived?
>
> **Pagan Egan:** Yes.
>
> **Sergeant Landry:** Had he ever seen your car?
>
> **Pagan Egan:** … Yes. In Moncton.

Landry shuffled through some papers, considering where to go next, and he decided to change tack. He'd noted, however, some hesitation in Pagan's answers about Henry Hebert although she'd tried to respond casually. He'd caught her off guard and maybe planted some seeds of doubt in her mind about her new boyfriend.

> SERGEANT LANDRY: Let's turn to your ex-boyfriend, Patrick McSheehy. Do you think he was involved in the kidnapping?
> PAGAN EGAN: No.
> SERGEANT LANDRY: Who broke up with whom?
> PAGAN EGAN: I broke up with him.
> SERGEANT LANDRY: Was he angry?
> PAGAN EGAN: No more than you'd expect with anyone. If you're asking if he's vindictive enough to try and set me up, he's not. I've never seen him act like that. And he's no criminal either.
> SERGEANT LANDRY: Several times in the recent past he's been spotted sitting in his car on your street, apparently watching your apartment. Mostly on weekend mornings. Did you know about that?

This was another bit of information that Wolf Byron had passed on to Landry. Pagan was again caught off guard, and again attempted to conceal it in her tone of voice.

> PAGAN EGAN: … No.
> SERGEANT LANDRY: Did Mr. McSheehy know that you owned two handguns?
> PAGAN EGAN: Yes.
> SERGEANT LANDRY: Did you know he's licensed to use restricted weapons?
> PAGAN EGAN: Yes.
> SERGEANT LANDRY: Did he ever have access to your car keys?
> PAGAN EGAN: Of course. We used to live together.

SERGEANT LANDRY: So he could have made a copy.
PAGAN EGAN: Um … obviously.

Something caught Landry's eye; Egan was definitely distracted, perhaps deep in thought. He waited and watched.

PAGAN EGAN: You asked me if I hated children.
SERGEANT LANDRY: Yes.
PAGAN EGAN: Is that a characteristic of the female pirate?
SERGEANT LANDRY: Yes.
PAGAN EGAN: Because I think that Patrick has a new girlfriend—a woman at work—and she's always saying how she hates kids, and I think she's sincere about that.
SERGEANT LANDRY: What's her name?
PAGAN EGAN: Cinders Cassidy.
SERGEANT LANDRY: If the two of them were standing side-by-side would you say that they were comparable heights.
PAGAN EGAN: What? Um … yes, I suppose so. And there's something else. In your summary of the crime a minute ago, you said that the pirates wore green gloves. Is that true?
SERGEANT LANDRY: Yes, they wore green gloves.
PAGAN EGAN: That's news to me. I heard nothing on the radio news about the colour of their gloves. In the original manuscript the gloves were green, but only there. After I sent the manuscript to Gillian Morris I changed the colour to red because I didn't want them to look like gardening gloves. You saw the synopsis that I kept in my desk. I'm fairly certain that I mentioned in there that the colour of the gloves was red. And, if Wolf Byron read the synopsis and modelled the crime on it, the pirate's gloves would have been red. Every aspect of the crime was exactly like the synopsis, so that one should have been as well."

Landry chastised himself. He'd read the synopsis. He'd noted the discrepancy in the colour of the gloves and took it to be insignificant.

SERGEANT LANDRY: So you're saying what?

PAGAN EGAN: That whoever did this crime read the original manuscript or was someone I talked to about it when I wrote it.

SERGEANT LANDRY: Sounds like you want to eliminate some people from consideration.

PAGAN EGAN: Well … on that basis I may have been off-base about Wolf because there's no way he could have known about the green gloves. … I told my mother about the book back then but I can remember the conversation and I'm absolutely positive that I didn't mention anything about the colour of the gloves. Why would I? So she couldn't have mentioned it to anyone else. Whoever did this had to have read the original manuscript itself or was someone I told about it at the time. But to tell you the truth, I doubt that I mentioned the colour of the pirates' gloves to anyone who I spoke to about the novel. It's an insignificant fact.

SERGEANT LANDRY: So who does that come down to? Who knew about the green gloves?

PAGAN EGAN: The literary agent. Maybe someone who worked with her. And Patrick. The book was up on my laptop for a long time. There could have been periods when I wasn't present; when I went to the bathroom or something. But even if not, I remember having detailed conversations with Patrick about the crime itself. He was very interested in the details of the computer transactions especially. He actually told me how to manage getting money to disappear through off shore bank transactions.

SERGEANT LANDRY: Would Patrick have known about your meeting with Henry Hebert on Saturday morning?

PAGAN EGAN: No. But he knew I'd be at my mother's in the afternoon. I told everyone at work that I eat lunch with. He could have guessed when I'd leave.

SERGEANT LANDRY: But you just said that there had to be a second car because you left home at 11:00 and the people in the kidnap car were firing at a police officer at 10:45 or so. Does either Patrick or Cinders Cassidy own a black Honda Civic so far as you know?

PAGAN EGAN: No. They'd had to have used another Civic with a fake plate or my second plate to make it look like I was guilty.

Later, back in the incident room—which he was using as his office—Landry leaned back in his desk chair and considered what he'd heard. He wasn't happy with the case against Egan. The timing didn't work to start with, but then again he only had her word for it that she was at home when the kidnapping was committed.

A more significant flaw in the case against Egan was the fact that she and Hebert were apparently together on Sunday and Monday—at least according to Jarrod Augustine—yet the Gallant children said there was always someone with them: the woman known as Grace O'Malley. Grace was certainly one of the participants in the robbery and her partner was a man, so not Egan.

And, now that he thought about it, the man couldn't have been Hebert either. Egan and Hebert were seen together by Morgan Macrae at the exact same moment that the two kidnappers were both present at another house with the children, right before they were released. That ruled out the possibility that either Egan and Hebert were working with Grace. Unless they were—singly or together—working in league with two pirate kidnappers

That would mean that there were three or four people responsible for the crime. Landry wasn't yet willing to believe that. He couldn't invent suspects to explain every discordant fact.

He told himself to go back to the beginning. There were two suspects only: Jack and Grace. And these two weren't Egan and Hebert.

So the bottle was spinning and it seemed to now be pointing towards Patrick McSheehy when it stopped.

Under normal circumstances his instinct would have been to be suspicious when Pagan Egan pointed towards her ex as the culprit. Not just because she might have an ulterior motive to do so but because a few minutes earlier she'd been convinced it was Wolf Byron who was to blame. By tomorrow she might be blaming someone else. She obviously liked to play detective—she wrote mystery stories after all—but even so, the case against Patrick McSheehy did have some merit.

Landry returned to the timing of the kidnapping.

For McSheehy to be guilty, one of two things had to have happened. McSheehy used Egan's car and she left home later than the 11:00 AM time that she says she left—giving him time to return it. Or McSheehy used a duplicate Civic.

Something occurred to Landry. If the kidnappers were out to implicate Egan they probably knew that she would be seeing Henry Hebert since it was a couple—a man and a woman—who did the crime. Implicating Egan alone wasn't enough. The ex-boyfriend Patrick was a stalker so it's possible that he knew about Henry somehow. That might even have been what set him off to get revenge.

A short while later, Landry interviewed Henry Hebert. His answers were exactly what Landry expected them to be. He even confirmed Pagan's version of the timeline—sort of.

Henry said, "The plan was changed. We were initially going to meet at noon. I'm not sure exactly when Pagan got to my place but it was around 11:30."

In a timely coincidence, Landry's phone rang shortly after the conclusion of his interview of Hebert. The officers canvassing Egan's neighbours finally had a hit—another sort of.

A senior citizen named Betty Simpson, had been walking her dog in the area on Saturday morning. Simpson hadn't been found earlier because she lived ten blocks from Egan, so out of the initial search area. Betty said that she saw the black Civic exiting Egan's driveway around 11:00 AM. The old woman said that even though she didn't have a watch her body clock told her it was 11:00. She knew because she was craving lunch and she always eats at 11:00. Seeing Egan's car —she didn't recall seeing the driver—caused her to turn around.

So a duplicate car had to have been used.

As things now stood, Patrick McSheehy might be a prime suspect, but there were too many ifs to jump to the conclusion that he was indeed involved in the kidnapping. He might even have an alibi.

He and his girlfriend, Cinders something or other, would have to be interviewed.

First though, Landry would attempt to obtain search warrants to check their homes for any evidence that the kids had been at either residence.

Landry got on the phone to Constable Michelle Ryan and directed her to compile a list of everyone in the Megumawaach area who owned a black Honda Civic. "The kidnappers," he explained, "possibly used a car like Egan's with a duplicate plate on it."

39

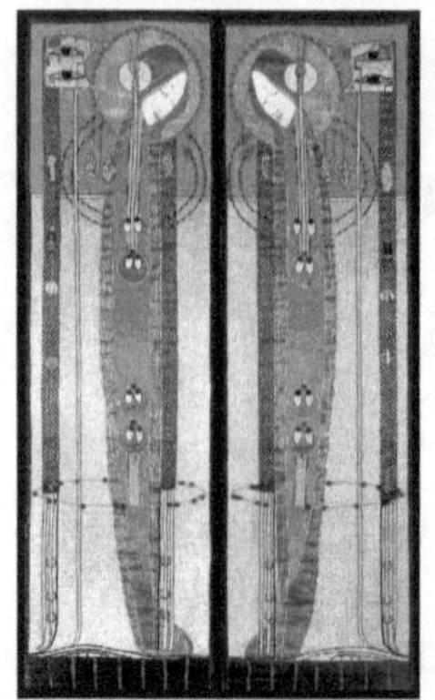

In his brief to the incident team on Tuesday afternoon, Landry told them that Pagan Egan had said that Cinders Cassidy and Patrick McSheehy were similar heights. "This needs to be confirmed. If what Egan says is true, it's potentially damning evidence."

Landry looked down at his notes. He'd obtained the heights of everyone whose name had come up so far. Vera Gallant was adamant that the two culprits were the same height. She said that at the time when she and the kidnappers were together in the house that she was trying to find things to help identify them at a later date. At one point, she said, the pair were standing side by side and she noticed that they were equal heights, and both of them were tallish.

Landry had noted that Wolf Byron was 5'11. Darla Abbott was 5'8 and Morgan Macrae 5'10. He wasn't about to mention these facts to the team lest it appear that he was suspicious of a fellow police office.

To the group, he said, "Henry Hebert is 6'0 and Pagan Egan is 5'5. There's no way that anyone would mistake them for being the same height." He wanted the team to see the dubiousness of any case against the pair.

After raising her hand, Constable Ryan was called on and said, "At the Gallant house, the landing inside the front door is over a metre deep. It's maybe four metres long since it runs the width of the sunken living room. There's a single step between the landing and the living room floor. Is there any chance that Vera Gallant could have been confused based on where people where standing? Maybe one person was on the step and the other was either on the landing above it or on the living room floor below it."

"Vera Gallant was insistent about the kidnappers being the same height. I asked her if the step might figure into things and she said 'no'. ... So, to conclude: McSheehy and Cassidy are now being transported here. We have search warrants for McSheehy's and Cassidy's property's."

After the meeting, something else occurred to Landry that might help to exonerate Pagan Egan: the black hair. Her hair had only been dyed black at Jarrod Augustine's parents' house. Augustine told them that in his statement, and the physical evidence bore it out.

So she'd dyed her hair black after a kidnapping that was done by someone with black hair. Only someone on the run who didn't know about Grace's hair colour—and the police hadn't given out that information to the media—would intentionally have tried to make themselves look more like the suspect ... unless they were trying to get caught of course.

Corporal Leslie Carruthers tapped on the incident room door.

"Come in," Landry called.

Carruthers opened the door and stepped inside. "Can I speak to you?"

"Go ahead."

"I was just thinking about this during your presentation to the team so nothing has been looked into. It's about the kidnappers copying their method from Pagan Egan's book. You said that Egan told you that only the Toronto literary agent and McSheehy would have known about the green gloves so he must have been involved. But when I spoke to Lindy Thatcher yesterday she told me that she knew all about the plot of the book. I don't know if Thatcher knew about the green gloves but she's a writer so she and Egan might have spoken about the book at some length."

"I thought that Thatcher had been eliminated ..." Landry considered Carruther's comments before proceeding. "It concerns me that Egan lied about who knew the plot of her book. It raises the question of why."

"Maybe she and Thatcher were involved. And we were wrong—I mean I was wrong—to eliminate Thatcher from consideration. I have a copy of Egan's new book on my desk.

I haven't read the whole thing yet but I was reading around in it last night. It's about a pair of women—lovers—who rob banks. And ..." Carruther's voice slowed for emphasis, "... and one of the bank robbers dresses up like a man and says nothing during the robberies."

Landry raised his eyes. "You said that Thatcher had an alibi for the weekend."

"Yes. She said that she was home with her wife."

"I'd like you to check her alibi. And then we'll need to look into her situation: her personal life, her work. Ask around. I'm not discounting the possibility that she could have been working with her wife or with Egan, but see if there's a man in her life who could have been her partner? A brother perhaps. Oh, and does she have a place where she could have held the children? Get Constable Woods to help you. He's been looking into Jarrod Augustine for me."

Landry was glad that he'd found a pretext to get Woods off of his assignment. Asking him to look into Augustine hadn't been Landry's wisest move. Given Wood's attitudes about Natives it wouldn't surprise him if he came back with a theory that Jarrod Augustine was the mastermind of the kidnapping plot. Woods was seriously overdue for more cultural sensitivity training.

As Carruthers was turning to leave, Landry called out, "And find out how tall Thatcher is, if she hates kids, and if she's ever dyed her hair black."

After Carruthers had left, Landry jotted some notes on his writing pad:

- *Was it possible the plan from the beginning was to release the kids? A possible reason for that (cooked up by Egan and Thatcher?): Since Egan was bound to be declared innocent this whole thing could have been a publicity stunt and not a real robbery. A way to promote her current book and to get the pirate novel published. I can see the dust jacket notes. "The plot of this book is so great that real criminals used it."*
- *Maybe the point of using E's plot wasn't to implicate*

her but a small group of people (because it was obvious that we would soon drop her as a suspect). E could have done this to lead us away from Thatcher because E knew we would take her word about who knew the plot of the book.

- *Murder on The Orient Express? i.e. is everyone part of the plan?*
- *There's no reason to seriously consider that Hebert staged the kidnapping with someone prior to meeting Egan on Saturday. Just because it's a possibility time-wise is not sufficient reason to entertain it as a possibility.*

40

When interviewed on Tuesday evening, Patrick McSheehy and Cinders Cassidy provided each other with alibis that couldn't be corroborated by anyone else.

During their initial interviews, both of them said that they left McSheehy's place at 8:00 AM the previous Saturday—the morning of the kidnapping—for a camping trip.

McSheehy parked his car on an overgrown trail leading to a cabin that his father and uncles built on fifty acres of bush owned by his grandfather. Among the family it was known as, 'the hunting camp'.

The couple returned to Megumawaach on Monday afternoon.

Landry had already dispatched a forensic team to the site of the hunting camp.

Cinders Cassidy was overwhelmed by her interview. She admitted to having made statements about not liking children but appeared bewildered about what was happening to her. Landry sensed that she was a good actress. He doubted the helpless female act.

When asked for details of the weekend she spent with McSheehy, Cassidy suddenly refused to answer any more questions without her lawyer present. Landry advised her that she didn't have this right in Canada but that they would take a break and then return for more questioning.

Patrick McSheehy, on the other hand, was belligerent.

Landry wasn't surprised about his attitude. It wasn't just that McSheehy had twice been arrested for bar fights when he was in college, it was that Landry recognized the strutting machismo of the bully. He'd seen it many times before.

During his interview with Sergeant Landry, Patrick McSheehy confirmed that he knew the basic plot outline of Pagan Egan's novel, *The Pirate Robbers.*

Sᴇʀɢᴇᴀɴᴛ Lᴀɴᴅʀʏ: Did you ever see Pagan Egan working at her novel on her laptop?

Pᴀᴛʀɪᴄᴋ McSʜᴇᴇʜʏ: Yeah, of course. She lived at my house.

Sᴇʀɢᴇᴀɴᴛ Lᴀɴᴅʀʏ: Did you ever read the manuscript?

Pᴀᴛʀɪᴄᴋ McSʜᴇᴇʜʏ: No, I like sci-fi.

Sᴇʀɢᴇᴀɴᴛ Lᴀɴᴅʀʏ: Pagan told me that you were interested in the details of the crime in the book.

Pᴀᴛʀɪᴄᴋ McSʜᴇᴇʜʏ: Not really. We talked about some of them. She wanted the kidnappers to … to avoid, ah, exposing themselves by picking up ransom money at a drop-off point. So instead, they get the ransom money by wire transfer and then make the money untraceable through further transactions. Pagan asked my help because I'm an IT guy who used to work at a bank.

Sᴇʀɢᴇᴀɴᴛ Lᴀɴᴅʀʏ: Do you understand why you're here?

Pᴀᴛʀɪᴄᴋ McSʜᴇᴇʜʏ: We're here because Pagan Egan is trying to set me up. And you believe her! She's not who you think she is: little Miss Prim And Proper. It sounds like she's got you wrapped around her little finger.

Sᴇʀɢᴇᴀɴᴛ Lᴀɴᴅʀʏ: Why would she set you up?

Pᴀᴛʀɪᴄᴋ McSʜᴇᴇʜʏ: Isn't it obvious? To pin her crime on someone else. She's obsessed with crime.

Sᴇʀɢᴇᴀɴᴛ Lᴀɴᴅʀʏ: I have a police report here of a car repeatedly parking just up the street from Pagan Egan's apartment, particularly on Saturday mornings. The driver apparently watches Egan's residence and never gets out of his vehicle. The make, model and license plate number of the vehicle all match your car. Why are you going there?

Pᴀᴛʀɪᴄᴋ McSʜᴇᴇʜʏ: There's a nature trail at the end of the street where I like to walk.

Sergeant Landry: Then why do you spend the whole time you're there sitting in your vehicle?

Patrick McSheehy: I don't. I walk around. I'm guessing that information comes from your boy Byron. I've seen him there. Maybe he's part of a ménage … part of a threesome.

Sergeant Landry: So you've figured out the name of the man leaving your ex's apartment. Was that your objective?

Patrick McSheehy: Yeah, of course. Jesus! I wanted to know if she was seeing someone else.

Sergeant Landry: And to record the times of her comings and going on Saturday morning perhaps?

Patrick McSheehy: That's bullshit. I'm being set up. I wasn't even in town. Ask Cinders!

Sergeant Landry: In a kitchen drawer, during our search of your house this afternoon, we found a set of keys for Pagan Egan's Civic. Did you borrow the vehicle last Saturday morning?

Patrick McSheehy: What? No, of course not. I didn't have her keys, or if they were there I didn't know about them.

Sergeant Landry: In a tote bag in your hall cupboard we found two pirate masks and a blue hair ribbon. It matches the description of one that was in the hair of Hélène Gallant when she was kidnapped. Our forensic team is looking at it now. Why is a ribbon belonging to Hélène Gallant in your house?

Patrick McSheehy: What! Oh, gimme a break. I know nothing about that. Nothing about any of that stuff. This isn't right. You need to listen to me.

Sergeant Landry: Also, I neglected to mention, that in the tote bag at your home there were two handguns. Their registration numbers match those of two handguns owned by Pagan Egan. How did these guns come to be in your possession?

PATRICK MCSHEEHY: No, no, no! This is all Pagan's doing. Did you ask her about the keys to my house? Maybe she still has one. Her and her boyfriend put that stuff in my closet.

SERGEANT LANDRY: Stop yelling. When exactly did Pagan Egan and her friend put something in your closet, they're in jail and there's no record of them being in Megumawaach since Saturday morning?

PATRICK MCSHEEHY: I'm not going to say anything else without a lawyer here.

Shortly after the interviews, word came back from the team examining the McSheehy family's hunting camp. It turned out to be a cottage-like two bedroom place with grey siding, not nearly so rustic as Patrick had made out. The beds in both bedrooms had recently been slept in but the sheets in the smaller bedroom were covered with urine stains. Whoever slept there had been a bed-wetter. DNA tests on the sheets and some hairs found there would confirm whether or not it was the spot where the Gallant children had been kept.

All those kids saw were trees, thought Landry. No water. Just like a hunting camp. ... The case was almost airtight. But was it too airtight? The fact that they were tripping over incriminating evidence, stuff that most people would have disposed of, pointed either to an overly self-confident criminal—convinced he would never be a suspect so had no need to dispose of evidence—or to someone who was being framed.

And there was still the problem with timing. McSheehy had a copy of Egan's car keys but it was impossible for her vehicle to have been in two places at the same time. There had to be a second Civic.

Immediately after the interview, Landry made a beeline for Constable Ryan, who was working the phone at her desk, to ask if another Civic had been unearthed.

"Sorry," said Ryan. "None of the car rental agencies have a vehicle that might be mistaken for Pagan Egan's. It's seven years old. I've made an initial list of the owners of black Honda Civics in the area, of the right vintage, and I'm calling them. So far, nobody has admitted to knowing either of the two suspects, and none of them think it's possible that their car could have been stolen and then returned. I'll expand the search area if I get nothing."

"Okay, keep at it," said Landry. "The car is the last piece of the puzzle to make a definitive case against that pair. Get me that car."

41 Wednesday

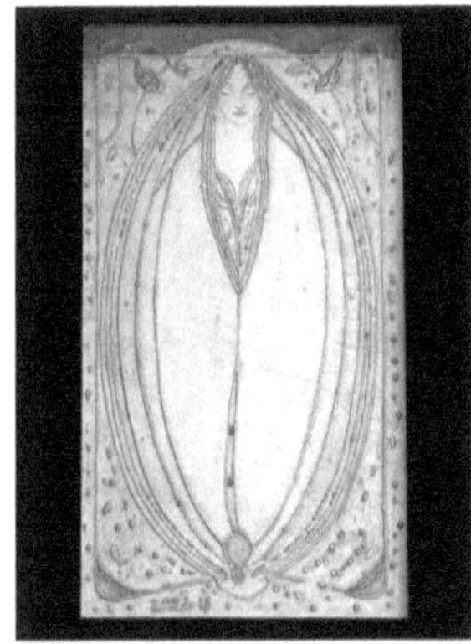

Just before lunch, Patrick McSheehy and Cinders Cassidy were charged with the kidnapping of Hélène and Anthony Gallant, and with extortion.

It was a strong case—with some problems. The pirate Grace—now assumed to be Cassidy—had been left alone much of the time. Presumably at the hunting camp. But where was McSheehy during those times and why would he have disappeared rather than being out and about showing his face around and making an alibi for himself? Plus there was the issue of the vehicle that had been used for the kidnapping. It still hadn't been located.

Problems aside, the evidence found at McSheehy's house alone was deemed sufficient to charge him and Cassidy.

Landry wasn't concerned that the news he received from Corporal Carruthers—just before the charges were laid—appeared to exonerate Pagan Egan being in cahoots with her ex, Lindy Thatcher. He welcomed it in fact. They needed to get rid of suspects, not add them, especially since they now had a solid case against McSheehy.

Corporal Carruthers reported that, "Lindy Thatcher was indeed home all weekend according to her wife. Her next door neighbours told me that they saw both of the women, multiple times, working in their backyard. On top of that, their house isn't grey and neither has a cottage or somewhere they could have held the kidnapped children. Thatcher confirmed what she said before: that she knew about the plot of Egan's first book, but she didn't hear about the green gloves and insists she's never spoken about the plot to anyone. She's a writer herself and that's just something she wouldn't do. Or at least that what she says. The possibility of

Thatcher being involved now seems highly unlikely."

Pagan was released later that afternoon. Henry, she overheard one of the cops say, had been released the day before for lack of evidence.

She wanted only to go home, shower, and sleep in her own bed. She hadn't managed much sleep during her time in jail.

The taxi dropped her off just as Darla was getting back from work, which was fortunate because Pagan had left her keys and wallet on Henry Hebert's kitchen table.

"He dropped them off last night. Your car too," Darla told her. "The stuff's on the kitchen counter. He left your car out front but I moved it to your parking spot."

"How did he get home from here?" Pagan asked.

"He said his neighbour was waiting outside for him so he had to rush off. He seems to be a nice man. He wanted to know if I knew how you were doing. He seemed genuinely concerned."

Darla was solicitous as well and insisted that she cook dinner for her and Pagan.

Pagan accepted the kindness but decided to first drive to the pharmacy. She wanted to get rid of her black hair.

She discovered that Henry had charged her phone so she checked for messages while sitting in her car in the Shopper's parking lot. First, she responded to her mother's request to call. Aisling was insistent that, if it should come to it that Pagan needed a lawyer, that she, Aisling, would pay for it.

Pagan was touched by the offer. She knew that her mother didn't make much money from her jewellery making business, so paying for a lawyer would mean selling things.

There was also a message from Lindy Thatcher, bringing Pagan up to date on her own dealings with the police.

It surprised Pagan that the police had found out about Lindy. She'd wanted her friend left out of their investigation, so hadn't mentioned her name to them. And she had phoned Lindy in the middle of the night so that not even Henry and Jarrod knew about her. Lindy was pregnant and Pagan didn't want the stress—in this case, from knowing she was part of a police investigation or from worrying about Pagan—to lead to yet another miscarriage.

Pagan felt guilty about all the grief she was causing everyone in her life. Not just Lindy, but for her parents, Jarrod, Darla, and especially Henry.

Henry had also left a message asking that Pagan call him when she was released. He'd left his message the previous evening. He assumed, he said, that Pagan would also be out of jail soon as well, and he hoped to hear from her.

Pagan was hesitatant about returning his call. Henry wasn't likely to know she'd been released so he wouldn't take it the wrong way if he received no call. She wanted to think about things.

It struck her as an incredible coincidence that Henry and the literary agent—who had the sole copy of *The Pirate Robbers* and who'd alerted the police about it—should be beside each other in a photograph. The odds against this must be astronomical, yet there they were. On the other hand, since both worked in the book trade in Toronto, it was plausible that they didn't actually know each other but just happened to end up standing side-by-side at a book launch.

Just because, as the detective said, Henry could have staged the kidnapping, she saw no reason to assume he did. What concerned her was Henry's contact with the police. Sergeant Landry had said that, "He can be violent," and he'd also said that Henry had been criminally charged—but not for what. She knew that Henry had some contact with police in the past. He was an activist. But she didn't know if he'd ever even been convicted. She also knew that activists were charged with a laundry list of offences that were soon dropped. Landry may have been simply trying to pull her strings. But, even so, she'd had enough of toxic masculinity for a lifetime and wanted to be sure that this wasn't part of Henry's make-up before she saw him again.

Pagan returned from the drug store, had a shower, then ate dinner with her roommate.

Darla was extremely interested in talking about the police investigation into the kidnapping.

Pagan was uneasy about the choice of subject since the last time they'd spoken she'd accused Wolf of being one of the kidnappers. She would apologize to Darla, in time, she decided.

As she pushed her spaghetti around her plate, not feeling the slightest bit hungry, Pagan listened and mulled over whether to mention to Darla that Wolf had a long-term lady friend. She decided that this was a conversation for another day—if ever—and put it out of her mind. She would play dumb if Darla asked her who she'd thought Wolf's partner in crime was when she was accusing him of being one of the kidnappers.

It turned out that Darla knew more about the facts behind the arrests of Patrick McSheehy and Cinders Cassidy than Pagan did. The information came courtesy of Wolf.

"The cops found something belonging to the kidnapped girl in a bag at his house," Darla said. "They found your guns at his place too, and your car keys."

"It seems so implausible though," said Pagan, shaking her head. "It doesn't strike me as being in character for either Patrick or Cinders."

"Well, we're often wrong about what people are capable of."

"I suppose."

"Speaking of which, I never told Wolf about you calling me from his house and that you suspected him of being a kidnapper. He doesn't know who broke in."

"Thank you. I'm sorry."

"You were in a desperate situation; not thinking straight. You're forgiven. Did the cops tell you that they have a record of Patrick parking just up the street, especially on weekend mornings? Wolf reported it."

"Yes … I had no idea he'd do something like that but it's not surprising, he's pretty jealous. Why didn't Wolf tell me?"

"He figured Patrick was watching someone but he didn't know who. If he knew Patrick was your ex I'm sure he'd have told you."

"What are the cops saying? Are they saying that the kids

were held at Patrick's place?"

"Apparently not. Wolf said they found some evidence that the kids were kept at a cabin in the woods that Patrick's family owns."

"The hunting camp."

"I think that's the place."

"Well Cinders does talk about camping a lot lately. But something else bothers me. The cops asked me about what time I left home on Saturday morning and I told them the truth. They figured Patrick must have used my car."

"They found a set of your keys in a drawer in his kitchen cupboard."

"I thought I'd lost those keys. Anyway, they said that Patrick and Cinders were shooting at a cop on Dube Creek Road around 10:45. It's hard to imagine Cinders even knowing which end of a handgun the bullet comes out of, but, that aside, the timing of the thing doesn't fit."

"I don't follow."

"Well, the car involved in the shooting was a black Civic with my license plate on it. The kidnappers either used my car and had it back by 11:00, when I left home, or they had a second car with fake plates. Patrick's car is nothing like a black Civic and neither is Cinders's. So what car did they use?"

Darla was thoughtful. "I thought you said that you were meeting your friend at 12:00 so you'd be leaving home at 11:30."

"That was the plan but I decided to make it earlier."

"So, you're saying that after the shooting, Patrick had fifteen minutes to drop the kids off where they were being held and then get your car back here. That would have taken how long?"

"From the hunting camp? A half hour maybe."

"And you're sure about the time you left?"

"I could be out a little bit. I might have left a little later than I think. But not a half hour later. I'm sure I glanced at the clock in the car—I always do—and it said 11:00 and change, like 11:02 or something."

Henry was having doubts of his own. He speculated that the police had used the fact that he barely knew Pagan to throw him off guard and get him talking against her. They'd spun a narrative to suggest that Pagan had a lover and the two of them were responsible for the kidnapping.

He knew the police were twisting things—he'd had some experience with this—but it was hard to have implicit faith that Pagan was being honest with him. She'd apparently been making secret phone calls in the middle of the night and, according to Landry, she had said during her interview that the only computer file of her pirate book was on the cloud. Yet Henry remembered Pagan saying that she had a copy of the book on a memory stick she kept in a safety deposit box. How do you trust someone who lies and hides things?

Next morning, as soon as she felt confident that HR Manager Mohini Patel would be in her office, Pagan phoned her.

Worrying that she might sound like a drama queen, but needing to ask, Pagan said, "Do I still have a job?"

Mohini laughed. "Of course. It's been all over the news that the police released you and arrested Patrick. It's quite a week you've had. How are you doing?"

"Okay. As well as can be expected I suppose."

"I can't imagine what you've been through. I don't have a problem if you want to take the rest of the week off, and next week too for that matter."

"Oh, no. I think it would be better to get back to work as soon as possible. Get out of my own head. I was wondering about coming in tomorrow."

"Really? Oh … ah … let me think. I suppose that would be okay but I need to speak to Blair. I suppose he might want me to send out a company memo."

"About what? That I'm returning?"

"No, not explicitly. It should also say something about how our colleagues are in the news and to remind people that we have counselling services available."

"You think people will think I'm guilty?"

"I don't know, honestly, but the place will be buzzing of course. I'll have to mention Patrick and Cinders. Maybe say … ah … that we have to let the justice system play out and that people are innocent until proven guilty. They both work here too. Geez, I'll run this by Blair. I want to tell people, before you return, to mind their own business. I don't want anyone to sass you. That it will be an HR matter."

"Thanks Mo. Should I call back to confirm everything's a go?"

"No, I'll let you know that it's okay after I speak to Blair."

At a few minutes past 4:00 PM, Mohini called back to tell Pagan that Blair had given the all clear for her to return to work but wanted a day to speak to everyone in the company. Instead of coming to work in the morning Pagan should come in on Friday.

In the evening, Pagan called Henry.

"Thanks for dropping off my car," she said. "I'll thank Jarrod when I see him on Saturday at the wedding."

"No problem. How're you doing?"

"Still processing all that's happening. It's dizzying and confusing. How was your experience?"

"The cops had little to say to me and I wasn't offering. I haven't had great experiences with the police on the whole."

"How so?"

"I've been to several demos where some of the cops were heavy-handed for no reason. I think they assume that environmentalists and Natives are terrorists. I've been arrested and man-handled. It's nothing compared to what some of the Native people around me had to deal with but … but there you go."

"They told me. Well not about the man-handling but about the arrests—like you were a violent person."

"I can imagine the picture they painted. You know how those things go, they break up a protest then charge protesters with trespass and resisting arrest—which means you laid there and let them drag you away—but nothing comes of the charges. They talked about you to me and suggested I was the helpless dupe of a conniving woman."

"Really!"

"Oh yes. A Jezebel. I think their tactic is to try and make people turn against each other so they'll feel betrayed and spill the dirt on the other person."

"That's what they did to me too. Showed me a photograph of you with the literary agent I sent my manuscript to."

"Yeah, isn't that wild? Both of us in the same picture. I don't know her. I vaguely recall her face but I never knew her name. That picture was taken at the launch of a book, whose subject is the environment, written by a novelist she represents."

Henry hesitated. He'd wanted to ask Pagan about her early morning phone call to an old flame, but now, on reflection, he realized that she was entitled to her privacy. It wasn't anything to do with him, or anything that hurt him.

"I'm going back to work on Friday," Pagan offered.

"Really? I'd have thought you'd want some time away to … to process. I can imagine your shock when they arrested Patrick. Do you think he did it and not Wolf?"

"I don't know. It seems that way. The kidnappers knew things about the original novel that only Patrick could know. People surprise you. Turns out he was stalking me and I had no idea. I would never have thought he could commit such a violation. So you never know."

42 Friday early AM

From *Irish Fairy Tales*

The woman with white hair came in the middle of the night.

Pagan was awakened by a crashing noise that reverberated throughout the apartment.

She was immediately out of bed and on her feet. The noise had come from the livingroom. Even without turning on a light, Pagan could make out the jagged edges of a gaping hole in the large front window. A shadowy lump of something lay on the rug.

She strode to the window. A figure below was climbing into a black car. A car much like her own. It was roaring off when the lights came on in the livingroom.

"What the hell was that noise?" said Darla from behind her. "Oh my God!"

"Someone smashed the front window." Pagan pointed to the boulder laying on the floor, "With that."

"Watch your feet," said Darla, seeing Pagan picking her way through the large shards to take up the rock.

"There's a piece of paper taped to this," Pagan said, twisting the boulder this way and that. "There's some writing on it. It says, 'Your dead bitch'." She handed it to Darla. "Nice eh? I wonder if this is a sign of what's to come for me. People who think I'm guilty."

Darla looked at the message. "Jesus! Keep away from the glass on the floor. Get your slippers on."

Pagan set the stone down and went to her room to put on slippers. By the time she returned, Darla was kneeling on a pillow in the midst of the glass, piling the large pieces on top of each other.

"I saw the person," said Pagan. "Maybe I should call the police."

"You saw the person? Did you know him?"

"I don't know. Maybe. It was a woman. I think I've seen her before but I didn't get a great look at her. She has bleached white hair and that doesn't ring any bells."

"Her?" Darla looked intently at her roommate.

"Yes. Tall. Drives a black car, same as my Civic maybe."

Darla shook her head. "Do you think it's a friend of Patrick's? Some lady jock from his gym maybe?"

"No idea. I guess I shouldn't be surprised at this sort of thing. I'm sorry."

"It's not your fault."

Pagan followed Darla's lead and dropped a pillow from the couch onto the floor. She knelt on it and began to pick up shards of glass. She said, "Hopefully they've gotten this out of their system. Do you think I should call the police?"

"Well, I think maybe you're right to treat it as a one off. Don't get someone in a lot of trouble for one bad night ... one stupid decision."

"So what do I do?"

Darla brightened. "Why don't you let me call Wolf. I can have him come by and take your statement—if that's what it's called—and let him handle it. Maybe he can keep the report to himself."

"He'd do that?"

"It can't hurt to ask."

Pagan held her breath as Darla made the phone call to Wolf. She was hoping he'd be at home and alone—or this evening would get much worse.

Wolf was up, and apparently in bed alone, but he agreed to come right over.

When he arrived, a short time later, Pagan blushed slightly at the sight of him remembering her phone call to Darla accusing him of kidnapping.

Wolf listened to Pagan's story while he helped her and Darla tape cardboard over the hole in their window. "And you didn't recognize the woman who did this?" he asked Pagan.

"No. She looked so familiar, I'm positive I know her from somewhere. It'll come back to me in time."

"I'll need to file a report in the morning, Sorry, I can't keep this to myself. You never know with these sort of people. They keep at it. When their identity comes to light, having a record of the things they've done can help if you want to get a restraining order against them and to make charges stick. Not saying that's going to happen here, or is even likely. Let me know if there's any other harassment, no matter how small: an email, a phone message, anything. And Pagan, I'm worried about you. Please promise me that you won't tell anyone about this incident, especially about seeing the culprit. You tell someone and they may tell someone else and so on till the person who did it finds out they were seen. The last thing we want is for the perp to think there was a witness who might be able to identify them."

The idea had ominous implications and Pagan nodded obediently.

43

The Turn of the Tide

On her way to work in the morning Pagan grabbed her set of keys from the peg inside the front door where she always hung them. I must have been exhausted last night, she thought, smiling to herself. She'd hung the key on a different peg than the one she always used.

She left a note for Darla to tell her that after work she was going to her mother's to help out with the wedding preparations and that she'd spend the night there. She added a sentence saying that she was going to the wedding with Henry, thinking the fact would please Darla, the person who was always on her case about getting out there and meeting someone new.

The first thing Pagan noticed when she started the Civic was that the time showing on her dashboard clock was a half hour slower than she expected. She checked the time on her phone. The car's clock was wrong. She wondered why Henry would have adjusted the time when he returned her car. He had no obvious reason.

Pagan entered the building by the front door and walked past the receptionist, who was talking on the phone.

She headed for the Traffic Department.

On her way, she passed Howard, going in the opposite direction, holding some papers in one hand; a work order for some department in the building no doubt. Howard worked with Patrick in IT and had always been pleasant to Pagan. Today however, Howard reddened and looked down at the carpet when he walked by.

"Hello Howard," Pagan said.

His response sounded like a grunt.

Pagan didn't know what to make of it and she might have

passed Howard's response off as being the result of someone distracted, until she passed Libby, a recent college graduate who worked with Cinders in Customer Service. Libby not only didn't reply to Pagan's greeting but scowled venomously at her.

My God, Pagan thought, are people blaming me for the bad actions of other people, or do they think I set them up?

Lynette, Pagan's young, part-time assistant in Traffic, hugged her.

At least one person's on my side, Pagan thought.

She decided to ask Lynette to pick up her lunch so she could eat in her car or at her desk rather than sit in The Cafe and be stared at.

Visits to the washroom were unavoidable but at least it was right beside the Traffic Department so Pagan could restrict her visits to times when the washroom seemed to be empty.

Pagan tried to focus on her work but soon realized it was useless. The latest phone call she'd received was still too much on her mind. Landry had called to ask if she had a key to Patrick's house.

Her guess was that Patrick was telling the cops that she was setting him up; that she'd planted the incriminating objects found at his place. Landry being interested in the key suggested that he was trying to confirm whether someone other than Patrick could have brought the stuff into the house.

Pagan had told Landry that she didn't have a key and he rang off. Her statement was true, insofar as Landry's question went at that moment. But sitting her in her office, mulling over the call, she suddenly remembered that she had kept her key to Patrick's house after moving out so she could return to pick up the last of her things. She and Darla made three trips. Later, when she looked for the key so she could take it to work and return it to Patrick, it was nowhere to be found. And she'd turned her room upside down. Thinking that it might turn up, she'd said nothing to Patrick about the missing key and he never mentioned it.

When Lynette returned from her lunch break she brought back a sandwich and a juice for her boss.

Pagan was glad to escape the office but, as she ate lunch while sitting in her car, she began to consider the ramifications of her car's clock being a half hour slow.

She called Darla at the copy shop. "Just a quick question. I noticed the clock on my car is almost a half hour slow. You said that Henry left my car in front of the house when he returned and you parked it round back. But I wondered, did you change the time on the clock?"

"I put your car around back but I didn't touch the clock. Is the time change significant?"

"It is. Remember I told you that I told the police I got to Henry's at 11:30, which means I left home at 11:00, which means that Patrick and Cinders would had to have had access to a car exactly like mine because they couldn't have gotten mine back to me by 11:00. If I actually left a half hour later it would mean that they could have used my car, which makes the case against them stronger."

"And that's a problem?"

"Well no. But now I'm in a bit of a panic because it could mean that I gave the police some wrong information. I was certain that I looked at the clock in the car last Saturday, but now I'm not so sure. If I now tell the cops I was wrong about the time I'm afraid they might think that I fiddled with the clock to set Patrick up. Like I want to make the case that it's fine if neither Patrick or Cinders had access to a car like mine because they could have taken mine."

"Didn't you say you had some trouble with your battery the day before the kidnapping?"

"Yes, the battery seemed to be dead after work so I called CAA. The guy that came said a wire from the battery to the fuse box had a bad connection because of rust or something and the contact was messed up because of it. He cleaned the connection and tightened the wire and the car started. You think it's possible that the clock went screwy because of that?"

"I'm no expert but it sounds plausible. So there you go.

Simple explanation. Your ex took your car after all. You should call the detective and tell him."

"I forgot to ask," Pagan said, during her call to Henry, "are we still on for the wedding?"

"Absolutely. I'm looking forward to it. Things still good between you and your mother?"

"Yeah. They were fine, even when I called her from Jarrod's on Sunday. As soon as she heard I was in trouble, everything else went by the wayside."

"And how are you fairing? How's your first day back at work going?"

"Strange. Some of Patrick's and Cinders's friends here seem to hate me. HR told people not to say anything to me about the police or the kidnapping, and no one has, but some people I passed in the hall either acted like I wasn't there or were extremely curt."

"Why? You did nothing wrong?"

"Exactly. I guess those are people who believe in their friends, so think that someone must be setting them up. Plus, I was all over the media being portrayed as a criminal and some people may not be ready to accept the opposite. It's all so otherworldly. I'm still trying to come to terms with Patrick and Cinders being charged, and now I have a supreme hater out there to boot."

"A what?"

"A hater. Someone threw a large boulder through our front window with a threatening note attached."

"Geez. Bloody cowards. All bullies are cowards and they're almost always men."

"You'd think so, but this was a woman. I caught a glimpse of her. I know her from somewhere. One of those people you see and then wrack your brains, saying to yourself, 'Where do I know them from?'. But so far nothing. It'll come to me though. Oh, don't mention this to anyone at the wedding. I promised a cop that I'd keep quiet about it so the person who did it won't find out they were seen. By the way, there's something I need to ask you. Did you adjust my car's clock?"

“No. Why?”

“It’s a half hour slow. When I was being interviewed by the police they told me that the kidnappers’ shoot out with the cops last Saturday was around 10:45 in the morning. And my car was supposedly there. It seemed to be a big deal when I said that I left home at 11:00.”

“Yeah, I can see that. It means they couldn’t have used your car.”

“Right. And neither Patrick’s or Cinder’s cars are anything like mine. So if I left a little later it makes it easier to make a case against Patrick since he could have taken my car. But I’m worried that if I call the police about it, maybe they’ll think I’m changing my story to set him up.”

“Well I didn’t change your clock and I didn’t notice the time being wrong when I returned your car. But in all honesty I probably didn’t even look at it.”

“What about when I arrived at your place on Saturday? Was it 11:30 like I said or was it noon?”

“Well, I can’t say for certain. I think it was more likely to have been 11:30 than a half hour later but I was outside in the garden when you got here so I might have lost track of time. Wouldn’t you have been checking your phone or a clock when you were upstairs getting ready?”

“Well, that’s the thing. Normally I’ll check the time on my phone when I’m at home. But I took my backpack to my mother’s. There’s a pocket on the side and I put my phone in there to keep my hands free for the wedding decorations I planned to take. So I probably didn’t check the time for a half hour or more before I left, and I would have gone by the car’s clock while I was driving. ... Now I don’t know what to do. Do I call Landry and tell him about the slow clock or not?”

“Well, if there’s even the remotest chance that it caused you to give him the wrong times then I think that you need to tell him.”

Pagan never got the chance to break the news to Landry. By the time she spoke to him he knew the whole story. The news about the slow clock had been transmitted to Landry via Grant Augustine. After speaking to Pagan, Darla had called

Wolf who reported the news about the clock to Grant.

It appeared to Landry that Wolf was becoming Pagan's conduit of information to the incident team. The previous morning he'd reported on an attack on Pagan's home by an unknown man.

The sergeant was surprised by Grant's information. He had a witness to the fact that Egan had left home at 11:00. But Betty Simpson it seemed, had made a mistake. Not surprising. She wasn't even wearing a watch at the time, nor could she tell who was in the car. A defence attorney would have made short work of her testimony. Paint her as a senile old woman. "This helps our case" he'd told Grant. "But I want everything in writing and submitted to me. I have yesterday's report from Wolf but I need this in a written report as well."

"I'll tell him."

44 Saturday morning

Under The Apple Tree

Landry was uneasy.

With the revelation that the clock in Egan's car was slow the timing issues with the case had been resolved. It meant that McSheehy had access to a Honda Civic—Pagan Egan's.

On top of that. Patrick had been watching Egan's place and knew her habits. And he knew about her wedding rehearsal. He had timed the kidnapping based on Pagan's schedule. He took the Civic, staged the kidnapping, and got the car back to her apartment before she left home.

So the timing issue was now settled. Deputy Police Chief Philpott would be thrilled. The force was already getting good press. The case against McSheehy and Cassidy was strong.

Yet Landry was still uneasy. He'd been up all night tossing and turning in bed, reviewing the facts in his thoughts, and he wasn't happy.

Everything implicating McSheehy and Cassidy felt staged.

The evidence against the couple was there but it was problematic. The two handguns found in a tote-bag at Patrick's had been scrubbed clean of DNA evidence. Why would they do this and then keep the obvious evidence of a serious crime? It made no sense. The whole point of cleaning them would be to destroy evidence. Landry reflected that, if it was him, the guns would have been sitting on the bottom of the ocean immediately after they were used.

And then there was the urine stained sheet found on the bed at Patrick's camp. Forensics had matched the DNA to that of little Anthony Gallant. A hair on the sheet was matched to his sister Hélène. But forensics had also shown that there were no urine stains on the mattress underneath the sheet. It told them that the stained sheet had been moved to the bed after it had dried.

"It's bullshit. I'm being set up." That's what McSheehy said during their interview. Was it possible this was indeed the case?

Landry opened the file on his laptop that contained his interview with Pagan Egan, and he began to review it. Something had occurred to him in the night. There was one exchange in particular that he needed to check on.

> **Sergeant Landry**: How many copies of the manuscript are out there?
>
> **Pagan Egan**: One. The one I sent to a literary agent in Toronto. I had it printed at a copy shop and it was so expensive—even with Darla's staff discount—that I didn't print any more.

He was right! Landry scrambled through the file on his desk that listed everything taken from the apartment of Pagan Egan when it was searched the previous weekend. Among the inventoried items was a receipt from a copy shop; the shop where Pagan's roommate Darla worked. On the note were written the words: "Pay me when you can."

"Stupid me," he said aloud. Pagan's manuscript had been photocopied, not by her, but by Darla Abbott. That meant that Pagan must have given Darla a memory stick with the file of the original book on it.

In other words, Abbott had access to the original manuscript so could have known that the pirates wore green gloves. And she also had access to the synopsis—written later —that indicated the colour of the gloves had been changed. These facts didn't in themselves upset the case against Patrick McSheehy but they raised the possibility that he was being set up—by Abbott.

Landry's working hypothesis said that only Patrick and the literary agent in Toronto knew about the green gloves. And that had been the basis for the assumption that Patrick and his girlfriend were the ones who staged the kidnapping. But what if there was someone else who knew about the green gloves, someone who wasn't supposed to? It would mean that that person could have staged the kidnapping and deliberately used green gloves to incriminate Patrick. It would mean that it was never Egan who was being set up by copying her novel's plot. It was always McSheehy.

Landry got Constable Roger Flynn on the phone and said, "I want you to find out everything you can about Darla Abbott—history, friends, old boyfriends—and check on her actions last Saturday."

In his excitement, Landry didn't think to also phone Constable Michelle Ryan and tell her to call off the search for a second black Civic.

The emergency morning meeting began with Landry explaining that Darla Abbott had access to the manuscript of Pagan Egan's first novel. It didn't exonerate the two suspects in jail but it did open the possibility that they had been set up. "I asked Constable Flynn to get us some background on Abbott." He turned towards him. "What do you have?

Not much of the information that Flynn shared about Darla Abbott differed significantly from the typical biography of any young woman.

Flynn also pointed to the timeline and mentioned that he'd confirmed that Abbott had been at work on the day of the kidnapping. Her only phone calls were to her boyfriend. There was, however, an interesting fact he'd dug up.

Darla Abbott, had once been romantically involved with a man named Frank Jackson, according to a 'bitter' former boyfriend of hers that he'd spoken to. There was a buzz around the table after Flynn informed the group that Jackson was a convicted bank robber, but the buzz just as quickly died when he reported that Jackson was now an inmate at Dorchester Penitentiary.

"Talk to him anyway," Landry directed the constable. "And I want Darla Abbott brought in for questioning. She could have been involved without having been one of the people who did the actual act."

The wedding was to be staged behind Aisling's house, on an area of lawn hidden from road traffic. Wildflowers had been cultivated in the area surrounding the lawn and they were currently at their most resplendent. Two raised garden beds along one perimeter housed an extensive collection of herbs. It was a joint project between Aisling and her dear friend Kate; a witch who used the wildflowers, herbs, and various roots found in the bush behind the house for her spells.

Pagan moved among the guests gathering in the backyard before the wedding. She greeted her aunts, uncles, and cousins who'd driven in from Toronto.

The only ones she knew well were her mother's sister Aoife and Aoife's husband, Hector. They drove down every five or six years.

Their daughter Brynn used to come with them when she was young. Pagan and Brynn had once playfully gotten themselves jammed together in a closet when they were twelve; an event that Pagan still remembered vividly since it was the first time she'd felt anything like sexual arousal.

By the time of Aoife and Hector's next visit, Brynn was eighteen and she decided to stay home; probably to party. And by the time of her aunt and uncle's next visit, Brynn was living on her own.

Pagan had met her mother's other two siblings, their spouses and kids, but it was so long ago that she remembered nothing about them. They were just people with faces that seemed vaguely familiar. One uncle reminded her of Nicolas Cage but that was about it.

Pagan was now a minor celebrity within the family and several asked her to sign the copies of her just released novel that Aisling had handed out; a new sort of task to Pagan and one that caused her to blush each time.

One of her unknown aunts approached her with the words, "Ah, la belle Pagan." Pagan had no idea why the French, but she didn't mind.

There were thirty chairs set out on the lawn, in a circle surrounding an apple tree. Pagan assumed the tree was a fertility symbol but she chose not to dwell on the idea and wasn't about to express any judgment of it. The circle, her mother had said, was a symbol of unity and wholeness, adding that the apple tree was home to her guardian spirit.

The older people were already sitting on the lawn chairs— or sprawling and leaning over them while chatting with those behind them or on one side or the other.

At one edge of the lawn a man sat cross legged on a blanket, singing traditional songs in Gaelic, employing Sean-nós singing, but sometimes taking up his guitar to perform more modern folk music.

The magician, he sparkles in satin and velvet,
You gaze at his splendour with eyes you've not used yet.
I tell you his name is Love, Love, Love.

Inside the house, in a corner of the livingroom, a young woman played a replica cláirseach [Celtic harp].

Aisling wasn't wedded to the idea of exactly replicating Celtic history so the arrangements were mostly modern. She put into practice whatever she felt was in the spirit of the ancient Celts, adapted to the modern world. "This isn't my religion," she told Pagan. "I'm not bound by any rules. I won't be going to hell for doing things in inappropriate ways."

A table was being set up with champagne and orange juice, but that was for later.

In spite of the activity and conversations, Pagan was distracted, her mind on criminal matters. There was something wrong with the case against Patrick but she couldn't figure out what it was. She just knew it.

The doubts were in the back of her thoughts even as she mingled among the family, hand in hand with Henry, introducing him, showing him off as well, since he looked handsome in a suit.

At one point Pagan wondered if the beard he'd recently

shaved off would have been short enough to fit under a pirate mask. She immediately felt guilty about the thought.

Jarrod's family was at the wedding. Pagan saw his sisters Beth and Ellie for the first time.

Ellie had arrived with her parents. Ellie with the dyed black hair. La belle Ellie.

All three of the younger children, the twins and Beth, had their mother's red hair. Only the eldest, Grant, had naturally black hair.

Jarrod looked older somehow. Must be the suit. At one point she glanced his way and discovered him watching her. He smiled and looked away, and she suspected that he was weighing the possibility that he'd misjudged her innocence in the kidnapping. 'Mystified'? 'Conjectural'? 'Uncertain'? 'Suspicious'? 'Dubious'?

The marriage began with a traditional Mi'kmaq smudging ceremony to purify the space and the wedding participants, and to drive away negative energies.

After Aisling and Jarrod brushed the smoke over their faces and bodies the 'Celtic' wedding ceremony commenced as Aisling had designed it. Jarrod and Aisling walked into the centre of the circle together while the harpist played solo.

The marriage couple were barefoot; in touch with the earth.

Aisling wore a gossamer summer gown of blue.

Jarrod wore a ceremonial Mi'kmaq knee-length robe with extensive, brightly coloured quill work along the collar, cuffs, lapels, centre and hem, as well as an elaborate design across the upper back.

The couple jointly managed the ceremony, beginning the ritual by swearing oaths to Land, Sea, and Sky—the three Celtic realms—an act that connected them to their ancestors and the gods.

Pagan felt surprisingly happy for her mother. Jarrod was no longer an alien child but a friend. She watched as the couple removed the rings on their right index fingers and placed them on their left hands. They then wrapped their wrists together with a ribbon, thus 'tying the knot'.

The ceremony was followed by the champagne and orange juice.

Aisling's friends who'd been engaged to serve dinner were soon cleaning up while rearranging the folding chairs around tables in the same space behind the house,

The bride and groom circulated among their friends and family.

Pagan and Henry circulated as well and found themselves speaking to Grant and Ellie Augustine.

"I'm sorry for using your black hair dye, Ellie," Pagan said. With a smile she added, "It was part of my brilliant disguise. I was trying to dodge the coppers, being on the run so to speak, and didn't know that I was dying my hair in the same colour as the woman they were on the lookout for." She laughed.

Ellie assured Pagan that all was fine and sympathized with her recent ordeal.

Grant was put off by Pagan's comment about, "being on the run." Pagan had made the force look amateurish.

"Let me know if you see anything that worries you," Grant whispered to Pagan as they began to move off. "I'm keeping my eye on the bush around here in case anyone shows up. And I'll make sure that patrol constables swing by your apartment and Henry's house regularly."

Pagan was surprised but grateful. "Thank you. The last thing we need in our lives is more disruption. More rocks through windows by ..." She stopped herself. She'd been about to say who the woman who threw the boulder through her front window was. It had been there, on the tip of her tongue, but now it was gone.

45

Flame

Grace got the call from Frank Jackson in the afternoon. He phoned from the penitentiary to tell her that the police had been to see him, asking about Darla.

"The cops have everything fuckin' ass-backward," Frank said. He laughed. "They think Darla and I were once a couple. I didn't tell them shit and I kept my mouth shut about you. I'll be out of here in four weeks and two days. You can pay me back then. You know what I like."

Soon after, Grace left the cottage. She headed for Frank's currently unoccupied shack.

There was no after-dinner dance at the wedding so people began slipping away. They were handed small evergreen trees in pots to plant when they got home. There was a note on each pot, written by Aisling, about the inter-connected consciousness and spirit of all parts of nature.

Pagan had felt frustrated the whole afternoon for not being able to talk to Henry about her experiences of the past week, her guilty feelings, and her doubts. It would have been too awkward to speak in a crowd while there were constant interruptions.

"I'll talk to you later," Pagan said whenever Henry brought up anything not connected to the wedding.

"Do you want to come to my house after?" Henry asked at one point.

"Yes."

Before they left Pagan used her old bedroom to change from her dress into casual clothes.

Henry and Pagan were soon back at their spot on the old couch in Henry's study. Pagan lay with her head on one of the armrests, her feet on the lap of Henry, sitting at the other end.

As they drank their first glass of wine, Pagan related the facts of the case against Patrick, insofar as she knew them.

"Sometimes life requires blind trust don't you think?" asked Pagan.

"Yes."

"Everything about the past week tells us that. We lose our faith in everyone we know so easily if prodded. It's not about loyalty, but about trust."

"The cops did their best to make us suspect each other."

Pagan considered Henry for a moment. "Do you trust me?"

"I do. I must. I think we all have to reconcile ourselves to our uncertainty about others and decide to trust based on our sense of the person. If we don't we'll spend our lives walking around with a metaphorical knife hidden up a sleeve waiting to be attacked."

The sipped their glasses of wine.

With a smile, Henry said, "So, did you have enough excitement this week?"

Pagan pretended to weigh the question. "No," she said, sighing as if sad, as if burdened by boredom.

"Well then ..." Henry lifted Pagan's feet from his lap, slid down off the couch and placed her feet on a cushion. On hands and knees he moved along, in front of the couch, and stopped.

"I know a way we could have some excitement." he said.

"You do? Don't tell me, it's Scrabble. I love the cut and thrust of Scrabble"

"That does if for me too but it wasn't exactly what I had in mind."

Henry's face was now only a few centimetres away from Pagan's.

"Oh, do tell."

Pagan rolled on to her side. They began to slowly kiss, soft and short kisses as if they were experimenting.

Eventually, Pagan said, "Should we retire to your bedroom?"

"Yes, absolutely."

You're being an idiot, Grant thought, she'll be fine. Still though, he couldn't sleep wondering whether Pagan Egan was safe.

Better swing by Hebert's place, Grant thought. He'd seen Pagan leave the wedding with Henry and drive away in his pickup. It would be no big deal to run over there in spite of the hour and the fact that a patrol constable would be passing by regularly.

Grant had built his house on the other half of his grandfather's old farm, across the road from Jarrod's half so, like Jarrod, he was a close neighbour of Henry. Better to check on Hebert's house than to keep tossing and turning.

He glanced at the illuminated hands of the clock on his bedside table. It was 2:00 AM.

He climbed from his bed and got dressed. He reset the alarm for 4:00 AM for another check.

The road was a lonely path in the darkness. The forest seemed to be sleeping but Grant had grown up in the country and knew there was always activity and watching eyes.

In her dream Pagan was walking by the water when she again saw the kelpie in the guise of a beautiful woman.

I know who you are, she thought. The kelpie was the same woman she'd seen on the night the boulder went through her front window. The tall woman with white hair on the street below—and her name was Grace.

This time, unlike their first meeting, the kelpie grabbed Pagan by the throat and forced her face underwater.

Terrified, Pagan struggled to breath.

It was Henry who woke up first though. He coughed, and then coughed again. His throat burned. He struggled to sit up, gasping and panting.

"Pagan, Pagan," he croaked. He reached out and took her wrist. "The house is on fire. We have to get out."

Henry pulled Pagan across the bed, in the direction of the door. He had her half out of the bed when she awoke. She fell to the floor.

"Shit," Henry said. He tried to reach down to pull Pagan to her feet. The effort caused him to stagger. He dropped to his hands and knees. His breathing came in loud, rapid rasps.

Pagan reached up to the edge of the bed. She struggled, Got herself up on her feet. Coughing repeatedly. Her eyes felt scalded.

The room was barely visible through the smoke. She saw a shape on the floor. Henry on his knees.

Pagan remembered something. Some wisdom from somewhere. Don't open a window. Oxygen feeds a fire. But oxygen feeds people too.

She picked up a pillow. Shook loose the pillow case. The small movement almost knocked her over. She stumbled towards the door. Stuffed the pillow case under it.

And then came the hard part. Henry was curled up. She reached down. Felt the surge of vertigo. Managed to grab him by the arms.

She dragged him away from the door. Across the room. Dropped him in front of the window.

Her hands fumbled along the frame. She found the latch. Fortunately a type she recognized. She shoved open the window.

Pagan punched out the screen. And then another hard part. She wrestled Henry up to a sitting position. His chin rested on the window ledge. A burst of air was immediately sucked into the room. It set him coughing.

"We have to get out the window," Pagan said. "Get up."

Henry struggled to his feet. With help. "Go, go," he mumbled.

"No, you first."

Henry obeyed. He sat on the window sill. He pulled his legs up. Dizzy, he fell backwards out the window. He tried to twist his body but to little effect. He landed mostly on his head. Had they not been on the first floor he might have broken his neck.

Pagan grabbed Henry's legs as he pitched backward. He was too heavy for her to stop his progress. Instead, she was catapulted out of the window. And landed on top of him. She rolled to one side. Onto the hard packed ground. The sparse undergrowth poking at her.

Get up, grab Henry, get away from here, she thought. But she felt pinned to the ground. She could feel the heat from the burning house. The air was breathable but she could taste the smoke in it.

Grant's vehicle rounded the last turn before Henry's house. He saw the flames through the trees. He jammed his foot down on the gas pedal.

As he wheeled into the yard, his headlights crossed over two bodies on the ground. Had the ground cover not been stunted and yellow he may have missed them. Survival in a fire was often a matter of luck.

Pagan felt the hands under her arms dragging her away from the house.

Grant returned for Henry. "Help's on the way," he told him.

He went back to Pagan and said the same thing.

She weakly grabbed his arm. Her voice was harsh as she softly said, "One is two."

"Okay," Grant said.

It was just then that the cruiser belonging to the constable on night patrol flew into the yard.

46 Early Sunday morning

From *Irish Fairy Tales*

There were people noises coming from right outside her basement bedroom window.

It was the second night of this and Hélène had had enough. She climbed from her bed and yanked open the curtains. There in the window well were three small children.

She yelled at them, "Go on now! Go away!" The children reluctantly climbed out of the hole and began to walk away, disappearing into the night.

Another person emerged from a dark shadow, the light spilling out from the window illuminating her face. It was a face that Hélène had never seen before but she know whose it was. She trembled in terror at the visage. The woman's hair was now white rather than black. And the expression on her face was pure malice. It was Grace O'Malley.

Grace slipped down into the window well and sneered at Hélène through the glass.

"Get out of here," said Hélène loudly. "Get the heck out of here or I'll hit you. I'll call the police."

Grace, continuing to sneer, said, "Go ahead. You'll never be rid of me. I think I'll stay right here. And there's nothing you can do about it."

Hélène was horrified by the face before her. It was inhuman. Pure malice. Pure evil. Hélène suddenly felt hopeless. There was nothing she could do to make Grace go away. She knew that even if someone struck Grace she still wouldn't go because she delighted in tormenting. Grace was here to stay.

"I won't tell on you if you go home," said Hélène calmly. A child's bargain. A better approach than making threats.

Grace laughed and shook her head.

And then Hélène's bedroom—actually on the second floor —was illuminated when the door opened and a light switch was snapped on.

Vera swept across the room. "Hélène," she said and sat down beside the small figure on the bed.

Hélène sat up, sweating and shaking.

"You were having a nightmare," said Vera. "I heard you yelling."

"It was Grace, mama. Only instead of black hair she had white hair. Her eyebrows were white and she was smiling wickedly."

"A nightmare, sweetie." She took the child in her arms.

"Stay here and leave the lights on please," said Hélène. "I want to keep my eyes open. I don't want to go to sleep or that pirate lady will be there again. I can't look at her. She scares me too much. I didn't know what to do to make her go away. I told her to go back to her house by the water but she wouldn't go. She said she'll always be here; that she'll never leave me alone."

Vera, continued to hold the frightened child. For the first time she fully realized how traumatic the kidnapping had been for her children. She chastened herself for being so blind. She'd been told the day before that her kids would need counselling but, as yet, she'd done nothing about it.

Vera wondered if this dream was something to relay to the police detective. Had Hélène seen Grace's face without her mask on after all?

"Don't worry dear," said Vera. "That awful lady pirate will never hurt you. She was just a bad dream."

"It was only the lady pirate with the black hair that I dreamed about. I'm not afraid of the other lady."

"The other lady? You mean the other pirate? The pirate man?"

"No mama, I mean the other lady pirate." Hélène smiled at her mother's denseness.

Vera drew back and looked her daughter in the eye. "You think that the person in the man's pirate mask was a woman?"

Hélène laughed. "Sometimes mama. One time the other

pirate was a man and one time it was a woman. Maybe she was the person that Grace used to phone. The one she called 'Annie'."

Remembering Sergeant Landry's request that she phone him if anything came up, Vera called his office number and left a message for him to phone her when he got in.

Landry called her back at 8:00 AM from the station.

He listened intently to the news that there were three pirate kidnappers: two women and one man. This was something that he'd have to consider; whether it was true and, if so, who was the third person.

"There's something else you might be interested in," Vera said, after she had provided Landry with all the details about the mystery woman that she had managed to get out of her daughter. "I recall your officer asking Hélène if she saw any water."

Landry said, "That's right, at the house where she was held. When we interviewed your daughter she told our sergeant that she saw no water, only trees."

"Well, last night, after the dream, Hélène said that she told the pirate lady to go back to her house by the water. Of course I noticed the contradiction between that and what she said at the interview so I asked her about it. Hélène said that you asked her whether she'd seen any water and she told you 'no' because she hadn't. But, she said, at night when it was quiet, she could hear waves lapping, like on the ocean or a lake. Oh, and she also said that sometimes she heard horses nickering and neighing."

47

From *Irish Fairy Tales*

Shortly before the morning meeting, the next-door neighbour of Patrick McSheehy's, Doris O'Keefe, phoned the police. Her call was directed to Corporal Leslie Carruthers since it related to the Patrick McSheehy case.

"I would have called you earlier," Doris told the corporal, "but I've been in Fredericton at my daughter's and didn't know what was going on with Patrick. I was just talking to Lyse Leblanc who lives on the other side of me and I was shocked to hear that Patrick was arrested for kidnapping those two small kids. Lyse said your officers had been around asking if any of us saw anything last weekend."

"Yes. And did you?"

"Well it was a long weekend so I guess Monday counts doesn't it?"

"It does. You saw something on Monday?"

"Yes. Not that it meant anything to me at the time but it was the first sign of life I'd seen next door in a couple of days."

"And what was that Mrs. O'Keefe?"

"On Monday morning—late morning it would have been —I went into my bedroom and happened to glance out the window. The window faces Patrick's driveway and side door. When I looked out I saw—a woman I think it was—in a black hoodie. She was at Patrick's side door and I saw her go inside."

"Did she use a key?"

"Well I couldn't see very well—she had her back to me and she blocked sight of the doorknob—but I think so."

"And you didn't see the person's face but you think it was a woman. you said."

"Yes. From her shape."

"Do you think it might have been the woman he's seeing now, Cinders, or his old girlfriend Pagan? I assume you've seen both of them."

"I have," said Doris, "but as I say I couldn't tell who it was. The woman just walked right in like she owned the place. Oh, and she had a blue backpack slung over her shoulder."

"And did you see a car?"

"No. Sorry, miss. I guess there must have been one in the driveway—or maybe on the road out front—but I never looked."

"Was the woman tall? Short?"

"I don't know miss. I was above her, looking down, so it's hard to say. If I had to guess I would say she was tall but I don't know. She could have been average height too."

Landry convened the incident team at 8:45 AM.

He brought everyone up to date about the fire and praised Grant for saving two lives.

The door opened and Corporal Carruthers slipped into the room. She looked at Landry sheepishly and mouthed 'Sorry'.

Landry continued what he'd been saying before the interruption, "Finding out who was responsible for the attacks on Pagan Egan is now at the same priority level as tracking the kidnappers was."

Landry looked at the faces around the table to ensure that everyone understood. "I have another bit of information to pass on," he continued. "I haven't sorted through it yet—it may be nothing—but I just got off the phone with Vera Gallant. She said that her daughter Hélène had a nightmare last night and when Vera went to comfort her the little girl said the dream was about one of the lady pirates. Yes, I said 'one of them'. Now the girl's saying that the male pirate was a man when she and her brother were abducted but that the person in the same pirate mask—the one who set them free— was a woman, and her name might be Annie."

"Do we think that's possible?" asked Constable Flynn.

"You did say that the girl was having a nightmare."

"True," said Landry, "but ..."

"... But if it's true, we now have a third person involved and at least some of our assumptions go out the window," Flynn completed his thought.

"Yes, yes, and there's something else that hurts our case. The little girl now says that the house where she was held was beside some water; either a lake or the ocean. She said she heard waves lapping and didn't tell us because all she was asked about was whether she saw any water. Oh, and she also said there were horses nearby. Said she heard them too."

As Carruthers was raising her hand to inform Landry of her conversation with Doris O'Keefe, a conversation which strongly indicated that McSheehy and Cassidy had been set up, Landry turned back to Constable Flynn and said, "Do you have anything more on Darla Abbott? You haven't brought her in."

Flynn cleared his throat.

"I'm having trouble finding her. She wasn't at home last night, at least when I was there. She wasn't at home this morning and hasn't returned my messages. Yesterday I went to the copy shop where she works but they say she booked off for the day."

"Okay, so we're nowhere on that end."

"But," Flynn said loudly, apparently annoyed at the interruption, "the copy shop manager said that Darla might be at her sister's. The manager dug out Abbot's file where her sister is listed as her emergency contact. But the phone number for the sister is out of service and she's no longer at the address given. She moved out four months ago and left no forwarding address."

"What's the sister's name?" asked Landry.

"According to Abbott's file, her name is Elizabeth Hughes. Abbot told the manager that she and Elizabeth are half sisters, hence the different last names."

"Jesus, I think I can help you with an address," interjected Constable Ryan, excitedly flipping through the papers laying on the meeting room table. "I've been checking up on the owners of black Honda Civics."

Shit, thought Landry, realizing he hadn't told Ryan to stop her search.

"There's dozens and dozens actually, since we expanded the search area, but there's one name here." Ryan stopped her search and pointed to a line on one of the pages. "A black Honda, the same year as Egan's, registered to a woman named Elizabeth Grace Hughes. The address looks to be a cottage on Faery Lake."

There was a murmur around the room before Landry said, "Grace. Could it be that simple? We dismissed Wolf Byron and Darla Abbott from consideration for a couple of reasons. First, because they didn't know the details of the original version of Egan's pirate book. Now it seems they might have known them. And secondly, because they were together in public when one of the pirates was with the kids. But what if they were both Calico Jack? Remember, that pirate never spoke. It could have been intentional, to throw us off."

Constable Grant Augustine said, "There's something I was waiting my turn to mention. I just phoned Aisling, Pagan's mother, and told her about the fire and that her daughter is in the hospital. She sort of flipped out—not surprisingly—but she managed to ask me if the fire was an attack on Pagan by the woman who threw the rock threw her window."

"That was a man," said Carruthers.

"That's exactly what I'm getting at. Who told us that it was a man? It was Byron."

"But why would he lie?" asked Carruthers.

"I can guess," said Grant. "I asked Aisling if she was positive that Egan said it was a woman who broke the window. Aisling said that she was. She said that Pagan told her that she recognized her attacker from somewhere and it was only a matter of time till she put a name to the face. Aisling also said that Pagan asked her to keep the information to herself because Wolf made her promise not to tell anyone so the culprit wouldn't find out she'd been seen. Maybe Wolf set the fire hoping to stop Pagan before she remembered. If Pagan identified the woman as Elizabeth Grace then Wolf's involvement would come out."

Landry said, "Egan wouldn't have known that the woman pirate went by the name of Grace since we kept it away from the media, but she may have met Grace, since she's the sister of her roommate. If was probably just a matter of time until Egan remembered who the woman was."

"The message on the boulder through the window wasn't meant for Pagan," blurted Roger Flynn. "The message was probably sent by Grace to her step-sister Darla, who betrayed her by returning the kidnapped kids."

"Do we know where Wolf is now?" said Landry. "He needs to be in custody—immediately!"

"God,"said Darren Woods. "I just saw him twenty minutes ago. He said he was on his way to the hospital to relieve Becca Wilson who's been guarding Pagan Egan's room."

With siren blaring Landry manoeuvred his car at high speed through Megumawaach. Heading for the regional hospital.

"They still haven't managed to get hold of Becca," said Grant Augustine. He was sitting in the passenger seat. Phone at his ear. Free hand on the dash. "They've alerted the hospital and told them to get some people to Pagan's room ASAP."

Landry focused on driving.

Grant said, "Pagan whispered something at the fire before she passed out. She whispered 'One is two'. I had no idea what she was talking about."

"She knew there were two Calico Jacks."

"She must have remembered who Grace was and figured out the rest of it."

"She was right about Wolf from the start, until I turned her off him. Find out what room she's in."

The telephone at the nursing station rang and rang. The hospital receptionist who'd taken the police call hung up. She would page the duty nurse.

Wolf had been watching Pagan through the window in the

door of her hospital room. She was sleeping with an oxygen mask strapped to her face. He concluded that whatever tests Pagan had been given must have shown she was oxygen deprived. No one will question if she dies from a lack of oxygen, he thought.

He'd kept one eye on the nursing station since he'd taken over guard duty. Waiting for an opportunity. It came in the form of an emergency. The duty nurse suddenly leapt to her feet and ran down the hallway away from him.

Perfect timing. Wolf knew everything would be fine. His mojo was working.

He stepped into Pagan's room.

Standing beside her bed, he reached behind her head and extracted a pillow.

A moment later a light began to flash on a panel at the unmanned nursing station indicating a medical emergency in Pagan Egan's room.

Landry jammed on his brakes.

He and Grant flung open the car doors. They bolted through the hospital's main entrance.

"Here, here," shouted Grant. He pointed towards a stairway.

The pair ran up the steps. Two and three at a time.

At the second floor, Grant broke into a run. The chair outside Pagan's room was empty. Wolf Byron's butt should be parked there. Landry ran too.

They burst into Pagan's room. Wolf Byron held a pillow over her face. Grant took two strides across the room. He threw himself onto Wolf.

The two men crashed into the bedside table. They ended up on the floor. Wolf instinctively curled himself into a fetal position. He soon grasped his dire predicament. He began to twist and punch at Grant. He growled in desperation.

Landry grabbed Wolf's legs.

"It's over Wolf," Augustine yelled. "Stay still."

"What the hell's going on?" barked the duty nurse, appearing at the door.

48

"No, no, she should be okay. They got to her just in time," said Leslie Carruthers, an hour after Wolf Byron's attack on Pagan Egan. "When I say 'okay' I mean she has a good chance of getting back to normal."

Carruther's car was stopped in Sobey's parking lot, pointing in the opposite direction to that of Patrol Constable Alicia Alexander. Their driver's side windows were a metre apart and open.

"How could Wolf have stooped so low?" said Alexander.

"How could anyone?" Carruthers amended. "Just keep watching for the black Civic."

"So not much has changed from last weekend when it was all about finding a black Civic," said Alexander. "Same car. New plate number."

Sergeant Landry stood in the hospital's lobby speaking to Deputy Police Chief Philpott.

"From what we know so far," said Landry, "it's clear that Elizabeth Grace Hughes is unstable. She has a long criminal record with violence and bizarre behaviour. Maybe she cracked under the pressure of holding the kids. Abbott would know her step-sister. I wonder if she figured Elizabeth had lost it and was a danger to the kids she was holding, and that's why she got them out of there."

"Which makes Grace a potentially very dangerous individual," Philpott said.

"Exactly."

"And we're doing everything in our power to find her."

Landry proceeded to outline the steps that the force was undertaking to track down Elizabeth Grace. He concluded by saying, "And we've seen nothing of the step-sister, Darla, either. They may be hiding together. Hopefully the public will step up. We've just sent a pair of cruisers to Wolf's house."

They turned and began walking to the hospital entrance. "Something occurred to me a few minutes ago," Landry said. Elizabeth's middle name is Grace. I did some research on pirates when the kidnapping began—or at least the names of the particular pirates involved, wondering if they were a clue to their identities. I came up with nothing. But as I just went over it now, in my mind, I realized that it's all in the middle names. Wolf's middle name is Jacques."

"Calico Jack."

"Just so. And Hélène, the little girl who was kidnapped, told her mother that Grace would speak on the phone to someone named, 'Annie'."

"Let me guess. Her step-sister Darla's middle name is Anne."

"I kid you not. And it's not just that. Calico Jack's wife—maybe it was his mistress, I can't remember—was named Anne Bonny."

"So, it's all their middle names."

"Yes. And what's more is that Anne Bonny, the pirate, used to dress as a man. ... The clues were there from the start but sort of impossible to discern."

"Did this gang know each other when they were kids?" asked Philpott. "I wonder if playing pirates was a childhood game revived by Egan's novel or if the book was the source of the game."

"I'd opt for the first possibility. They all grew up together. Remember that guy in Dorchester we looked at, Frank Jackson? I read the detailed report of the meeting with him. He said that he hadn't seen Darla in years. Constable Woods, who interviewed him, said in his report that Jackson has the name 'Blackbeard' tattooed on his forearm."

"The famous pirate. Now don't try to tell me this Jackson's middle name is Blackbeard."

"No, but his middle name is Edward and Blackbeard's birth name was Edward Teach. I just looked it up."

"Here's a thought," said Philpott with a smile on his face.

"I remember a bit about Blackbeard from when I was a kid. He was one of the famous pirates of the Caribbean. Maybe all these pirates operated in that region. Anyway, do you remember the location of the offshore account the ransom money was to be paid into?"

Landry nodded. "The Caribbean."

"Maybe they fancied themselves as real pirates of the Caribbean."

"So this whole thing could have been just a game for them, to see if they could be real pirates. Jesus!"

Darla backed her blue Sentra out of Wolf's driveway and set off for her parent's cottage.

The car radio was on, tuned to a local country station but her phone was still turned off as it had been since Friday night. She'd needed to tune out. No work. No kidnapping. No bank robbery. No Grace. No attacks in the night. No anxiety. No police. Nothing for the whole weekend.

Darla had slept well, both nights; till noon on Saturday and till 9:00 AM this morning. She could feel her system recharging.

She felt that she'd recovered enough to confront her sister. Darla dreaded that meeting because of the uncertainty about how Grace would respond to seeing her—but it was something that had to be done. Grace had a propensity towards violence and almost no discernible impulse control, but until the other night, she'd never directed her rage at Darla.

Darla hoped that Grace had moved on from those sorts of feelings. Peace between them was necessary to put the failed kidnapping and robbery in the past.

Wolf had already headed off to work. He'd also gotten up and left home some time in the night. His attempt at coming and going silently was unsuccessful. Darla had heard him leave and an hour or so later she'd awakened when he returned. Her guess was that he'd gone to either check up on Grace or to watch her apartment in case Grace paid a return visit.

Darla suddenly felt buoyant, like she'd taken a shot of serotonin. Things were only going to get better. Plus, the radio was playing a sad country song and few things made her happier than that.

Darla was alerted to the police presence at Grace's cottage well before she arrived.

The grey cottage was in a valley and from the top of the hill Darla spotted the two cruisers sitting in the driveway. She immediately swung her own vehicle onto the driveway of a horse farm on the south side of the road, near the top of the hill.

A wave of anxiety swept over Darla as if her whole future had suddenly made itself manifest. Nothing was over. Nothing was better. Everything was going to get a whole lot worse.

And there she sat, heart pounding, hands shaking, trying to talk herself down. Maybe the cops weren't there because of the robbery. Maybe Grace had been out doing something stupid. God knows it would be like her.

Darla debated whether to continue to Grace's cottage or to turn around and hope the cops hadn't spotted her turning around to avoid them.

She decided that her best course of action was to drive up to her parent's cottage and demand to know what was happening. A good offence is the best defence, as they say.

But, she thought, what if the police were looking for her as well as Grace? She put through a call to Wolf to ask what was happening. He didn't answer so she left a message.

Next she called the phone they'd bought for Grace. The call went directly to voicemail.

Darla drove towards the cottage.

When she got there she didn't even slow down. She went right by. Grace was nowhere to be seen. Her car wasn't in the driveway. And there was no sign of the police officers.

A short time later Darla pulled her vehicle to the side of the road. She again called Wolf and Grace. There was still no answer from either.

She cursed under her breath. What to do?

Her phone rang and since she didn't know the number she ignored it. Soon she got a beep to indicate the caller had left a voicemail.

Darla called up the message and listened. The old man spoke slowly and deliberately.

"Hello Darla. It's Barney Marks, your neighbour. I thought that you should know—I mean if you don't—that there's cops parked in the street in front of your house. I was told they're in your apartment. Anyway I heard on the radio that your boyfriend Wolf was arrested and the cops are looking for you so I thought you might want to know about all the action here. Take care and if you need help with anything let me know."

Darla began to cry. She had never let herself believe that the robbery would come to this. Wolf had assured her over and over that it would be fine.

The whole damn scheme had been for her sister. Grace had begged them to participate in her 'game'.

Telling Grace the plot of Pagan's novel about the pirates had been a mistake. Grace had gotten all fired up about copying the crime in the book, and then it became an obsession. It would be a lark, Grace insisted, and easy money. Finding the pirate novel meant that copying it was her 'destiny'.

Initially both Darla and Wolf had laughed at the idea but in time they'd relented. The plan was foolproof, Wolf said— over and over. Plus he needed the money. He was house poor. Most of all, he said, that he owed it to Grace to help her. He'd concocted and been involved in the first crime she'd been arrested for and Grace had gone to jail to protect him. It was the start of Grace's downhill slide. Grace had been in and out of jail since then. If he hadn't gotten her into crime, her life might have been much better.

Darla too had her own guilt to deal with when she thought about Grace. About the way she'd reacted to her sister's problems after a youthful incident when Grace shot a yard full of raccoons. She'd told her friends that they weren't really sisters and then proceeded to ignore Grace. It was just teenage insecurity but if she hadn't turned a blind eye to her sister's problems maybe things would have been different.

But what had gone wrong? The cops had arrested Wolf. They must have done it when he was at work since they hadn't come by his house, where she'd been.

And now they were at Grace's and at her own apartment too. Was it possible they knew everything about the kidnapping? It had to be the case.

And where was Grace? She had to find her so together they could come up with a story.

She's at Frank's, Darla thought. Frank was Grace's long-time friend, sometime boyfriend. He was a sleazy creep, and a drug dealer who Grace was trying to keep away from. But he was in prison at the moment and it wasn't as if Grace had any other options of where to go.

Darla turned left, just past the last of the village houses. She drove along a dirt road that she followed for maybe five hundred metres before turning right. She went down a narrow driveway. Two grooves worn between overgrown grass.

She drove for a hundred metres or so before parking in front of a low to the ground wooden bungalow with drab grey barn board siding. The place seemed even more squat than it actually was because there was no visible foundation and the high grass reduced the discernible walls to something like a metre and a half. The parking area was just a bit of weedy grass between the end of the drive and the house.

Darla sat in her car and surveyed the house.

Grace wasn't here although the grass was trampled so she likely had been. Maybe she'd return.

And then Darla remembered the horses.

When they were kids, Grace loved to walk up the road from the cottage, to the top of the hill. The entrance to a horse farm was there and Grace loved horses. She was mesmerized by the sight of them and had told Darla many times that she felt that she was a reincarnated horse.

But Grace didn't cross the road and walk to the farm itself. Instead, she stayed on the lake side. It was where a wide and steep walking path began. The owner of the farm and his family would ride their horses down the path to drink at the lake.

Grace never went down the trail. Instead, she would climb the high rocky cliff above the lake. There she would sit, her legs draped over the edge, to watch and wait for the horses to come.

They showed up daily—Darla had forgotten the time of day—and when they arrived Grace was radiantly happy.

If her sister was going to prison for a very long time—and surely that's where they were all headed—and she had one place in the world to see and savour beforehand, Darla knew that the bluff overlooking the lake would be the spot.

49

The Kelpie

Grace sat on the rock at the edge of the bluff overlooking Faery Lake, her feet dangling into the void. She'd sat in this exact spot hundreds of times over the years, dreamily watching for the horses to walk down the public access lane and drink at the lake. Nothing had ever fascinated her more. Nothing had ever given her a greater sense of peace.

Darla approached as silently as possible. She was startled by her sister's appearance. The sun on her bleached hair created a radiant effect. She had never seen Grace looking so beautiful.

Without turning her head, Grace matter-of-factually said, "Hello Annie."

"Hi Grace."

"I guess this didn't turn out so well."

"It doesn't seem so. Maybe we can make this better somehow. Turn ourselves in once we know what the cops have, then tell them the same story. We can make up our stories now to cover any eventuality of what they might ask."

"Do you mean rat on Calico Jack? Blame him? I don't roll like that. Never have."

"I know that. I remember that time you were all together at the scrapyard. Neither you or Frank turned him in."

"But I don't think it's reciprocal," said Grace. "I mean, I don't know why Jack would try to kill your girl Pagan but the fact the cops are now looking for you and me means he's trying to blame us for it. Seems he fucked it up like he does everything else."

Darla sucked in her breath and gasped. "He tried to kill

Pagan? That's what he was arrested for?"

Grace, continued to look out over the water. "Oh, I see you didn't know."

Darla was at a loss for words and stared off into space. Eventually she said, "Wolf wouldn't do anything to hurt you. If he tried to kill Pagan it was because she saw you from the apartment window the night you threw the boulder through it and she knew your face. She couldn't place who you were immediately but it was only a matter of time. Wolf kept talking about it. He was really worried you'd get caught."

Grace didn't respond and Darla began to pace.

"We'll stick together, the three of us," Darla said.

"And then you'll blame me."

"What? No. We've been protecting you. We planted the evidence to implicate Pagan's dirt bag ex boyfriend, like we agreed. And then I turned back the clock in her car so the cops wouldn't go looking for your car. What Wolf did was for you too."

"I'm not going to the cops," Grace said emphatically.

"They'll find you sweetie."

"Not where I'm going. I'm going home."

For the first time Darla noted her sister's intense gaze at the water, twenty metres below.

"You can't mean that. It'll be okay. The two of us will turn ourselves in and say nothing. Get a good lawyer and let her make a case for us. Or maybe we can hide at Frank's for a bit. When things calm down, we can sneak into the States."

Darla walked across the rock cliff and stopped beside her sister. She held out her hand and said, "C'mon Grace."

For the first time, Grace turned her head up towards Darla. She smiled dreamily and got to her feet. She reached out her arms to Darla.

Grace was taller than her sister. The same height as Calico Jack in fact. And she was stronger too. When she hugged her Annie, Grace squeezed tight, and then, with Darla in her arms she plunged sideways over the cliff.

The impact of the water stunned Darla!

She hung limply beneath the surface of the lake. Alone.

Grace no longer held her.

Turning her eyes upward, Darla saw the sunlight through the water. She kicked her feet. When her face broke the surface she sucked in oxygen. She looked about for Grace. There was no sign of her.

A flash of something caught her eye. A riderless black horse stood in the shallow water by the end of the trail. The horse was watching her. Darla hadn't, until then, known that any horses were watering.

She frantically scanned the shoreline hoping to spot someone, anyone, who could help her find Grace. No one was there.

Darla made three dives but there was no sign of her sister under the water either.

She slowly swam back to shore. Her beautiful and troubled Grace was gone.

Glancing along the shoreline, she saw that the black horse had disappeared as well. And in the next moment she caught sight of the police officer scrambling down the horse trail. He'd been driving away from the grey cottage when he spotted Darla's Sentra parked at the side of the road

50 Two weeks later

Finis

Grant stood in the doorway of Pagan's flat, shifting back and forth from one foot to the other.

"I'm in a rush. Just thought I should bring the two of you up to date," he said after declining Pagan's offer to come inside the apartment.

Pagan and Henry listened expectantly.

"They still haven't found Grace's body after an extensive search of the lake, but we're not giving up."

The day after Grace went into Faery Lake, Aisling had told Pagan that, "They'll never find her because there's nothing to find. She's a kelpie who's now gone home."

Aisling wasn't alone in her belief. A startling number of people in the area—startling to both Pagan and Henry that is —now seemed inclined to accept this less than rational explanation for Grace's disappearance.

Pagan recalled the one time she'd met her roommate's sister. Grace had black hair, an odd sense of humour—dark and morbid—and a horsey laugh. But even so ...

"So it turned out that your idea, that Wolf was behind everything, was correct," Grant said to Pagan. "And it sounds like you were dismissive of Darla being involved because you were friends. That too had some some foundation. They both told us that Grace wanted to frame you for the kidnapping but that Darla pushed back. She agreed to use your novel's plot only on the condition that they set up Patrick McSheehy—who she gathered was not a nice man, and a stalker to boot. ... You know, in the end, I almost admire their planning. Darla and Wolf watched Patrick so knew he was now spending his weekends at his camp with a woman, so he was no longer watching your place. Apparently you told her about Patrick's hunting camp. Darla figured the two lovebirds would be there when the kidnapping occurred, so they'd have no alibi."

"Incredible," said Pagan.

"Apparently they planned to do the kidnapping earlier that Saturday morning while you were at home so it would look like Patrick stole your car. They were right in assuming that we would soon dismiss you and Henry as suspects because there would be too many holes in the case against you. And that's when they would look at Patrick."

"Because of the green gloves," said Pagan.

"Exactly. They thought that if they made it appear that he had used your car that it would appear that he had been trying to set you up. But there was an accident on the highway when they drove north and they were so late with the kidnapping that it conflicted with when you had actually left the house."

"Plus, I left earlier than planned."

"Right again. The problem for them was that Grace and Wolf went ahead with the kidnapping anyway. Apparently Grace insisted. ... Oh, and trying to kill you was all Wolf's doing. Darla knew nothing about it. After her step-sister put the rock through your front window you said that you might be able to eventually recall where you'd seen her face. Darla was willing to bet that you wouldn't, but Wolf who became obsessed with the idea. That's why he tried to kill you."

"Thank you again for what you did," said Pagan. "I'm going to trust my instincts more in the future. I knew Wolf was behind it and Darla wouldn't purposefully try to hurt me."

"How's the house going?" Grant turned towards Henry, brightening, relieved of the burden of the words he'd been carrying.

"Fine, good," Henry said. "They've finished tearing down the old place and are starting to rebuild. We had a big hand in the design. The doctor's told us both that we need several weeks to recover so we aren't taxing ourselves. We live here now and drive out to watch the progress on the new place every day."

"I noticed a couple of solar panels at your house before. I

guess you'll have a whole whack of them now."

"Not necessarily," Pagan said. "When you build a house from scratch you can cut down on how much power you need. When we designed the place we decided on triple pane glass, the best insulation available, and to include it everywhere, top to bottom. We wanted to make the house as airtight as much as possible. Combined with huge south facing windows for passive solar heat we don't feel that we will need much energy at all for heat or hot water."

"Clever."

Henry elaborated on the other features of the house but stopped short of explaining that, since the plan was for both he and Pagan to move into the house, that the new design included two studies.

Nor did he mention that the brick outbuilding at the front of the property, facing the road, was to become a publishing company and bookshop. He and Pagan planned to publish local stuff like cookbooks, trail maps, books on regional herbs and legends, poetry, short stories, kid's books, and even experimental work. The possibilities for titles were endless since everyone was a potential author.

They reasoned that if only five copies of each book were printed at a time, it wouldn't require a huge capital outlay. And if no copies sold, then Pagan and Henry wouldn't be out much money. Some books might even be given out free. This would be a labour of love for publisher and author since no one was going to get rich off it. They reasoned, however, that by sheer volume of titles, it might bring in a bit of income for them over time. More importantly, it could be a means for people in the community to share their wisdom, stories, and history with each other.

Pagan had no way of knowing if these changes in her life were the right moves—and they were likely just the first of many more—but her instincts said yes and she was determined to trust them. Empirical evidence by itself could only take you so far.

After Grant left, Henry said to Pagan, "So you saved me

from the fire. Will you write me as a damsel in distress?”

“’A damsel in distress’? No, not a ‘damsel’. Instead of ‘damsel’ would ‘lord’ be better? Maybe ‘knight’? … ‘Squire’? … ‘Lad’? … ‘Gentleman’? … Maybe ‘bachelor’?”

Henry, who was following through on his promise to learn French, said, “I think that ‘damsel’ comes from a French word and the male equivalent is ‘damoiseau’.”

“Aren’t you the wordsmith,” said Pagan. “You might be of some benefit to have around after all, even if I have to save you over and over.”

Notes

All the characters in this book are fictional and any resemblance to any actual person is purely coincidental.

When I began writing this novel I recalled that Giles Blunt set his Cardinal mysteries in the fictional city of Algonquin Bay (rather than the real North Bay) and his reasons for doing so: to allow for greater artistic freedom and to eliminate the possibility of mistakes. I believe that his referencing the original inhabitants of the area in his city name was a mark of respect.
With these things in mind, I chose to set this novel in the fictionalized city of Megumawaach—rather than Miramichi. Megumawaach is therefore not Miramichi.

"Megumawaach: The literal translation, according to [John Clarence] Webster, "people of the country." Micmac land. The country of the Micmac. Webster concludes that the word Miramichi is probably derived from Megumawaach."
From "A Selection of Micmac Words" (A Supplement to the Historical Essay *"The Micmac Of Megumaagee"*).
http://blupete.com/Hist/Gloss/IndiansWords.htm

The quote on the title page is from Anne Brigman's book *Songs of a Pagan*, freely available online:
Anne Brigman. *Songs of a Pagan*. The Caxton Printers Ltd. Caldwell, Idaho. 1947.
https://collections.library.yale.edu/catalog/10187372

As a matter of interest, her book *Wild Flute Songs* is available here:
https://collections.library.yale.edu/pdfs/10187358.pdf

The book referenced on page 110 is:
Anne-Christine Hornborg. *Mi'kmaq Landscapes*. London. Routledge. 2008.

The song lyrics quoted on page 207 are from:
Donovan Leitch. *Sunny Goodge Street*.
https://www.azlyrics.com/lyrics/donovan/sunnygoodgestreet.html

Image Credits

The art images used are, for the most part, associated with the Celtic Revival.

The illustrations by Arthur Rackham are from:
Irish Fairy Tales. James Stephens. *Irish Fairy Tales*. London. Macmillan & Company Ltd. 1920.
Gutenberg Edition Ebook. https://gutenberg.org/files/2892/2892-h/ 2892-h.htm#linklink2HCH0017

Cover:
Craig Strahorn. CC0 1.0 (license link https://creativecommons.org/ publicdomain/zero/1.0/deed.e) Public Domain.
https://commons.wikimedia.org/wiki/File:Spooky_Trees_(Unsplas h).jpg
Title page:
Luke Braswell. CC0 1.0 (license link https://creativecommons.org/ publicdomain/zero/1.0/deed.e) Public Domain.
https://commons.wikimedia.org/wiki/File:Where_to_go %3F_(Unsplash).jpg
Preface:
Anne Brigman. Infinitude. Public Domain.
https://commons.wikimedia.org/wiki/File:Infinitude_(022440).jpg
Chapter 1:
Ewelina Karezona Karbowiak. Woman hair over face Bristol. CCO 1.0 (license link
https://creativecommons.org/publicdomain/zero/1.0/deed.e)
https://commons.wikimedia.org/wiki/
File:Woman_hair_over_face_bristol_(Unsplash).jpg
Chapter 2:
John Duncan. Drawing of the Irish Mythological Hero. Public Domain. https://www.wikiart.org/en/john-duncan/drawing-of-the- irish-mythological-hero
Chapter 3:
AnonMoos. Triskele-Symbol-spiral-five-thirds-turns.svg flipped horizontally. Public Domain. https://commons.wikimedia.org/wiki/ File:Triskele-Symbol1.svg
Chapter 4:
John Duncan. The Fomors (or The Power of Evil Abroad in the

World). Public Domain.
https://www.wikiart.org/en/john-duncan/the-fomors-or-the-power-of-evil-abroad-in-the-world
Chapter 5:
Charles Rennie Mackintosh. Part Seen Part Imagined. Public Domain.
https://www.wikiart.org/en/charles-rennie-mackintosh/part-seen-part-imagined-1896
Chapter 6:
Arthur Rackham illustration for *Irish Fairy Tales* by James Stephens. Project Gutenberg Ebook. 2008. Public Domain.
https://gutenberg.org/files/2892/2892-h/2892-h.htm
Chapter 7:
John Everett Millais. The Bridesmaid. Public Domain.
https://www.wikiart.org/en/john-everett-millais/the-bridesmaid
Chapter 8:
Gary Henry (collaboration with Edward Atkinson Hornel). The Druids: Bringing in the Mistletoe. Cropped. Public Domain. https://www.wikiart.org/en/george-henry/the-druids-bringing-in-the-mistletoe-collaboration-with-edward-atkinson-hornel-1890
Chapter 9:
Joyce Compton and Clara Bow in *The Wild Party*.
Public Domain.
https://commons.wikimedia.org/wiki/File:Joyce_Compton-Clara_Bow_in_The_Wild_Party.jpg
Chapter 10:
Gilbert Reeves. Public Domain. Crop of
https://commons.wikimedia.org/wiki/File:EAST_FRONT_-_Greenhouse_Service_Station,_522_South_Main_Street,_Woodstock,_Cherokee_County,_GA_HABS_GA,29-WDSK,1-1.tif
Chapter 11:
John Duncan. Helene Schlapp. Public Domain.
https://www.wikiart.org/en/john-duncan/helene-schlapp
Chapter 12:
Dillon Family. Gráinne Mhaol Castle. Public Domain.
https://www.flickr.com/photos/nlireland/17087792645
Chapter 13:
Anne Brigman. The Masterpiece. Public Domain.
https://commons.wikimedia.org/wiki/File:The_Master-piece_(125850).jpg

Chapter 14:
Sergei Prokudin-Gorskii. Head Study (reclining woman in white blouse and blue skirt). Public Domain. Cropped. https://commons.wikimedia.org/wiki/File:Reclining_red-haired_woman_in_white_blouse_and_blue_skirt_(by_Sergey_Prokudin-Gorsky,_ca._1910).jpg

Chapter 15:
Lily Yeats. Landscape at Night embroidery. Public Domain. https://commons.wikimedia.org/wiki/File:Lily_yeats.jpg

Chapter 16:
Frances Benjamin Johnston. Public Domain. https://commons.wikimedia.org/wiki/File:Nude_piper_posed_on_rocks.jpg

Chapter 17:
Charles Rennie Mackintosh. In Fairyland. Public Domain. https://commons.wikimedia.org/wiki/File:Charles_Rennie_Mackintosh_-_In_Fairyland_1897.jpg

Chapter 18:
Evelyn De Morgan. The Dryad. Public Domain. https://en.wikipedia.org/wiki/Dryad

Chapter 19:
AnonMoos. Triple Goddess Symbol, composed of waxing crescent, full moon, and waning crescent (outlined version). Public Domain. https://commons.wikimedia.org/wiki/File:Triple-Goddess-Waxing-Full-Waning-Symbol.png

Chapter 20:
Frances Macdonald. Floral Design. Public Domain. https://www.wikiart.org/en/frances-macdonald-macnair/floral-design-1901

Chapter 21:
Bessie MacNicol. The Goose Girl. Public Domain. https://commons.wikimedia.org/wiki/File:Bessie_MacNicol_-_The_Goose_Girl_1898.jpg

Chapter 22:
Ann Macbeth. The Huntress. CC BY-SA 3.0 (license link https://creativecommons.org/licenses/by-sa/3.0/). The original is in ccolour. https://en.wikipedia.org/wiki/File:The_Huntress_by_Ann_Macbeth_Studio_Magazine_vol_27_(1903).jpg

Chapter 23:
AnonMoos. Spiral Goddess symbol of modern neo-paganism (this

variant with shortened vertical height). Public Domain.
https://commons.wikimedia.org/wiki/File:Spiral_Goddess_symbol
_neo-pagan_2.svg
Chapter 24:
John Duncan. Force and Reason. Public Domain.
https://www.wikiart.org/en/john-duncan/force-and-reason-1939
Chapter 25:
Thomas Millie Dow. The Kelpie. Public Domain.
https://commons.wikimedia.org/wiki/File:The_Kelpie_by_Thomas
_Millie_Dow.jpg
Chapter 26:
Craig Strahorn. Spooky Trees. CCO 1.0 (license link
https://creativecommons.org/publicdomain/zero/1.0/deed.e) https://
commons.wikimedia.org/wiki/File:Spooky_Trees_(Unsplash).jpg
Chapter 27:
Frances Macdonald. Girl in a Tree. Public Domain.
https://www.wikiart.org/en/frances-macdonald-macnair/girl-in-a-
tree
Chapter 28:
Charles Rennie Macintosh. Landscape. Public Domain.
https://www.wikiart.org/en/charles-rennie-mackintosh/landscape-
1927
Chapter 29:
Anne W. Brigman. Soul of the Blasted Pine. Public Domain.
https://en.wikipedia.org/wiki/Anne_Brigman#/media/
File:Soul_of_the_Blasted_Pine_(Brigman).jpg%20%20Soul%20of
%20the%20Blasted%20Pine
Chapter 30:
John Duncan. Public Domain. https://www.wikiart.org/en/john-
duncan/unknown-1
Chapter 31:
Margaret Macdonald. The White Rose And The Red Rose. Public
Domain.
https://commons.wikimedia.org/wiki/File:Margaret_MacDonald_-
_White_Rose_And_Red_Rose.jpg
Chapter 32:
Fouquier. Magpies. Public Domain. https://www.flickr.com/photos/
fouquier/51041627538/in/photostream/
Chapter 33:
Public Domain. CCO 1.0 (license link
https://creativecommons.org/publicdomain/zero/1.0/deed.e) https://

commons.wikimedia.org/wiki/File:Pirate_Flag_of_Jack_Rackham.
svg
Chapter 34:
Alice Boughton. Public Domain.
https://commons.wikimedia.org/wiki/File:Alice_boughton_two_wo
men_under_a_tree.jpg
Chapter 35:
Arthur Rackham. Illustration in Irish Fairy Tales. Public Domain.
https://commons.wikimedia.org/wiki/File:Irishfairytales01step_007
9.jpg
Chapter 36:
Clarence Hudson White. The Bubble. Public Domain.
https://commons.wikimedia.org/wiki/File:Clarence_hudson_white2
.jpg
Chapter 37:
Annie French. Summer Time. Public Domain.
https://commons.wikimedia.org/wiki/File:Summer_Time_by_Miss
_Annie_French.jpg
Chapter 38:
John Duncan. Unknown. Public Domain. https://www.wikiart.org/
en/john-duncan/unknown
Chapter 39:
Margaret Macdonald. Embroidered Panels. Public Domain. https://
www.wikiart.org/en/margaret-macdonald/embroidered-panels-1902
Chapter 40:
Arthur Rackham. Illustration in Irish Fairy Tales. Public Domain.
https://gutenberg.org/files/2892/2892-h/2892-
h.htm#linklink2H_4_0013
Chapter 41:
Charles Rennie Mackintosh. Décor de la salle à manger (House for
an art lover, Glasgow). Public Domain. https://www.wikiart.org/en/
charles-rennie-mackintosh/d-cor-de-la-salle-manger-house-for-an-
art-lover-glasgow-1901-2
Chapter 42:
Arthur Rackham. Illustration in Irish Fairy Tales. Public Domain.
https://commons.wikimedia.org/wiki/File:05_A_man_who_did_not
_like_dogs._In_fact,_he_hated_them._When_he_saw_one_he_use
d_to_go_black_in_the_face,_and_he_threw_rocks_at_it_until_it_g
ot_out_of_sight.jpg
Chapter 43:
John Duncan. The Turn of the Tide. Public Domain.

https://www.wikiart.org/en/john-duncan/the-turn-of-the-tide
Chapter 44:
Bessie MacNicol. Under The Apple Tree: Public Domain.
https://en.wikipedia.org/wiki/File:Bessie_MacNicol_-
_Under_The_Apple_Tree_1899.jpg
Chapter 45:
Anne Brigman. Flame. Public Domain.
https://commons.wikimedia.org/wiki/File:Flame_(125850).jpg
Chapter 46:
Arthur Rackham. Illustration in Irish Fairy Tales. Public Domain.
https://commons.wikimedia.org/wiki/File:11_The_Hag_of_the_Mil
l_was_a_bony,_thin_pole_of_a_hag_with_odd_feet.jpg
Chapter 47:
Arthur Rackham. Illustration in Irish Fairy Tales. Public Domain.
https://commons.wikimedia.org/wiki/File:Irishfairytales01step_027
9.jpg
Chapter 48:
Clarence Hudson White. Rose Pastor Stokes. Public Domain.
https://commons.wikimedia.org/wiki/File:Rose-pastor-stokes-by-
clarence-h-white-1909.jpg
Chapter 49:
Herbert James Draper. The Kelpie. Cropped. Public Domain.
https://en.wikipedia.org/wiki/Herbert_James_Draper#/media/File:T
hekelpie_large.jpg
Chapter 50:
Anne Brigman. Finis. Public Domain.
https://commons.wikimedia.org/wiki/File:Finis_(022440).jpg